PENGUIN  CLASSICS

THE ROAD THROUGH THE WALL

SHIRLEY JACKSON was born in San Francisco in 1916. She first received wide critical acclaim for her short story "The Lottery," which was first published in *The New Yorker* in 1948. Her novels—which include *The Sundial, The Bird's Nest, Hangsaman, The Road Through the Wall, We Have Always Lived in the Castle,* and *The Haunting of Hill House*—are characterized by her use of realistic settings for tales that often involve elements of horror and the occult. *Raising Demons* and *Life Among the Savages* are her two works of nonfiction. She died in 1965.

RUTH FRANKLIN is a book critic and a contributing editor at the *New Republic.* Her writing also appears in *The New Yorker, The New York Review of Books, Bookforum,* and *Salmagundi.* Her first book, *A Thousand Darknesses: Lies and Truth in Holocaust Fiction,* was a finalist for the 2012 Sami Rohr Prize for Jewish Literature. She is currently working on a biography of Shirley Jackson.

SHIRLEY JACKSON

The Road Through the Wall

Foreword by
RUTH FRANKLIN

PENGUIN BOOKS

PENGUIN BOOKS
Published by the Penguin Group
Penguin Group (USA) Inc., 375 Hudson Street,
New York, New York 10014, USA

USA | Canada | UK | Ireland | Australia
New Zealand | India | South Africa | China
Penguin Books Ltd, Registered Offices:
80 Strand, London WC2R 0RL, England
For more information about the Penguin Group visit penguin.com

First published in the United States of America by Farrar, Straus 1948
This edition with an introduction by Ruth Franklin
published in Penguin Books 2013

LIBRARY OF CONGRESS CATALOGING-IN-PUBLICATION DATA
Jackson, Shirley, 1916–1965.
The road through the wall / Shirley Jackson ; foreword
by Ruth Franklin.
pages ; cm.—(Penguin classics)
ISBN 978-0-14-310705-7
I. Title.
PS3519.A392R63 2013
813'.54—dc23
2013005495

Printed in the United States of America
1 3 5 7 9 10 8 6 4 2

Contents

Foreword

"My goodness, how you write," John Farrar wrote to Shirley Jackson after receiving the manuscript of *The Road Through the Wall*, her first novel. It was July 1947, almost exactly a year before the appearance of "The Lottery" in *The New Yorker* would make Jackson the most talked-about short story writer in America, but her career was already off to a promising start. The previous few years had seen nearly a dozen of her stories published in *The New Yorker*, as well as other respected magazines. After Jackson gave birth to her first child, a son, in 1942, the family relocated to Vermont so that her husband, the literary critic Stanley Edgar Hyman, could teach at Bennington College. There Jackson began writing *The Road Through the Wall*.

Jackson once told her daughter Sarah that "the first book is the book you have to write to get back at your parents. . . . Once you get that out of your way, you can start writing books." The parental crime to be avenged may have been simply the Jacksons' effort to provide their daughter with a typical suburban childhood—to which she was by all accounts spectacularly unsuited. The novel is set in the fictional California town of Cabrillo, which bears certain similarities to Burlingame, where Jackson grew up: a middle-class suburb within commuting distance from San Francisco, with its majority-WASP population beginning to show the stress of an influx of newcomers, including Catholics, Jews, and Chinese. And certain incidents—in the first scene, the protagonist, Harriet Merriam, comes home to discover that her mother has been reading her private writings—may be drawn from Jackson's life.

But it would be wrong to suggest that *The Road Through the Wall* is predominantly autobiographical. An ensemble novel with a large cast of characters, the book narrates the happenings on a single street from the perspective of a dispassionate onlooker. If it draws upon Jackson's experiences as a girl, it does so mainly to the extent that she was an uncommonly close observer who speculated, based on details real or imagined, that beneath the sunny surfaces of her neighbors' lives there lay darker secrets: infidelity, racial and ethnic prejudice, and basic cruelty.

The last point extends especially to the novel's children, who are treated with at least as much gravity as the adults and are well their equals in connivance and inhumanity. The story centers around Harriet's struggles to fit in with the other children on the block, and her short-lived friendship with Marilyn, another outsider. (Friendship between girls and women is a central theme in nearly all of Jackson's novels, and she is a particularly close observer of the small rituals by which these intimacies are created.) But Marilyn's family is Jewish, and the prejudice of the other neighbors—always expressed subtly, in the politest terms—is unmistakable. When one family organizes the children on the block for a Shakespeare reading, for instance, they exclude Marilyn out of false concern that she will be offended by *The Merchant of Venice*. Finally, Harriet's mother tells her to break off their friendship. "We must expect to set a standard," she says. "However much we may want to find new friends whom we may value, people who are exciting to us because of new ideas, or because they are *different*, we have to do what is expected of us."

We have to do what is expected of us: It is hard to think of a better definition of conformity. One of the novel's surprises is the essential role that women play in enforcing society's expectations. *The Road Through the Wall* exists almost entirely in the world of women and children: Nearly all the action takes place after the men have gone off to work. It would be a stretch to call it a feminist novel, not least because Jackson seems to have had an allergy to the word. Still, the way she portrays certain of her characters' attitudes strikingly anticipates the movement to come: One neighbor regards herself as "something more than a housewife," and is scorned by the others for putting on airs. But no escape is possible from the hothouse of hostility in which these women exist. The psychological intrigues that dominate their lives turn out to be far from superficial: In fact, they have the power to bring down the neighborhood. Things start to fall apart not long after Harriet's rejection of Marilyn, and the pace of disintegration accelerates until the novel's disastrous conclusion.

The novel includes well over a dozen characters, but Jackson's control over her material is superb. She parcels out scenes in perfect rhythm, maintaining the book's taut atmosphere. Every description is carefully calculated for what it reveals, both about the character to whom it refers and the person whose attitude it represents. When Marilyn sneaks into the home of Helen Williams, the girl who is her chief tormentor, as the family is moving out, she notices the poor quality of the furniture and regrets having been so easily intimidated: "Helen dressed every morning for school in front of that grimy dresser, ate breakfast at that slatternly table . . . no one whose life was bounded by things like that was invulnerable." Jackson's readers will recognize here the early flutterings of her interest in houses and their furnishings as expressions of psychological states: One unfortunate family lives in "a recent regrettable pink stucco with the abortive front porch . . . unhappily popular in late suburban developments." (In an astonishing, almost throwaway aphorism, Jackson comments: "No man owns a house because he really wants a house, any more than he marries because he favors monogamy.")

Compared to *The Haunting of Hill House* or *We Have Always Lived in the Castle*, Jackson's masterful late novels, *The Road Through the Wall* is a slighter work. But it is marvelously written, with the careful attention to structure, the precision of detail, and the brilliant bite of irony that would always define her style. There are wonderful moments of humor, as when one of the neighborhood girls, seeking to decorate her living room with some high-class art, accidentally orders a set of pornographic photographs. And the Merriam

household is an all-too-convincing portrait of familial dys-
function. After Harriet's mother discovers her daughter's secret writings, she forces Harriet to burn them in the furnace
while her father sits obliviously at the dinner table: "Seems
like a man has a right to have a quiet home," he grumbles to
himself. Later Harriet and her mother will spend afternoons
writing together: Mrs. Merriam writes a poem titled "Death
and Soft Music," while Harriet's is called "To My Mother." A
childhood poem in Jackson's archive bears a similar title.

The Road Through the Wall was published by Farrar, Straus
in January 1948 to a largely unappreciative audience. Critics
were put off by the book's unpleasant characters, its grim
tone, and its violent conclusion. But some recognized Jackson's
inimitable gift for diagnosing the "little secret nastinesses" of
the human condition. Jackson, it seems, was not discouraged
by the reviews. At any rate, she was hardly dissuaded from
using her fiction to tell her readers unpleasant truths about
themselves. Those who were nonplussed by this first depiction
of a small town in which the residents gradually undo one
another must have been utterly astonished by the thunderbolt
that came next. But for readers with the sense to take Jackson
seriously from the start, "The Lottery" was a natural sequel—
and a deserved vindication.

RUTH FRANKLIN

The Road
Through the Wall

PROLOGUE

The weather falls more gently on some places than on others, the world looks down more paternally on some people. Some spots are proverbially warm, and keep, through falling snow, their untarnished reputations as summer resorts; some people are automatically above suspicion. Mr. John Desmond and Mr. Bradley Ransom-Jones and Mr. Michael Roberts and Miss Susannah Fielding, all of whom lived on Pepper Street in a town called Cabrillo, California, thought of their invulnerability as justice; Mr. Myron Perlman and possibly Mr. William Byrne, also of Pepper Street, would have been optimistic if they thought of it as anything less than fate. No man owns a house because he really wants a house, any more than he marries because he favors monogamy, but all these men were married and most of them owned houses, and they regarded themselves as reasonable and unselfish and even, to themselves, as responsible. They all lived on Pepper Street because they were able to afford it, and none of them would have lived there if he had been able to afford living elsewhere, although Pepper Street was charming and fairly expensive and even comfortably isolated. The town of Cabrillo, in 1936, was fortunate in housing such people as Mr. Desmond and his family.

The Desmonds had lived on Pepper Street longer than anyone else, because when Mr. Desmond was able to build his home (he rented the first house he lived in with his wife) he chose a good location in a neighborhood not yet developed but undeniably "nice." The Desmond house was on the corner of Pepper Street and Cortez Road, facing Pepper Street, with a large garden to the side along Pepper Street and tall blank windows on the Cortez Road side. The tall windows belonged on the inside to the Desmond living-room where the family sat in the evenings, and the Venetian blinds were always closed after dark. When the Desmonds moved in, their daughter Caroline had not been born, and the hedge around the visible sides of the house was inches high. By the time Caroline was three, the hedge was waist high and required the services of a boy every Saturday to keep it trimmed. Beyond the hedge the Desmonds lived in a rambling modern-style house, richly jeweled with glass brick. They were the aristocracy of the neighborhood, and their house was the largest; their adopted son Johnny, who was fifteen years old, associated with boys whose families did not live on Pepper Street, but in neighborhoods where the Desmonds expected to live some day.

Next door to the Desmonds, on Pepper Street, was the orchard of apple trees which successfully hid the house of crazy old Mrs. Mack, and beyond that was the Byrne house where fourteen-year-old Pat Byrne and twelve-year-old Mary lived under Mrs. Byrne's rigid faith, and from which they issued every morning with faces glowing from hard soap. Their house was a recent regrettable pink stucco with the abortive front porch made of a mantel over the front door and a slight unreliable iron railing on either side of the one step, a front porch unhappily popular in late suburban developments. Mr. Byrne had not built this house, neither did he own it, but he paid the rent for it regularly.

Next door to the Byrnes were the Robertses. Mike Roberts had been a cavalry officer in 1917 and had felt ever since that life without his horse was restricting. His wife had helped the architect with the plans for their house, and it began with bravado and ended weakly with a flat ugly goldfish pond never finished in the back yard. In front it had a sweeping wide concrete porch upon which bougainvillea would not grow— although the Perlmans next door had it in profusion—and was thickly surrounded with bushes which were inadequate to disguise the fact that the roof was colonial, the windows modern, and the whole a gaudy yellow. The Roberts family had two children, Art and young Jamie. Art Roberts and Pat Byrne were free with one another's houses, and had once built a telephone of tin cans and pieces of string between their bedroom windows.

The Perlmans were the only Jewish family on Pepper Street, and lived sheltered under their masses of bougainvillea. They lived in a house which they rented, although it must have had the proper number of bedrooms and adequate closet space, since they never moved. The Perlmans' driveway was barely separated from the vacant lot next door by a grey picket fence; from their dining-room windows the Perlmans would survey the reaches of empty grass and shortcut paths which ended at Winslow Road, cutting north and south across Pepper Street's east and west. There was another vacant lot just across Pepper Street; it lay next to the Ransom-Jones house, which was then roughly across the street from the Perlmans'.

Mr. and Mrs. Ransom-Jones and her sister lived on Pepper Street, probably, because like Mr. Desmond they were not rich enough to live in the style they coveted and not proud enough to live in opposition to it. They devoted themselves, instead, to a garden which swept up from the sidewalk to the end of their lot, compensating for the tiny house, which might have been quaint and cottage-like, but was inadequate by Ransom-Jones standards. The Ransom-Jones garden, however, stretched so far that the house was almost hidden from its neighbors, and it was necessary for Mrs. Ransom-Jones to leave her front door and walk halfway down the stepping-stones before she could see the street. The Donalds were the Ransom-Jones's neighbors, pushed so far down the block by the garden that they were almost directly across the street from the Byrne house. Mr. Donald was another one who only rented his house; it had never occurred to him to build a house of his own, and so he spent all his life living in the patterns set out by other more enterprising men. His present house, which suited him and his family admirably, was made of bricks put together in a square, ample enough for Mr. and Mrs. Donald and their three children, and pretentious enough for Mr. Donald's wife and daughter to feel at home.

The one thorn in the side of the Donald women was the

house-for-rent, which crowded them boorishly, in contrast to
the Ransom-Jones garden; it went up for rent regularly and
was never suitably tenanted during the Donalds' residence;
one completely unsatisfactory family after another moved in
and then out. Mrs. Donald suspected, and said publicly, that it
was because the landlord rented it too cheaply for Pepper
Street standards; it was a white elephant, she said, because it
was badly planned and dreadfully dark. Someone obviously
aiming at another effect than he got had intended it to be
beautiful rather than comfortable; it was a thin greyish building with, blessedly, four thick trees crushed between itself and
the Donald house, and a wall made of rough stones cemented
together between itself and its other neighbor, Miss Fielding.
The front of the house was also built of the same rough stones;
Mrs. Donald had remarked accurately that it looked like a
reform school.

Miss Fielding paid her rent and was never known to dislike
her house and had probably never looked carefully at the outside of it. Pepper Street was one of the few neighborhoods
where an old single woman like Miss Fielding could live alone
in a house that suited her. By some architectural sleight-of-
hand, Miss Fielding's house seemed to be set high above ground,
as though she were living in a tree, or on a houseboat: there
was a long flight of shallow steps shielded by a stone balustrade, and at the top the incredibly small house perched, with
its small windows and door looking kittenishly down at the
street. Miss Fielding had a little front porch with a continua-
tion of the stone balustrade protecting it from falling down
into the street, and the whole was colored white, with green
frames around the windows and doors; it was on the front
porch that Miss Fielding sat, day after day, with her cat—one
of the Ransom-Jones's Angel's kittens—on her lap. The small
space of ground in front of this house was bare earth, but her
neighbors forgave Miss Fielding this on consideration of the
steps, which were really too much, they thought, for a woman
her age.

The Merriams had the corner of Pepper and Cortez opposite
the Desmonds, but the Merriam house made no attempt to

compete with the grandeur of the Desmond semi-modern. For one thing, the Merriams lived officially on Cortez Road, that being where their front door was. For another, Mr. Merriam, although he owned his house and would not live in a rented one, owned other houses at various places in the county, and lived in this one because it was the slowest to rent, and the least likely to sell. It had been built before the Desmond house by about ten years, and remodeled when Mrs. Merriam took it over; consequently it had the appearance of age which none of the other houses in the neighborhood had attained as yet. It was grey and weatherbeaten, and, since it had been modeled originally after someone's grandfather's manor-house, looked even older than it was.

Finally, next door to the Merriam home, defiantly on Cortez Road, was the house inhabited by the Martins, a stolid family who lived where they had to and held on to what they had; the house belonged to old Mr. Martin and his wife, grandparents to George and Hallie Martin, fourteen and nine years old, children whom Mrs. Merriam found regrettable; she would have preferred to keep her own fourteen-year-old, Harriet, far away from the Martin children, but this was almost impossible, since both Harriet and the Martins played communally with the other children in the neighborhood. Moreover—and this was one of Mrs. Merriam's objections—the house next door was also the dwelling of young Mrs. Martin, mother to George and Hallie, who worked as a waitress somewhere downtown. The house itself was yellow, and ended with two apple trees by the back door; it was a step downward from the Merriam house, and certainly not fit to go around the corner on to Pepper Street.

Because Cabrillo was perhaps thirty miles from San Francisco and was, in 1936, halfway between a suburban development and a collection of large private estates, and because Pepper Street was, in turn, on the borderline between these two, it possessed an enviable privacy; beyond the Martin house, and running along behind all the houses on the south side of Pepper Street, was a heavily wooded section, probably unexplored except by the Pepper Street children, which included a dried-up creek and ended far south in a golf course. Backing on the houses of the northern side of Pepper Street—that is, the Desmonds' to the Perlmans'—was a row of apartment houses which in turn faced a main highway. Pepper Street was rarely troubled with invasions from this quarter, probably because the apartment houses and the people who lived in them and the cars traveling the highway were all intent in another direction, toward the center of town, with little concern about what went on in back of them. One of the apartment houses had stolen around the corner near the Desmond house to have an address on Cortez Road; it had even gone so far as to stretch a numbered awning out across the sidewalk, but people rarely went in or out that way, preferring the larger, double-awninged entrance on the highway. This apartment house, the Merriam house, and the Martin house were the only three places in the world to have addresses on Cortez Road. On the side of Cortez Road opposite these three was the wall.

The wall was the limit of a large estate which had originally encompassed all the property around Pepper Street, and which had been sold off lot by lot. At present the wall ran down one side of Cortez, along the highway for a block, and then up the corresponding street on the other side; it was a thin high brick wall, taller than Mr. Donald, who was the tallest man on Pepper Street, and never scaled within the history of the neighborhood. It was called the wall, and the highway was called the highway, and the gates were called the gates. These stood at the head of Cortez Road, where the wall reached its own estate and became self-important, having more ground to circle than a city block. The gates were square piles of brick on either side of the street, with no bars between, nothing to indicate that they were a barrier, but they were an effective end to Pepper Street life. Beyond them lived the rich people, on a long curving road from which you could not see any house; beyond them was a neighborhood so exclusive that the streets had no names, the houses no numbers. The people who owned the wall lived there; so, although no one knew it very surely, did the people who owned some of the houses on Pepper Street, and the man who owned the bank that owned the house-for-rent. Mr. Byrne's employer lived there; so did Hallie Martin's future husband.

The sun shone cleverly on Pepper Street, but it shone more bravely still beyond the gates; when it rained on Pepper Street the people beyond the gates never got their feet wet; beyond the gates all the houses were marked "No Trespassing."

In any case, at two-thirty in the afternoon, Pepper Street was very quiet and pleasant, with the California sunlight of early summer almost green coming through the trees, almost painful straight from the sky. The trees lining Pepper Street on either side, which the children called locusts and the parents regarded vaguely as peppers, had spent the spring through with tiny pink blossoms, meeting to make a bedroomish arch overhead for a month, and then, suddenly, turning green and leaved, abandoning the pink blossoms overnight, so that the street was rich with pink blossoms underfoot. For a few days the pink blossoms would be everywhere—in the gutters, on the lawns, tracked into pleasant living-rooms, lying on the tops of bags of groceries carried home—and then they would vanish, again overnight, and the trees would continue to be greener and greener until school started in the fall, and then the street would be full of leaves and the trees bare all winter, preparing new pinkness for the spring.

The pink blossoms were underfoot now on Pepper Street, which made middle June almost certain. Mr. Ransom-Jones and Mr. Merriam and Mr. Desmond had all breakfasted in their homes by early morning sunlight before driving together to San Francisco, as they did every morning. Old Mr. Martin, who left before dawn for his greenhouses, regarded the warm weather as encouraging for the roots of growing things. Miss Fielding's cat liked the weather, and so did little Caroline Desmond.

It was the last day of school; fortunately the weather was to continue warm and fair until the end of summer, when school began again.

CHAPTER ONE

Mrs. Merriam came to her back window, which saw Miss Fielding's house and Pepper Street beyond, and looked anxiously down Pepper Street. Mrs. Merriam's clock had stopped; it was easier to look out the back window than go upstairs to the bedroom clock. Mrs. Merriam's kitchen had a built-in electric clock (and a built-in dishwasher and a built-in refrigerator) but the electric clock had broken long ago, and when the refrigerator broke and the electrician came to fix it Mrs. Merriam could have him fix the clock. So that when the living-room clock stopped Mrs. Merriam was without the time downstairs.

At quarter-past three Mrs. Merriam had gone back to her sewing, but she heard the children coming up Pepper Street. They came from Winslow Road, from the school, and they came past the vacant lots first and then down past the Ransom-Joneses on one side and the Perlmans on the other (Marilyn Perlman, however, was always home last, because she left the school a few minutes after everyone else, and walked home alone), and then they passed the Robertses and the Byrnes on one side and the Donalds on the other, and the Roberts boys dropped off, and Pat Byrne, and Tod Donald went home while Virginia Donald and Mary Byrne came along the street slowly with the girls, Harriet Merriam and Helen Williams, and the girls stood on the corner of Pepper and Cortez and talked while the boys went home to leave their jackets and receive from their mothers an apple or a piece of cake, or, in the case of Pat Byrne, a glass of milk and two graham crackers. Miss Fielding heard the children coming when they reached the Donalds' house; she went inside with the cat, and lay down on the living-room couch. Mrs. Merriam, who was anxious, heard the children when they passed the house-for-rent, and from her back window saw Harriet coming down the street, carrying her books, along with the other girls, while the two Martin children, always the least enthusiastic and with the farthest to go, hesitated constantly—George outside the Desmond house till Johnny Desmond put his head out of the kitchen window and said, "Go on home, Martin," and Hallie, who was only nine, around the group of girls on the corner, trying artfully to get a word into the conversation, until the group broke up and Hallie came tagging up Cortez Road with Harriet.

Mrs. Merriam prevented herself from going to the door to meet Harriet; she sat in the long light living-room with the basket of sewing on the floor beside her, unaware that with her tall thin body silhouetted against the big window, and her narrow severe head bent slightly to the sewing, she looked bleak and menacing after the cheerful sunlight outside. She heard Harriet say, " 'Bye, Hallie," and come noisily up the front steps and open the door with a crash. Mrs. Merriam kept her eyes down on her sewing; Harriet would know she was offended. She heard Harriet's steps in the hall, and then the hesitation that would be Harriet in the living-room doorway, recognizing that her mother was offended.

"I'm home, Mother," Harriet said. "No more school till September." It was her nervous voice, trailing off at the end of the sentence with a little giggle. Harriet was a big girl, large-boned and stout, and Mrs. Merriam braided Harriet's hair every morning and dressed her in bright colors. For the last year or so, from twelve to almost fourteen, Harriet had begun to speak awkwardly when she was uneasy, missing her words sometimes, and stammering. Mrs. Merriam thought of it as Harriet's nervous voice, and it made her own voice even more precise.

"I see you're home," Mrs. Merriam said. "That is, I *heard* you."

Harriet looked down at her large feet, in heavy-soled oxfords. "I'm sorry I slammed the door," she said.

"Of course you are," Mrs. Merriam said. She leaned over

and selected a spool of thread from the sewing-box beside her on the floor. "You always are, afterward."

Harriet waited for a minute, politely, and then said, "Can I go on down to Helen's? They're waiting for me. I just wanted to tell you I was home."

"You *can* go to Helen's," Mrs. Merriam said. She heard Harriet's gusty sigh of relief, and added daintily, "but you *may* not."

"Why?"

Mrs. Merriam tightened her mouth over her sewing. "I think you know what you've done, Harriet."

"Mother," Harriet began, only what she finally said was, "M-m-m-mother," and she stopped helplessly.

"Please, Harriet," Mrs. Merriam said. "There's nothing to talk about. Go to your room."

"But—" Harriet began. Then she said, "Oh, Lord," and started heavily up the stairs.

"You might spend the time writing letters," her mother said, raising her voice slightly.

The word "letters" carried Harriet hastily up the stairs and into her room; if there had been a lock on the door she might have been able to lock herself in, but she slammed the door violently, and then walked miserably over to her desk, although she knew, had seen from the doorway, that it was open. The slant-top, which should have been securely locked, was dropped down to make the table surface, and Harriet's small papers and notebooks lay as she kept them, mercilessly neat, put back in the pigeonholes, perhaps even put back more carefully than Harriet, who loved them, ever did. Harriet went to the bed and looked under the pillow; the key was there, where it belonged. Harriet sat down heavily on the bed and said aloud, "What shall I do?" not because it was meaningful to her, or because she was concerned about what to do—she knew now, without question, the eventual series of acts to be forced from her—but because "What-shall-I-do?" seemed the formation of sounds most likely to apply to a situation like this.

From where she sat on the bed she could see out of the window which looked down on the corner of Pepper and Cortez;

Hallie Martin, eating what seemed to be a doughnut, was rounding the corner, apparently bound for Helen's. For a minute Harriet thought of calling to Hallie ("All is discovered"? "Burn the evidence"?), and then she said, "What shall I do?" again and got up and went over to the desk.

She put her hand lovingly on top of it; it had been a present from her father, who probably supposed that her mother had a key to it, from long knowledge of her mother. Harriet sat down in the desk chair and picked up the letter she had begun last night; her mother had set it open in the center of the desk, the only thing left out of place. It was a letter to George Martin, and it was written on shiny pink paper, and it began, "Dearest George." Helen set the style; it was the way love letters were written, she said, and sometimes Helen's letters to Johnny Desmond began, "Dearest dearest Johnny." Harriet had chosen George to write to because he was dull and unpopular and she felt vaguely that she had no right to aim any higher than the one boy no one else would have; if she understood this feeling at all, she thought of it as "George always liked *me* best."

Virginia Donald was writing to Art Roberts, and Mary Byrne was, cautiously, writing to her own brother. Hallie Martin carried the letters around, and Helen had written one for her to James Donald, who was seventeen and in third year high and the neighborhood hero. Hallie gave her letter to James Donald one evening when he came home at dinner time from football practice at the high school, and he read it while Hallie lurked excitedly on Helen's front porch; and when James tore the letter up and dropped it in the gutter Hallie sneaked down and got the pieces and took them home. "They *always* do that," Helen said wisely. "Men who don't care, they're callous."

Harriet looked down at the "Dearest George" on the pink paper, and read on, in her own writing, "Let's run away and get married. I love you and I want to—" The letter ended there, because Harriet had not been able to think of what she wanted to do with George; Helen's letters ended, "kiss you a thousand times," but Harriet could not bring herself to write such a thing, at least partly because the thought of kissing George Martin's dull face horrified her. She felt, although she had not confessed it to Helen, that she could possibly bear to kiss James Donald's face, but then Hallie had already written to him. Harriet tore the letter up slowly and threw it into the wastebasket. It was written, it had been read, she had no doubt that her mother would remember the words, and it was unpleasant to look at.

It was when she reached out for the other papers in the desk that she began to cry. She took down a notebook with "Poems" written on the front of it in pink and blue letters, and turned the pages slowly, reading and trying to pretend that she was her mother reading. The notebook labeled "Moods" she put aside unopened; it was dedicated "To my unknown hero," and perhaps if she did not read it now, her mother would not have read it earlier. There were more notebooks, one called "Me," which was the start of an autobiography; one named "Daydreams."

"Pat," Mrs. Byrne said softly, "you're not drinking your milk."

"I've got to hurry, Mother," Pat said. He put the books down on the table and picked up the milk to drink it standing.

Mrs. Byrne reached out one of her hands, chapped and red from much housework, and took the glass away from him. "That's not the way my boy does," she said. "Sit down, son."

Mary Byrne looked up from her crackers and milk. "For heaven's sake sit down or get out," she said. She was small and anemic and she had sinus trouble and she sniffled when she talked. Mr. and Mrs. Byrne both loved her dearly, but Pat was tall for his age and dark and almost handsome; both Pat and Mary were top of their classes in school, but Mary wore glasses and her hair straggled on her neck. "Golly," Mary said, "other people are in as much of a hurry as you are."

"I'm going to the library," Pat said. "Artie and me."

"You can drink your milk first," Mrs. Byrne said. "Mary, finish before you go out."

"What's for dinner?" Mary asked. She moved her chair to see what Mrs. Byrne was doing at the sink. Her brother poked her arm, and she turned.

Pat gestured with his head at his mother, her back toward them, and took the folded papers out of one of his books. "Yours," he mouthed at her.

Mary's letters were written on blue paper; she recognized them and picked them up, thinking from her brother's clandestine attitude that she might risk a knowing grin, but his eyes were looking away and his mouth was turned in disgust. Mary Byrne added another brick to her hatred for her brother and said, "Thanks." She put the letters in to the pocket of her dress and said, "'Bye, Mom," as she left the kitchen. Pat watched her go out the door into the front hall and then he said quietly, "Mother?"

"Pat darling," said his mother without turning around.

"Listen," Pat said quickly, "I don't want to be a tattletale, but you better stop Mary from writing letters to boys."

His mother turned, paring knife in her hand, and regarded him. "And what kind of letters is Mary writing to boys?"

Pat looked down at the table, at his hands moving nervously. "Letters," he said, and wriggled. "*You* know."

"And how do *you* know?" his mother said.

Pat's face was red, and his voice went more and more quickly. "All the girls are doing it. It's that Helen Williams. I just happened to see the letters."

"And what boys?"

Pat stood up and picked up his books, but he said, "That's the trouble. I don't know *what* other boys."

"I'll speak to Mary," his mother said. "But you mind your own business after this."

"But it's dirty," Pat said.

"I'm not worried," his mother said. "I want you to be a gentleman. A *real* gentleman. Don't go out without your jacket."

Pat hesitated and then said, "I didn't mean to tell on her."

"That's my fine fellow." His mother put down the knife and came over to kiss him. "Now don't get all interested in the library and forget to come home for dinner."

Mrs. Byrne had her potatoes pared and set on top of the stove, and the string beans cut and ready to start, when the phone rang. Drying her hands on her apron, Mrs. Byrne went into the hall and picked up the phone.

"Hello?" she said, and the telephone said steadily, "Hello, this is Josephine Merriam. Harriet's mother."

"Of course, Mrs. Merriam." Mrs. Byrne bowed politely to Mrs. Merriam at least once a day. "How are you?"

"I am very much disturbed, Mrs. Byrne, and I think you ought to know the facts immediately, which is why I called. Our daughters have been doing some rather indiscreet things."

"Yes?" said Mrs. Byrne.

"This morning," Mrs. Merriam went on, "I happened to discover a letter my daughter had written to one of the neighborhood boys. It was a childish," and Mrs. Merriam laughed shortly, "but improper letter. She tells me that the other girls in the neighborhood have been writing the same kind of letters."

"Mary?" Mrs. Byrne said.

"Mary indeed," said Mrs. Merriam. "And Virginia Donald, and of course, the source of it all, Helen Williams. I don't know, naturally, whose *fault* it is," she said lingeringly, "but of course I think the girls should be spoken to."

"Of course," Mrs. Byrne said. "I'll speak to Mary, of course."

"Harriet also tells me," Mrs. Merriam said, "that your son has been *getting* letters."

"Who from?" Mrs. Byrne's voice was suddenly flat.

"I think *he's* the person to tell you *that*," Mrs. Merriam said. "I'm sorry, Mrs. Byrne, to be the one to tell you."

"You couldn't do anything else," Mrs. Byrne said.

"After all, my own daughter is in it too," Mrs. Merriam said.

"I'll speak to Mary," Mrs. Byrne said.

Marilyn Perlman came into the house quickly, opening the front door with her key. She put her books down on the hall table and read the note sitting there: "Dear, have gone to Mrs. White's, back about five. If anyone calls take message. Love,

Mother." Marilyn wondered vaguely why her mother always ended even the slightest notes formally; her father had once told her solemnly that the notes left for the milkman always ended, "Yrs. sincerely, R. Perlman."

The Perlmans' home was probably the wealthiest-looking on the block, although presumably the Desmonds had more money than the Perlmans, and Mrs. Merriam was vaguely noted for her "taste." The Perlmans' living-room was pale green and beige, and Mr. Perlman liked to see a wood fire in the fireplace, although the Donalds had theirs stacked with imitation logs, and the Byrnes had a grate with a red light behind it. When Marilyn came into her living-room she was able to take a book from a bookcase; it was a limp-leather bound volume of Thackeray, but Harriet Merriam, after all, spent Saturday morning dusting the photograph album which lay on a side table in the Merriams' living-room, and the first secular book in the Byrne house was Pat's copy of *Robinson Crusoe*.

Marilyn was reading through Thackeray for words; from *Vanity Fair* she had gleaned "adorable" and "fearsome" and "horrid"; from *The Virginian* she already had half a dozen. Her word for today was "storied"; it had turned up in English class in school, and Marilyn had written it on the margin of her English book, for copying later.

With the Thackeray under her arm, Marilyn went into the kitchen and opened a bottle of coke, and took the bottle and the book out to the front porch. The Perlmans' porch was heavily screened by vines, and in the glider Marilyn was hidden and secure to watch the movement of people up and down the block. She knew some of the people very well; the Ransom-Joneses across the street, and Harriet Merriam, toward whom she felt a respectful sympathy, and James Donald, whom she loved desperately. The Perlmans were far down the block from the Desmonds and Helen Williams, but Helen Williams was a terror to Marilyn and young Mrs. Desmond an ogress. Mrs. Desmond cut Mrs. Perlman on the street, almost certainly not intentionally, but Helen Williams followed Marilyn around the schoolyard, into the schoolroom, and up and down the halls. At home, Marilyn rarely went past the center of the block; to go below the Donald house meant probably meeting Helen. One day, at the noon recess, Helen and a group of friends had found Marilyn reading in an empty classroom and sat down around her, and Helen said, "Perlman, we've been looking for you." (Thinking about it, on her own front porch behind the vines, thinking as she did almost daily, Marilyn remembered the sudden sickness, looking up from her book to see Helen and, cruelly, Harriet Merriam.) "We've been wondering," Helen said, looking at the other girls, who laughed, even Harriet, "we've been wondering about Christmas."

"What about it?" When Marilyn remembered herself in this scene, she saw herself as small and frightened and ugly; Harriet, on the other hand, remembered herself as dirty and fat and overbearing; and perhaps Helen Williams, if she thought of it, remembered *herself* as friendly and teasing.

"Well," Helen said elaborately, "in about ten months it's going to be Christmas again, and you know around here at Christmas on the last day of school all the kids give each other presents." The story had not been planned; so much might be Harriet's defense; the girls listened to Helen with smiles and some wonder. "And we thought," Helen went on, watching first Marilyn and then the other girls, "that maybe when we all got together to draw names for the Christmas presents you maybe would think it was nicer of us just not to put your name in. So you won't be embarrassed."

For so long a story it had very little point; Harriet was confused and looked at Helen, frowning. Marilyn put both hands down on the open pages of her book and looked around at Helen and at Harriet frowning and at the other girls, one of whom was fidgeting toward the door, and said, "I don't know why you want to do *this*."

Helen laughed. "Maybe you have two Christmases," she said. She turned around to the other girls, to Harriet, and said, "Marilyn has *two* Christmases. One of her own and one she gets in on with us."

"I don't get it," one of the girls said, and the one edging toward the door said, "Come *on*."

"Marilyn knows what I mean," Helen said.

It was the feeling of having them all around her that bothered Marilyn; they were all together, and when one of them left they would all go, even Harriet. They were all looking at Marilyn at once, and she could only look at one of them at a time. She looked at Harriet and said, "If you're through, I can go back to my book. I was studying."

"I'll tell you all about it," Helen said. She stood up and gathered the other girls and led them out. Perhaps she stopped them outside the door, in a little group in the hall, perhaps she wrote it in a note and sent it around the schoolroom, perhaps it was nothing at all, but Marilyn was afraid of her, and when she wanted someone to die it was always Helen Williams.

She finished her coke and read her Thackeray, and went inside with the book and the empty bottle at half-past four. She put the book back in the bookcase and the empty bottle on the back porch, and went upstairs to her own room, which was the prettiest place she knew, and out of her top dresser drawer she took her notebook and sat down on the bed with it. She opened it to the first blank page, and "storied," she wrote, and "grisly."

Mrs. Roberts was a big woman fortunate enough to be married to a big man, and when Mr. and Mrs. Roberts sat down at either end of their dinner table, the dining-room seemed full and the table setting dwarfed. Jamie Roberts, their younger son, showed signs already of continuing the family tradition: he was broad-shouldered and long-legged, at ten, and looked so emphatically like his father that Mrs. Roberts frequently addressed all her remarks to him when she was quarreling with her husband.

Artie, the older boy (and Mrs. Roberts supposed always that it was because she had never really wanted Artie and then only kept on to have Jamie because Artie was such a disappointment) looked like Mrs. Roberts's brothers and uncles, small and thin and pale, with colorless hair and eyes and the mouth that in Mrs. Roberts's Uncle Frank was always half-open. It was difficult for anyone as hearty as Mrs. Roberts to see a puny son at her dinner table and not be angry; Artie was already fourteen years old, and Mrs. Roberts honestly despaired of making a man of him. She and Mr. Roberts both spoke to him gently, when they remembered, because secretly they were both a little afraid that a boy who read books instead of playing baseball might someday turn on them with a dreadful sure knowledge that would cut away their confidence and their muscles and leave them insecure and frightened, their stronger son as weak as they.

"*Eat*, Artie," Mrs. Roberts said. "You've got to get some meat on you."

"Little exercise," Mr. Roberts said. He put down his butter knife and looked at his older son appraisingly. "If you'd get outdoors more and get a little exercise, you wouldn't look like a bag of bones."

"I eat," Artie said defensively to his plate.

"Artie would rather play with the girls," Mrs. Roberts said jovially. "What's this I hear about you and the girls, Artie?"

"Artie?" Mr. Roberts said.

Jamie looked up with his mouth full, turning his head around the table to hear every word. "Artie?" he said thickly.

"Our son," Mrs. Roberts said formally down the table to her husband, "has been getting love letters from some young lady."

"Good for you," Mr. Roberts said. He laughed and pointed his finger at Artie. "Make them chase you," he said.

Artie knew that across the table his brother's broad face was shining with unbelieving delight. "That silly stuff," Artie said inadequately. He felt himself blushing, his face hot and horrible, and there was a sudden gleeful shout of laughter from his mother and father and brother.

"Look at him," Jamie howled. "Look at Artie!"

"Why, Artie," his father said. "Kiss and tell?"

When the laughter died down Mrs. Roberts said with apparently meaningless amiability, "Well, just the same it's nice to see the *girls* doing the chasing for a change."

"John," Mr. Desmond said soberly, "your mother has asked me to speak to you." He had taken Johnny into a corner of the living-room where no one usually sat, in a spirit of manly formality. Johnny sat on a stiff chair, looking his father in the eye, his expression all attention. Mr. Desmond, who found the experience completely enjoyable, went on gravely, "It's a serious responsibility, John. The responsibility of a father talking like this to his son. And you know you *are* truly my son." Mr. Desmond laid his hand on his son's knee for a minute, and found his own eyes almost tearful. "A *man*, John," Mr. Desmond said, "must never take admiration lightly, whether it comes from a silly young girl, or a maturer young lady, or even from a mother or sister or aunt. It is the duty of a *gentleman*, John, to regard all this admiration as a compliment. It *is* a compliment, John," Mr. Desmond went on very earnestly, "in the very deepest sense of the word. I'm *proud* to know that my son is admired. We must never dismiss the emotions natural to the feminine heart—" Mr. Desmond stopped to chuckle paternally, and lost the thread of his sentence, so he began again, "You'll find, as you grow older, John, that many women will feel the same way, and you must never dismiss—"

Helen Williams grabbed her little sister by the hair and shook her wildly back and forth. "Did you tell?" she said. "Did you go and tell, you bad, bad girl?"

Mildred stared wild-eyed. "Grandma," she whispered.

"*She* can't hear you," Helen said. She shook her sister again. "*No one* can hear you. You tell me now, did you tell on me?"

"Grandma," Mildred whispered again. "Mommy."

Disgusted, Helen let go of her sister and looked down on her, with her hands on her hips. "You just listen to me," she said in her normal voice, "if you ever tell on me again, if you ever tell anything, I'll cut out your tongue and I'll slice off all your fingers and I'll cut a big hole in your stomach with a carving knife and I'll hit you with a hatchet."

"Look," Pat Byrne said viciously to his sister, "You cut it out, do you understand?"

"Cut what out?" Mary Byrne said innocently.

Pat looked around to make sure that his father was still

reading his paper in the living-room and that the kitchen sounds were going on peacefully where his mother was finishing up the dishes. Pat and Mary were in the hall, and because Pat spoke almost in a whisper Mary kept her voice quiet. "You just cut it out," Pat said.

"Pat," Mr. Byrne called harshly from the living-room, "Mary! No secrets whispered around this house!"

"I don't know what you're talking about," Mary said. She put out her lower lip and turned her back to walk away, but Pat pushed her shoulder and she turned around, her face ready to call her mother.

"You cut out all this dirty stuff," Pat said. He put his face close to his sister's and said again almost helplessly, "You just *cut it out*, that's all."

"You're crazy," Mary said. "I didn't do anything."

"I don't want any more of those dirty letters," Pat said. "I don't care what happens, don't *you* write any more to *me*."

Hallie Martin walked slowly down the block, scuffing the loose sole of her shoe through the pink flowers, cautiously experimenting with a side tooth that might very well be coming out. She stopped for a few minutes, open-mouthed, across the street from the Desmond house, watching little Caroline moving around the flowers. Caroline was little and delicate and clean, and Hallie was lean and dirty and wet-faced, and after a minute Hallie moved on down the block without crossing the street.

Hallie, who was nine years old, Jamie Roberts, who was ten, and Mildred Williams, who was seven, were the youngest children around except for Caroline; they were an in-between generation, awed and overruled by the thirteen- and fourteen-year-olds, expecting in their turn a younger generation to bully and educate. If Hallie had crossed the street and stood outside the Desmond yard, Mrs. Desmond would have come out on the side porch to sit quietly until Hallie was gone away; if Hallie stayed Mrs. Desmond would finally take Caroline indoors.

"Old Caroline," Hallie said to herself as she went down

toward Helen's, where the older girls would be, "old Caroline wets her pants."

At Helen's house you didn't bother to ring the bell or call Helen outside; you opened the door and went in, walking around inside the house until you found whomever you were looking for. Mrs. Parnatt, whom the children called Old Lady Parrot, and who was Helen's grandmother, spent most of the day in a back room with the door locked; when she came out to the bathroom or to the kitchen to make herself coffee they saw an old woman with a tiny head and shoulders and huge from the waist down; an aged Pekinese following her in and out of her room. The dog's name was Lotus, and when the girls were in Helen's room next to her grandmother's, they could hear the old lady crying over the dog, or sometimes stamping around the room and screaming because the dog had fouled the rug.

"That dog snaps," Helen was fond of saying to her friends. "Some day she's going to hit him with a chair or something and he's going to bite her hand off."

When Harriet Merriam came to the house—the other girls thought this was funny and tormented her with it—she would open the door a crack, peering down the long dark hall inside to see if the grandmother's door were open. If the door were open that meant that Lotus was abroad, and Harriet would wait outside. "I don't want him to snap at *me*," she said reasonably.

"If he snapped at *me* I'd kick him in the head and kill him," Hallie said wisely. "That's how you kill dogs anyway, kick them in the head."

"You just kick my grandmother's dog," Helen said. She laughed. "My *grandmother* would bite you."

In Helen's room at the back of the house were old fashion magazines and pictures of movie stars and collections of lace and ribbons the girls used to dress up in; Helen's mother worked in the city, and she bought Helen neat young girl's clothes which Helen decorated with bows or lace collars or five-and-ten jewelry and wore to school. Sometimes the girls at Helen's house would go into the dark front room where Helen's mother sat alone in the evenings, and play records on the phonograph and dance together. Once or twice they brought George Martin in to dance with them, although he was clumsy and had to be bribed with penny candy before he would stand up patiently for a minute or two and walk around the floor holding one of the girls.

"When I go live with my *father*," Helen said frequently, "I've got to know how to dance and how to dress pretty, because my father is going to take me out a lot and we're going to travel and everything."

"Where is your father?" someone, probably Harriet, would ask, and perhaps Virginia Donald would add respectfully, "You're terribly lucky."

"My father goes everywhere," Helen said. "Maybe Paris, or New York. Paris is where they have men who kiss your hands." She giggled, and it made the other girls giggle too. With a lace shawl over her head, Helen stood up and curtseyed, holding out her hand. "Why, Mr. Paris," she said in a high voice, "you mean you want to kiss *my* hand?"

Hallie stood in back of her, shouting, "Why, Mr. Johnny Desmond, you mean you want to kiss *my* hand?"

And Helen said seriously, "Boy, I'm not going to stay here much longer. I'm going to find my father pretty soon now."

The Williams family was moving soon; Mrs. Williams had mentioned to Miss Fielding, who was the only person out-doors in the very early morning when Mrs. Williams left to catch her bus to the city, that it was too hard to try to get back and forth every day, and she wanted to put the girls into a city school. Miss Fielding told Mrs. Desmond, who said timidly that perhaps it was just as well. Little Mildred Williams, Mrs. Desmond said, was entirely too sweet and kind to be away from her mother all the time, and Mrs. Desmond added, with a stronger note to her voice, that perhaps the grandmother (out of respect for Miss Fielding's age Mrs. Desmond did not say "that almost bedridden old lady," as she did later to Mr. Desmond) was not quite—Mrs. Desmond lifted her hand gently—not *quite* the person to deal with dear little Helen.

The word that dear little Helen had for Mrs. Desmond was "horse's behind." "Thinks she owns the world," Helen said.

Helen's little sister Mildred came home the last day of school
and went immediately out into the back yard, where for the
last month or so she had been building an elaborate playhouse,
partly underground, dug out with a spoon, and partly put
together with pieces of board salvaged from vacant lots and
other back yards. The playhouse was just big enough for Mildred to crawl in and lie down, and her dolls were in there and
what pillows and dishes she could take from her own house.
"It's for my mommy and me," she told Mr. Donald over the
fence. "When Helen and Gram go away my mommy and me
will live here."

The afternoon that Harriet's mother found out about the letters, Hallie found Helen alone in the living-room, dancing solemnly around to "Missouri Waltz" on the phonograph. Hallie
fell into line behind Helen, imitating her and saying, "Bet when
you find your father you'll be the best dancer there."

"I'll dance all day long," Helen said. "I'll never stop dancing
till I'm hungry and then I'll eat ice cream and chicken and
chocolate creams."

"I wish I could go with you," Hallie said.

Helen stopped dancing and fell down on the couch. Hallie
lifted the needle off the record and set it aside. She came over
and sat down next to Helen and said, "Listen, Willie, can't I
go with you?"

"You want to know something?" Helen said dreamily.

Hallie nodded, leaning forward.

"Don't tell," Helen said, and Hallie nodded again. Helen
looked around sharply, and Hallie crossed her finger over her
heart, and Helen said impatiently, "Don't do that, baby. Swear
on your honor."

"I swear on my honor," Hallie said obediently.

"Well," Helen said, "you know where I was last night?"

Hallie shook her head, her mouth a little open.

Helen laughed excitedly. "Well," she said, "I went out for a
walk and I went over down by the stores."

"Why?"

"I don't know," Helen said vaguely, "I just *felt* like going
that way. And you know this guy, the one in the gas station,

the one we stopped and kidded with once?" She waited while Hallie nodded again, and then went on, "Well, he was there and we got to talking and he says he'll take me to the city some night and we'll go somewhere and dance."

"*I* don't know, sweetie," Dinah Ransom-Jones said to her sister, "I really don't know, you have such a *sense* of flowers."

"But it's *your* garden, dear," her sister said gently. "You'll be here a good deal longer than I will."

"Brad always says the flowers look prettier when you do them," Mrs. Ransom-Jones said.

"But I won't do them always," her sister said. "He loves the way you plan them."

"Sweetie," Dinah said, "you've just *got* to decide. Nothing *ever* goes well around here unless you help. You know that."

"Well." Her sister hesitated. "Over *there*, then." She pointed to a far corner of the garden, near the street hedge.

"Really?" Mrs. Ransom-Jones said. "You really think *there*?"

"Not if you have a better place," her sister said.

"Of course not," Mrs. Ransom-Jones said. She picked up the gardening basket and the bag of bulbs. "Don't you lean over," she said, "I don't want you overtiring yourself."

"It doesn't matter, really," her sister said.

Mrs. Ransom-Jones moved with determination, and her sister said, quickly, "Not *that* way, dear. By the street hedge."

"Oh." Mrs. Ransom-Jones stopped and looked around. "I thought you said over *here*," she said.

"Well, I *did* say by the street hedge," her sister said, "but if you have a place you like better. . . ."

"Of *course* not, sweetie," Mrs. Ransom-Jones said. She started off again toward the corner of the garden. "Brad will think this is wonderful," she said. "That's just the spot for shy flowers."

"He loves everything you do," her sister said, following.

It was evening, and the kids were all outside; Harriet could see them from her bedroom window, Miss Fielding could see them from her chair on the porch, Marilyn Perlman could see them from the living-room window, past her father's head bent over papers at the desk. Early evening and twilight were always longer on Pepper Street than anywhere else; dinners were early up and down the block so the children could play longer; even Miss Fielding, who did not play, felt uncomfortable sitting down alone to her dinner later than anyone else, hearing the noise of dishes being washed at the Merriams'. Mrs. Perlman served dinner early because Marilyn might want to play with the other children.

They played tag and hide-and-seek and long involved games with a line across the street from curb to curb and elaborate systems of bases and penalties. Mr. Desmond, who walked out for the evening air, met Mr. Roberts halfway down the block, and together they stood on the sidewalk and watched the game.

"If those young animals could put half that creative ability into their school work," Mr. Desmond commented drily.

"Healthy kids," Mr. Roberts said. "Good to see."

They stood quietly in the half-darkness, smiling vaguely. Past them their own children and the children of their neighbors moved swiftly back and forth, following some ancient ritual of capture and pursuit, dance steps regulated as far as the placing of the feet. With a wild howl little Jamie Roberts made a capture in the gutter near his father, and Mr. Roberts took the pipe out of his mouth to say, "Good boy, Jamie." He lifted his eyes to where, across the street, his older son sat with Pat Byrne on the Donalds' lawn. They were half-watching the game, half-talking. Mr. Desmond followed his attention, and said quietly, "That's a very good boy, that Art of yours. Bright kid."

Mr. Roberts sighed and turned to watch Jamie shrieking up the street.

"I guess just anywhere where you could find a job," Art Roberts was saying. "Anywhere not here."

"They send you right back," Pat Byrne said. "You can't get a job because you're too young, and they send you right back."

"In another year, maybe," Art said. "I could say I was eighteen."

"They take you in the navy at sixteen," Pat said, "I *think*."

Hallie cornered Helen for a minute, away from the glow of the street light, and said insistently, "Are you going to take someone? A friend?"

"I don't know what you're talking about," Helen said, turning away.

"Tell me," Hallie said insistently. "You said to him you'd take a friend?"

Helen looked down on the top of Hallie's head. "I said I'd take a *friend* with me, not a dirty little baby."

James Donald came out of his house, spoke to Art Roberts and Pat Byrne on his way down to the sidewalk. He was all dressed up, and when Mr. Roberts and Mr. Desmond saw him they smiled at one another and waved across the street to him. He stood uncertainly for a minute and then crossed over to where they stood and said, "Evening, Mr. Desmond, Mr. Roberts."

"How're you?" Mr. Desmond said. "And your family?"

"Dad's not well again." James turned, hands in his pockets, and surveyed the game as though he belonged with Mr. Desmond and Mr. Roberts instead of with the kids in the street.

"Got a date?" Mr. Roberts said cheerfully.

James moved nervously, and swallowed. "Thought I'd go out for a while."

"Young men," Mr. Roberts said, and he and Mr. Desmond laughed.

James straightened his shoulders and laughed with them.

"Have a fine time, son," Mr. Roberts said, and began to walk on. "Good night," he said over his shoulder, and James and Mr. Desmond both said, "Good night."

"Come in and see me some evening," Mr. Desmond said to James. He smiled tolerantly and added, "Sometime when you're not so busy."

"Thank you," James said awkwardly, "I'd like to."

"Still set on architecture?" Mr. Desmond asked.

"Guess so," James said.

Mr. Desmond put his hand on James's shoulder for a minute before he turned away. "Good fellow," he said. "You come in and see me."

"I will," James said. He watched Mr. Desmond go down the street, and then he looked ostentatiously at his watch and began to walk in the other direction, proudly aware that the children in the street were watching him over their game. He had not gone as far as the Perlmans' house when he heard footsteps behind him and Helen Williams caught up with him.

"Hey, James Donald," she was yelling.

He turned with dignity and waited, his head held back and his arms folded across his chest in a manner strongly reminiscent of Mr. Desmond. "You running away from me?" Helen asked.

"You're very much mistaken," James said.

Helen looked up at him from under her eyelashes. She was very blond and wore her hair in a long straight bob, and when she bent her head down her hair fell softly along her cheeks. "You never came over to see me at my house like you said you would," she said.

"I don't have much time any more to play with the kids," James said.

Helen put out her lower lip; all her gestures were very much exaggerated because she practised them alone in front of a mirror. "I wouldn't play with the kids, either," she said meaningly, "if there was anything else to do."

James looked at his watch again. "Well," he said.

"Where you going?" Helen demanded.

"I am going," James said elaborately, "to an orchestra rehearsal at the high school. Now are you happy?"

"Bet you got a girl there," Helen said to his back, and when she saw his shoulders tighten she said more loudly, "You got a girl at school, James has got a girl."

When he was past hearing her she turned and went back to the game still going on. Tod Donald ran up to her and said loudly, "We missed you, Willie, you don't want to talk to my old brother."

"Let me alone," Helen said. "I'm going home."

"I suppose I should be used to this by *now*," Mrs. Merriam said. She took out her clean handkerchief and put the damp one down on the table next to her. "After all," she said, "I've been your wife for eighteen years, Harry, and I think by now I deserve a little consideration. Every sort of humiliation and insult. . . ." With a wail she lifted the clean handkerchief and began to cry again.

"Oh, Mother," Harriet said irritably, and her father began heavily, "Josie, honey."

"Don't *call* me that," Mrs. Merriam almost screamed. Harriet looked at her father, but he turned his face away and sighed.

"I try to make my daughter into a good decent girl in spite of—" Mrs. Merriam sobbed, "—in spite of everything, and I work all day and I worry about money and try to make a good decent home for my husband and now my only daughter turns out to be—"

"Josephine," Mr. Merriam said strongly. "Harriet, go upstairs again."

Harriet went upstairs away from her mother's sorry voice. Her desk was unlocked; instead of eating dinner, she and her mother had stood religiously by the furnace and put Harriet's diaries and letters and notebooks into the fire one by one, while solid Harry Merriam sat eating lamb chops and boiled potatoes upstairs alone. "I don't know what it's all about," he said to Harriet and his wife when they came upstairs. "Seems like a man ought to be able to come home after working all day and not hear people crying all the time. Seems like a man has a right to have a quiet home."

Alone in her room again Harriet sat down by the window. Outside, the eucalyptus trees in the first rich darkness were quiet and infinitely delicate, a rare leaf moving softly against the others. Harriet was accustomed to thinking of them as lace against the night sky; on windy nights they were crazy, pulling like wild things against the earth. Tonight, in their patterned peacefulness, Harriet rested her head somehow against them and stopped thinking about her mother. Lovely, lovely things, she thought, and tried to imagine herself sinking into them far beyond the surface, so far away that nothing could ever bring her back.

"Harriet," her mother said from the foot of the stairs. Her voice was steady. "Harriet, dear, come downstairs."

Harriet came down the stairs, hitting every step violently with her great shoes. Her mother waited at the bottom, newly powdered and very tall and gracious. "Dear," she said, "I want to apologize."

In the living-room her father was reading the paper. His face was very tired and his mouth stiff, but when Harriet came in with her mother's arm around her he looked up and said, "Now everyone's happy," and went back to his paper.

"Your father," Mrs. Merriam said meekly, "has made me feel that I have been too severe with you today. I was very much upset, of course."

"Oh, Mother," Harriet said. Now that her mother was calm Harriet felt at last like crying. She loved her mother again, as one should love a mother, tenderly and affectionately. She put her arm around her mother and kissed her. "I'm sorry," she said.

Her mother patted her shoulder. "We'll spend more time together from now on. Reading, and sewing. Would you like to learn to cook, really *cook*?" she added brightly.

Harriet nodded, and her mother laughed deprecatingly. "We can write together, too. I used to write poetry, Harriet, not very *well*, of course, but that's probably where you get it."

Warmly Harriet smiled at her mother, and thought how pleasant it always was after these scenes, how for a little while the three of them would live together in vast amiability.

"You'll show your mother everything you write, of course," her father said.

"Everything," Harriet said earnestly. The room was so quiet, so friendly.

"And we won't see that Helen Williams any more," her mother said. "Now that there's no more school, there's no need for my girl to run around with that sort of person."

"She's not going to be here much longer, anyway," Harriet said. "She's going to live with her father."

Mrs. Merriam raised her eyebrows delicately and said, looking obliquely at her husband, "And perhaps next year, some really *nice* private school."

There was a long silence, and then Mrs. Merriam sighed and went on, "I'm not going to punish you any more, Harriet. As I said, I feel that some of this is my fault."

"I'm really sorry," Harriet said. She put her head on her mother's shoulder, and her mother touched her hair lightly.

"I'll try to make it up to you, dear," Mrs. Merriam said.

"I do not know why," Mrs. Roberts said with a deadly level voice, "I really do not know why a grown man is not capable of conducting his affairs so that his women know their places."

"I don't know anything about this 'women' business," Mr. Roberts said sullenly.

"Arthur took the message," Mrs. Roberts went on. "*Arthur.* Someone named Jeanie." She said "Jeanie" with a great casual gentleness, as though the name itself were precious to her.

"Arthur wouldn't know," Mr. Roberts said. "Why don't you mind your own business?"

"It is my business." Mrs. Roberts stopped and said, "Be quiet. Here come the children."

Artie and Jamie hurried in, taking off jackets as they came. Mrs. Roberts called Jamie over to her and pushed his hair back out of his eyes. "Both boys look mostly like you," she said reproachfully to her husband.

"Why weren't you playing with the other fellows tonight?" Mr. Roberts asked Artie.

"Talking to Pat." Artie had his foot on the bottom step, his hand on the stair rail. He waited.

"You might come in and talk to your mother and father once in a while," his father said.

"I was just going upstairs to read." Artie came reluctantly into the living-room and sat tentatively on the piano bench.

"If we'd been going to a movie you'd be down here fast enough," his father said.

"Mike," Mrs. Roberts said.

Artie looked at Mr. Roberts solemnly. "There was a phone call for you," he said. "Some dame wanted you."

"Bedtime, darling," Mrs. Roberts said to Jamie. "Artie, you may go upstairs now. Turn off your light in half an hour."

She went to the foot of the stairs with both boys. "I'll be up to kiss you good night," she said. She watched them up the stairs, and then turned back to her husband.

CHAPTER TWO

Nobody ever noticed Tod Donald very much. He was a quiet boy who had spent nearly thirteen years trying hard to be moderately good at what his older brother James was able to do naturally and effortlessly. James was tall and pleasant-looking; Tod might be tall some day, but at thirteen he wore a perpetual nervous smile which deepened occasionally into apprehensive trembling, and he was what his brother James called "a bad sport." Tod had learned, painfully, to ride a bicycle and play football and rollerskate; no one had ever taught him anything; but when Tod sat on his front steps or walked off to school or joined in a game or brought out his bicycle, no one waited for him or asked him to wait. No one ever chose him for a side in a game; he was always allowed to merge himself undesired into one team or another, never allowed to bat in the baseball game.

Perhaps if Tod's father had been more interested in his children he might have favored Tod beyond anything he could feel for either James or Virginia, but Stephen Donald (perhaps, once, he had been very much like Tod, never like James) had no pity to waste on anything so distant as his youngest child. There was no recognition, now, in any look Stephen Donald gave the world; he had absorbed too much disappointment already to jeopardize himself needlessly for his children.

James Donald privately regarded his younger brother as an imperfect copy of himself, and was as irritated by Tod as he might have been by any cruel, pointed parody. Much of James's athletic sense of good and evil was invested in Tod; Tod was inefficient and a bad sport, which was evil; he was smaller, and could not be struck, which was a delineation of good.

Consequently, James never required himself to include any form of evil in his own personality; such things belonged naturally to Tod, and were accepted numbly by Tod as his portion.

Much more, however, of Tod's lack of independent existence was due to his sister Virginia, who was a year older than Tod and his contemporary in a narrower sense than James—she played with the same children, and she hated Tod as she hated everyone upon whom it was not necessary to intrude her ingratiating personality. Tod was used to having his sister ignore him before the other children, and to hearing her say, "Don't let Toddie play, he does *everything* wrong."

The other children followed Virginia's example, because she was tacitly assumed to know, being Tod's sister. If Virginia had called Tod names, or refused to play with him, he would have gained prestige as a participant in a family fight, but when she seemed to believe sincerely that he had never wholly existed, he was lost. If he had been able to do any single thing better than either his brother or sister, he might have won some small place in the neighborhood hierarchy, or perhaps even in school; as long as he was the patient, desperately-clinging minority of the family, he had to be content with the opinion his family were known to have of him.

However, one day during the early summer he came close to winning a foothold. The older children were lying in the heat on the Donalds' front lawn, the only spot where Tod could rightfully assume a position anywhere near the heart of the circle. Helen Williams was holding forth on her father; she had just sent her baby sister home crying, and she was saying, "And when I go to live with my father, Mildred will have to be in a nunnery."

"What's wrong with a nunnery?" demanded Mary Byrne. She looked for her brother, her support on all theological questions, but he was in the street playing catch with George Martin. "Why do you say a nunnery like it was a punishment sort of?"

"A nunnery," Helen explained patiently, "is a place where

they put you and you never get out as long as you live. And sometimes they starve you," she added convincingly.

"That isn't true at all," Mary said with the conviction of inside information.

Helen turned the corners of her mouth down and looked around at her audience. "Let's hear *you* say what a nunnery is."

"It isn't like that at all," Mary said. "I bet your sister would like it in a nunnery even."

"Where they starve you?" Helen said. "Not Mildred, not Mildred at all. She eats like a pig."

"I eat like a pig too," Virginia Donald said dreamily. "I ate almost a whole apple pie once. You should have seen me eat a whole apple pie."

Tod was on his own front lawn. "I ate a whole mince pie once," he said, giggling.

According to neighborhood ethics, there was only one person who could lead the attack on Tod on his own land. His sister turned slowly to look at him and then back to the other children. "He never does anything really," she said.

"You never did it," Helen said. "Your sister says so."

"I did so," Tod began weakly, but Mary Byrne said, "I don't believe you could eat even one piece of mince pie."

"Even a piece as big as a ant," Hallie Martin said.

Having nine-year-old Hallie join in against him was the lowest indignity. Tod stood up, said, "Guess I'll get in the ball game," and walked down to the street while his sister said, "Tell more about nunneries, Willie."

Tod stood for a few minutes waiting to be asked to play ball, but neither George nor Pat offered to include him. As an indication that he would play if asked, Tod picked up a handful of stones from the gravel driveway and began tossing them into the bushes. After a minute he tossed one at George's foot and laughed weakly when George said, "Cut it out, Toddie."

He threw another so that it landed about a foot from George, and George looked at him crossly and hesitated for a minute before throwing the ball, as though debating whether or not to walk over and give Tod a lesson in interference. When he decided against it and went back to the game, Tod was afraid to throw any more pebbles in that direction and faced directly around to throw at the girls. He was possessed of as strong a desire for punishment as he had ever achieved, but he wanted more for his penalties than tapping George Martin on the ankles with a pebble. He threw a pebble at his sister and hit her in the arm, and she said, "Hey," and looked around; if it had been any of the other boys who threw it she would have been in a fantastic exaggerated rage and would have stood up, most likely, and found rocks of her own, but she only said, "Oh, run *along*, will you, Toddie?"

Tod threw his next pebble at Hallie Martin because she had spoken up against him, but he missed her and she laughed at him.

"Toddie," Virginia said sharply, "if you don't cut it out you can just go and stay in the house."

His sister had no right to give him orders, particularly not in a tone indicating that she expected them to be obeyed. Possessed by a sort of frenzy, Tod threw a handful of pebbles together, as hard as he could, into the group of girls on the lawn, and Mary Byrne howled and fell over backward, her hands over her face.

"Tod Donald," Virginia shouted, "I'll tell Mother on you!"

It was glory of a sort, and Tod ran up to Mary and stood next to her while she lay on the ground crying. "I'm sorry, Mary," he said. "I'm *awfully* sorry."

Pat Byrne pushed him aside and said impatiently, "What's the matter now?" and Helen Williams said, "Tod put Mary's eye out with a rock, that's all," and Hallie began to wail, and someone went running for Mary's mother, and Pat said, "*Toddie* did?" and George Martin said, "Golly," over and over again.

Mrs. Byrne came running across the street, and the children stood silently while she knelt down beside Mary on the grass and pulled Mary's hands away from her face. Tod, wondering vaguely what happened to people who put other people's eyes out with rocks, said, "I'm sorry," again, and Mrs. Byrne let her hands drop in relief and said, "She's got a little scratch on her cheek; she's no more hurt than a fly."

"Someone was throwing rocks, and she got in the way," Pat said.

"You children shouldn't be throwing rocks," Mrs. Byrne said, standing up. Mary sat up and wiped the tears off her face. "You'd think she'd been killed."

She started back across the street, and Pat said, "Come on, George," and they went back to their ball game. "I knew she wasn't much hurt," Pat said, "when I heard how she was hollering."

"I'm certainly glad you weren't really hurt," Virginia said to Mary.

"I'm sorry, Mary," Tod said.

She looked up at him, surprised. "That's all right, Toddie," she said. "You didn't mean to do it."

"What were you aiming at?" Virginia asked cruelly. "A window?"

"I only wish," Mrs. Roberts said crossly, "that the summer was over and school was starting again. Sometimes I think—" Her voice trailed off as she leaned over her workbox to choose a thread.

"I don't know," Mrs. Desmond said gently.

"Well, *Caroline*," Mrs. Merriam said. She looked sweetly down at Caroline, who sat on a small stool between Mrs. Merriam and her mother, absorbed in a collection of bright scraps of ribbon she was cutting into pieces. "Caroline is simply an angel."

"She loves to come here," Mrs. Desmond said to Mrs. Merriam. "You treat her as though she were grown-up."

"No need for *you* to worry about school for a while," Mrs. Roberts said.

Mrs. Desmond laughed and let her embroidery lie on her lap. "I don't know what I'll *do* when Caroline goes to school," she said. Mrs. Desmond always did embroidery while Mrs. Roberts and Mrs. Merriam darned socks and mended torn sweaters; it would have been incongruous for Mrs. Desmond, with her small delicate hands always so near Caroline's blond head, and her pale face so like Caroline's, to sit with great socks or spools of darning cotton on her lap. Mrs. Desmond brought her sewing in a lacquer box, and Caroline had a miniature lacquer box filled with her bright ribbons. Mrs. Roberts and Mrs. Merriam had no objection to seeing their own sufficiently ladylike hands dealing competently with heavy mending, but either of them would have been faintly surprised at Mrs. Desmond's doing it; it was an unexplained aristocratic principle.

"Caroline is just an angel," Mrs. Merriam repeated. "Aren't you, darling?" Caroline looked up gravely, and Mrs. Merriam said, "She's an angel."

"Boys, now—" Mrs. Roberts said, holding up a middle-sized brown sock, fearfully torn at heel and toe.

"I don't know," Mrs. Merriam said. "Harriet's almost as bad. Sometimes I worry about her," she went on confidentially, "about her being so heavy, I mean. It's very hard on a girl."

"Harriet's a nice girl, Josephine," Mrs. Desmond said. "She'll outgrow it in time." Her soft voice made Harriet sound slimmer.

"I was very heavy at Harriet's age," Mrs. Roberts said. She straightened her shoulders and took one hand away from her sewing to pull down the front of her dress where it had a tendency to blouse. "I can't say I completely *outgrew* it—" she laughed richly "—but I guess I *tamed* it."

Mrs. Desmond and Mrs. Merriam smiled, and Mrs. Desmond said, "I always used to admire girls who could really *wear* clothes. Caroline and I will always have to go around in pale colors and ruffles." She made a small face and looked fondly down at her daughter.

"But Harriet is getting to an age where it's really important to her," Mrs. Merriam said.

"When she gets interested in *boys*, Josephine," Mrs. Roberts said emphatically, "it won't take her long before she starts cutting out candy and potatoes and begins to watch her figure. I *know*," and she laughed again.

"Did you girls," Mrs. Merriam said carefully, looking down at her sewing, "did either of you girls hear anything about this silly business?" She looked at Mrs. Desmond and Mrs. Roberts, and said, "I mean, the letters the girls were writing to some of the boys?"

"Artie was in on it," Mrs. Roberts said, with a note that sounded like pride. "One of the girls had a crush on Artie. Can you imagine, Marguerite," she went on, looking helplessly at Mrs. Desmond, *"Artie?"*

"Some day Artie is going to surprise you," Mrs. Desmond said. "He's a very quiet boy, but that type usually turns out well."

"Well, *you* don't need to worry," Mrs. Merriam said unhappily. "I was never so *shocked.*"

"These things happen," Mrs. Roberts said philosophically.

"I really couldn't believe it of Harriet," Mrs. Merriam said. "Those letters—I saw one—they were *disgusting.*"

"The ones Artie got were silly," Mrs. Roberts said, "but I wouldn't have called them exactly disgusting."

"Who wrote them?" Mrs. Merriam asked quickly.

Mrs. Roberts shrugged. "The Donald girl," she said.

"I'm not surprised." Mrs. Merriam set her sewing aside and leaned forward earnestly. "I don't know what you think of that girl," she said, "but I think she has more to do with these things than anyone knows."

"There's no real harm in Virginia," Mrs. Desmond said.

"Well, I know her," Mrs. Merriam said, and tossed her head angrily. "I'd be the last person to defend Harriet—I think her conduct was absolutely *disgusting*—but I'd be inclined to think that nothing at all would have happened if certain young ladies around this neighborhood weren't a good deal too *mature* for their own good."

"Well, Helen Williams—" Mrs. Roberts said.

Mrs. Desmond snipped off a long length of blue embroidery thread and held it out to Caroline. "Here you are, darling," she said. Then she said to Mrs. Merriam, "I don't know very much about Helen, of *course*, but I think that kind of person is very often more sinned against than sinning."

"I don't think she's done anything really *bad*," Mrs. Merriam said, shocked.

"It's just that she's so much older, mentally, Marguerite, than the other girls," Mrs. Roberts said. "It's a shame they've gotten to know her so well."

"Well, *Harriet* won't know her any longer," Mrs. Merriam said.

"I don't think it's entirely wise," Mrs. Desmond murmured, "to keep girls apart. As soon as they know someone is bad for them—"

"I didn't even mention it to Artie," Mrs. Roberts said.

"Well, a boy. . . ." Mrs. Merriam stood up. "How about some tea?"

"Oh, don't bother," Mrs. Desmond said.

"Really," Mrs. Roberts added.

"No trouble," Mrs. Merriam said, as though she had not planned anything. "It's all ready."

She went into the kitchen, and Mrs. Roberts said, "I think she's a little hard on Harriet sometimes."

"I suppose she takes it very seriously," Mrs. Desmond agreed.

"You know," Mrs. Merriam said, coming busily in from the kitchen with a full tray which had obviously been sitting out there waiting, "You know, it seems strange to have only the three of us this week."

"Sylvia Donald had to take Virginia to the dentist," Mrs. Roberts said. "I don't know *what* happened to Dinah."

"Probably that poor woman had another spell," Mrs. Desmond said. "It must be a terrible thing to have to take care of an invalid like that."

"Worse than children," Mrs. Roberts said heartily. She threw her sewing aside and came over to Mrs. Merriam's tea tray, which she inspected critically. "Those *wonderful* sandwiches, Josephine."

"Next week you'll all come to my house," Mrs. Desmond said. "Aren't you *nice*?" as Mrs. Merriam presented a slim glass of milk to Caroline.

"The sweet child," Mrs. Merriam said. "She sits there so quietly and never says a word."

"One thing about you," Mrs. Roberts said enthusiastically to Mrs. Merriam. "You always have the most *wonderful* sandwiches."

"They're *only* cream cheese with a little sherry," Mrs. Merriam said. "I'll write it down for you."

"Are you *sure* you'll be all right, sweetie?" Mrs. Ransom-Jones asked earnestly. "I can very easily—"

"Not at all," her sister said. "I wouldn't dream of it. I'll be fine."

"But I just feel so sort of *guilty*," Mrs. Ransom-Jones said. "You so much worse and all."

"I'll be perfectly all right," her sister said. "You go right ahead."

Mrs. Ransom-Jones smoothed the long black skirt of her evening dress; her dark hair was pulled up on top of her head instead of gathered at the back of her neck, and she looked very dignified and sure. She put her hand on her sister's forehead and said, "I'm sure you'll be all right. If we hadn't planned it for so long."

"You couldn't know I'd be worse," her sister argued. "Don't give me a single *thought*, dear."

"Brad would be terribly disappointed," Mrs. Ransom-Jones said. "If he were only coming home instead of meeting me in town."

"You *look* perfectly lovely," her sister said. "He'll be proud of you."

Mrs. Ransom-Jones touched her earrings. "The Roberts boy is very reliable. You know him."

"Of course, dear," her sister said. "Just don't worry."

"I've left the doctor's name and telephone number on the hall table," Mrs. Ransom-Jones went on, counting on her fingers, "and your emergency medicine is right beside it. And he can always call his mother and father if there's anything."

"And the Donalds are home right next door," her sister said.

"I'll call during the evening," Mrs. Ransom-Jones said. "We can get home at any time in less than half an hour."

"You'll be late, dear," her sister said. "You don't have to wait till the boy comes."

"I'd *feel* better," Mrs. Ransom-Jones said vaguely. "Now are you *sure*—"

The doorbell rang, and she took up her evening bag and gloves as she went to the hall. "Hello, Arthur," her sister heard her say. "You're very nice to come."

"That's all right, Mrs. Ransom-Jones," Artie said. "I was just going to read anyway."

"It's just that my sister had another attack two days ago." Mrs. Ransom-Jones dropped her voice, but her sister could still hear her. "She has to be very quiet, and I just wanted someone here in case anything should—" She hesitated slightly. "In case anything should happen," she repeated.

"I see," Artie said.

"Here's the doctor's name and telephone number, and Lillian's medicine, which she gets if she *should* happen to have another attack, and the telephone number where we'll be, and—"

"I can tell him all about it, dear," Lillian said, raising her voice. "Don't you bother."

Mrs. Ransom-Jones came in, bringing perfume and the sound of black velvet moving softly. "Well, sweetie," she said.

"Good night, dear," Lillian said, raising her face. "I'll most likely be asleep when you come in."

"Good night," Mrs. Ransom-Jones said. "I'm sure everything will be fine," she said to Artie in the doorway.

"Have a nice time," Artie said politely. "Hello, Miss Tyler."

"Hello, Arthur," Lillian said. Mrs. Ransom-Jones waved from the doorway and went out, closing the door very gently. Lillian sat back and smiled at Artie. "She does worry *so*," she said.

Artie sat down gingerly. He had been in the Ransom-Jones house before, but never in a position of responsibility. He felt proprietary about the tapestry chairs standing carefully against the walls, about the oriental rug, the thick scarf on the piano. He knew Miss Tyler as a person of authority, a grown-up in his children's world, someone his mother knew, and now he was in charge of her; he sat back more comfortably and smiled at Miss Tyler on the couch. "Can I get you anything?" he asked.

"No, indeed." Miss Tyler smiled back at him, tenderly, as though drawn away from an enchanting reverie. "They do have such good times together," she said.

Artie smiled again, blankly.

"Brad and that woman," Miss Tyler said. "My sister."

"Have you lived here long?" Artie asked idiotically. He had understood that Miss Tyler would be in bed, an invalid, and he was to read quietly until Mr. and Mrs. Ransom-Jones came home, alert only for an emergency that would require the medicine, the doctor, the various phone numbers. But Miss Tyler sat on the couch across from him, looking fragile in a lavender negligee, and he was, atrociously, condemned to polite conversation until Miss Tyler should remember her duty and go obediently to bed.

"He brought her here when he married her," Miss Tyler said. She looked up at the ceiling, around the walls. "They've always lived here. You can tell by the flowers." Artie stared, and she said tolerantly, "Flowers grow best when they have always been tended by the same hand. My sister and I planted this whole garden. It was a wilderness." She nodded her head vehemently. "It was a real wilderness at first."

"You've certainly made it look good," Artie congratulated himself; the remark had made sense, it belonged in the conversation, it was complimentary.

"When I was *your* age," Miss Tyler said, and laughed lightly. "It must have been twenty years ago," she said, "I used to tend an acre of roses all by myself. Lady Hamiltons." She looked at him vaguely. "You wouldn't remember that far back," she said.

"I'm afraid not." Artie was troubled with thoughts of his responsibility; she ought to be going to bed soon, that was certain; he had a grave burden on him. ("Shall I help you to bed, Miss Tyler?" "Don't let me keep you up, Miss Tyler," "You ought to rest now, Miss Tyler.") "Miss Tyler," he began, but his voice was weak and he stopped.

"Such a pretty wedding," Miss Tyler was saying. "She carried armfuls of my roses. *My* roses."

"You have beautiful roses here," Artie said. It was the same kind of remark as before, the kind he was proud of.

"*I* never married," Miss Tyler said. "Young men like you—how old are you, dear? Eighteen? Twenty?"

Artie cleared his throat. "Miss Tyler," he said. ("Shall I help you to bed, Miss Tyler?")

"Young men like you passed me by," Miss Tyler said. "Brad was the only one."

"That's too bad," Artie said. That was the kind of remark he was not proud of.

"Well," Miss Tyler said soberly, "it's time I retired. You don't mind?"

"Of course not," Artie said. "Can I get you anything?"

"Thank you, no," Miss Tyler said. "You won't be bored?"

"No, no," Artie said. "I have to read this book."

He stood up when she did, standing back respectfully to let her pass him. "Will you help me?" she asked suddenly, and swayed a little so that he was frightened when he ran forward and took her arm. "Over there," she said. "I have my room downstairs now. There's a bathroom and everything." He helped her into the hall and she stopped at her doorway. "My sister is so kind," she said, leaning her head against the closed door. Then she took her arm away from him gently and said, "Thank you very much, Arthur."

"Can you manage all right now?" Artie said. He felt a very real sympathy, not quite realizing that it was because he could walk perfectly well, could run if he wanted to, could go upstairs fifty times a day. "Please let me help you."

"I'm perfectly all right now," Miss Tyler said.

Artie realized with hideous embarrassment that she was waiting for him to go before she opened the door to her bedroom. He backed away, gasping, "Good night, then," and Miss Tyler waved one finger roughishly at him. "You *gay* young men," she said.

Artie, sitting tentatively on the edge of one of the tapestry chairs in the living-room, listening for the sound of a fall or a scream, heard her say tenderly, "Always some rash young fool, my darling dear," and then she was quiet.

He read his book, finally, accustomed to the silence, never leaving the living-room except for one tiptoed journey down the hall to see if he could hear her breathing. After an eternal minute outside her door he came back to his chair and read peacefully until Mr. and Mrs. Ransom-Jones came home shortly after one.

"Everything's been fine," he said.

"I *knew* she'd be all right," Mrs. Ransom-Jones said, "that's why I didn't bother to call." She gave him a quarter.

"When I grow up," George Martin said to his grandfather, "I'm going to drive a truck. A ten-ton truck."

"First you grow up," his grandfather said. He nodded sagely. "First you grow up," he said. "Once," he went on slowly, "I thought I would be a doctor, myself. Now I am a gardener." He nodded again, as though a point had been proved. He was sitting on a broken box in the Martins' back yard, wild growing things in profusion around him and the morning sunlight heavy on his old head. It was his custom to sit here Sunday mornings when the weather was good, and regard phlegmatically the garden which belonged to him and which he never had time to cultivate; except for George's abortive efforts and an occasional fussing over by the children's grandmother, the back yard was allowed to run a wilderness. In one corner, near the Merriams' fence, was an aged plum tree which no longer bore plums; next to it was the rabbit-house built by George, where one sickly rabbit had perished miserably the summer before. There were two more plum trees and an apple, the plum trees all barren and the apple given to wry unpalatable fruit. The rest of the yard was wild grass, weeds, and junk, and a climbing rose tree which grew up the back of the house and caught at the grandfather's shoulders when he sat on his broken box.

George was building something again; it was to be either a

skate coaster or a wagon. He had nailed an orange crate on to a board and was busy trying to fit two halves of an old skate onto it for wheels.

"If I had a truck, you know what I'd do?" George continued in an even singsong that corresponded rhythmically with his work; when he became most careful, in some delicate operation, his words slid out and became long and breathless; when he worked steadily along, hammering or measuring, he spoke evenly and smoothly. Occasionally he looked up at his grandfather, to prove some important statement, and then the sunlight touched his eyes and mouth, and gave him an expression of intelligence usually lacking in his vacant face.

"You know what I'd do?" he insisted, turning to look at his grandfather. "I'd run it right into old Missus Merriam's house and I'd run right over her. Run over Missus Merriam, run over Missus Merriam, and I'd run over Misssssssssster Meeeeeeeeerriam." This became very long because George was trying to straighten a skate wheel. Then his voice quickened again. "And I'd run over old Harriet and I'd run over old Missus Merriam. If I had a truck that's what I'd do."

The sun made the old grandfather sleepy, and he half-closed his eyes. He found it difficult to understand much of what his grandchildren said; they spoke so quickly, and with such strange words, and the tongue itself was still alien to an old man. When George looked up at him, the grandfather smiled and nodded, exactly as he had smiled and nodded at the immigration officials forty years before. "You grow up," he said sleepily.

"When I grow up," George went on, "I'm going to have a tractor."

"Tractor?" the grandfather said.

"I'll run into the whole world and kill them," George said. "And Missus Merriam." He began to sing, monotonously, "Old man Kelly had a pimple on his belly and it tasted like jelly."

His grandfather stirred in the sun, and the leaves of the climbing rose rustled gently.

"Old man Kelly," George said. "How'd you like to run a streetcar, Gramp?"

His grandfather opened his eyes and smiled.

"Boy," George said. "Clang, brrrrrrrrrr, clang, clang." He left his work and moved about the yard, pulling imaginary levers, steering a desperately maneuvering machine, ringing the bell. "Clang, clang," he shouted. "Clang."

With a faint surprise, the old grandfather watched. A leaf of the rose tree touched his cheek, and he reached up and pulled the leaf around to look at it. Scrutinizing it carefully, he called, "George, come, boy, to me."

George stopped careening around the trees and came over to his grandfather. "What you want, Gramp?" he said. He kicked at his skate coaster to come over and stand next to his grandfather.

"See?" the grandfather said, holding the leaf close to George's face. "See?" He pointed to a tiny spot on the leaf. "Not good," he said.

Harriet Merriam and Virginia Donald walked down Cortez Road arm in arm. They were going to the nearest store, three blocks away, where they would each buy a popsicle and then walk home again. They were passing the big apartment house on the corner of the highway and Cortez when a man, hurrying into the building, ran into Virginia and knocked her nickel out of her hand. "Darn it!" Virginia said loudly, and the man, who had said, "Pardon me," and hurried on, turned and came back to them. "Is something wrong?" he asked.

"I lost my nickel," Virginia said. She was looking around on the sidewalk and did not see that the man was Chinese, but Harriet saw him and pulled Virginia's arm. "You can have *my* nickel," Harriet said. "Come on, Virginia."

"It was my fault," the man said. "Let me make it good." He took a handful of change out of his pocket, and Virginia said, "No, no, please," before she looked up and saw him. Then she said, "Of course not," very coldly, and took Harriet's arm again.

The man smiled at them sadly. "I insist on giving you the nickel," he said. He had selected a nickel from the change in his hand and now he put the rest of the money back in his pocket and held the nickel out to Virginia. "It was my fault, after all," he said.

Virginia hesitated. "You can have my nickel," Harriet said again.

"Such a charming young lady," the man said. "And I have troubled you." He held out the nickel, more urgently. "You would be very unkind to refuse," he said.

"Thank you," Virginia said. She took the nickel, and the man bowed and said, "Thank *you*. Now I feel less clumsy."

Harriet thought that he had forgotten how much of a hurry he was in before; he stood there as though anxious to talk to them, his head on one side and his smile courteous and expectant. He was excellently dressed, as well dressed as Mr. Desmond, and there had been a lot of money in the change he took out of his pocket. Virginia said, feeling the expectancy in his face, "Do you live here?" She waved at the apartment house.

He turned and looked at the house curiously. "Yes," he said. "Yes, I do."

"I've never been inside," Virginia said. "Is it nice?"

"Very bad taste," he said. "No modesty."

"I remember when they built it," Virginia said. "Do you, Harriet?"

Harriet shook her head, continuing her steady faint pull on Virginia's arm.

"That was when we were kids," Virginia said. "We used to play here when they were building it."

The man listened intently, and nodded when she was through talking. "I have lived here for two years now," he said. "Perhaps some day you will visit me and see the inside of the house."

Harriet made her pressure on Virginia's arm more violent, but Virginia said, "Thank you. Some day I'd like to."

"Perhaps you would like to come to tea some day," he said. "With your charming friend, of course."

Virginia pulled back as violently against Harriet, and said, "Thank you. We *would* like to."

The man thought for a minute, and Harriet said, "Virginia, we've got to *go*."

Then the man said, "Perhaps a week from today?" He looked at them, and his smile faded. "No?" he said as politely. "Another time, then."

"We'd *love* to," Virginia said hastily. "I was just trying to think if we were busy that day."

He smiled again. "Next Tuesday, then," he said. "About four. I'll meet you right outside here, so that you won't be uncomfortable, coming in by yourselves."

"Thank you," Virginia said. She yielded slightly to Harriet's tugging, moving slowly along the sidewalk after Harriet while she talked. "It's very nice of you," she said. "We'll be here."

"Thank *you*," the man said. He bowed to them and then went into the house, in a hurry again.

"Virginia," Harriet said, "you must be *crazy*. Stopping to talk like that."

"What could he do to us?" Virginia said. "He gave me a nickel."

"Suppose someone saw us?" Harriet said. "Suppose my mother had come by?"

"What of it?" Virginia said. "We were looking for my nickel, is all."

"You're not going to go next week?" Harriet said, frightened by something in Virginia she did not understand.

"I may," Virginia said, turning down the corners of her mouth tantalizingly. "*Helen* would go."

"I won't," Harriet said.

"Anyway," Virginia went on, "I found mine. Look." She held out her hand with two nickels in it. "We can get gum," she said.

"You shouldn't have," Harriet said uncertainly.

"What of it?" Virginia said again. "It doesn't hurt to take money from a Chinaman."

"I'll bet this old thing used to be deep enough for swimming," Pat said.

"That would be something, swimming right next to home," Art said, "right around the corner almost."

They were lying in the deep grass in the old creek bed. Above them on either side were the steep banks, grown over with moss and grass and high above the eucalyptus and fir trees heavy and ending far up in the sky. The old creek was the border of the golf course which spread over a vast area near Pepper Street; the golf course belonged to the better neighbors beyond the gates, but because golf courses are large and the better neighbors only played on this one and never tried to live there, the fairways were allowed to meander democratically past the strict border line of the gates and touch, formally, the neighbors on the other side, even to the extent of permitting young boys like Pat and Art on its fringes. They could have caddied on the course if their fathers had not opposed their working, but they would have had to go around through the gates and up the long road where no home was permitted to be visible, around in a great circle to the clubhouse, barely distinguishable from the edge of the creek. Starting from the clubhouse and following dutifully along with bags of clubs, they might have approached the creek from the better, or well-tended, side, might have reached the place where they were lying now, in search of erring golf balls. (It is a known fact that George Martin once retrieved a golf ball from the creek bed, and kept it to play with, although the act was eventually, in neighborhood conclave, accepted as stealing.) The golf course was in no sense a forbidden heaven to the Pepper Street children; James Donald had been, correctly dressed, to the clubhouse for dinner, and Mr. Desmond played on the golf course regularly of a Sunday; as a member, he had even taken Mr. Roberts occasionally.

What the golf course represented, actually, was a reminder that within the sphere which the people who lived on Pepper Street allowed themselves, there was a maximum and a minimum attainment; Mr. Desmond, for instance, belonged to this club and another in the city, and a further club in which he played squash, but before long Mr. Desmond intended to promote himself beyond the gates; John Junior and Caroline would grow up in a house not visible from the street; they might even have a tennis court and be called rich. Mr. Byrne, on the other hand, preferred bowling and performed every Saturday night with as select a group of men as those with whom Mr. Desmond played golf, although Mr. Byrne's friends lived without the gates and never planned to live within. To Mr. Byrne and his friends, Pepper Street was the ultimate goal and they reached it with as much satisfaction as Mr. Desmond would reach his home inside the gates and, eventually, his estate outside town. At present Mr. Byrne and Mr. Desmond met as equals and respectful acquaintances; eventually they would be as far apart as they had been when they started, although probably equally wealthy. Pat Byrne and Johnny Desmond would almost certainly meet at some expensive university, but all they would have in common would be the old times on Pepper Street and recollections of the creek, not the golf course.

Except that there was the faint chance of being brained by an overzealous golf ball, the creek was very nearly ideal for a neighborhood hideout. Mildred Williams had never been there, nor had Caroline Desmond, nor Marilyn Perlman, but they were the only ones. The creek was filled with big stones for making walls, with heavy grass for sod fights; it was called the creek only by courtesy, for it was a long time since water had flowed there. Sometime in the far distant past a tree had fallen across the widest part of the ravine, from the vacant lot on the one side to the golf course on the other, making a dangerous bridge. James Donald was the only person—it did much to establish his neighborhood reputation—ever to ride across this log on a bicycle; Pat and Art, and Helen Williams, who would do anything a boy could do, could walk across it upright; Johnny Desmond had run across it once and fallen into the grass below, breaking his arm; Tod Donald and such younger children as Jamie Roberts were able to inch across it on their stomachs. Mrs. Merriam did not know of its existence, Mr. Roberts approved of it enthusiastically, and Mr. Desmond, although the children were unaware of the fact, had once walked across it dead drunk in the middle of the night, starting from the golf-course side.

Pat lay in the grass on his back with one arm over his eyes, and Art sat up, his arms around his knees. They spoke only occasionally, without much regard to communication, in a sort of pleasant comfort that came partly from their great familiarity with one another, and mostly from the feeling of ground and grass under them and trees and sky overhead, with no houses to be seen. Pat twisted a blade of grass in his fingers, feeling it more tangible than food, than books; he saw the sky overhead as arched personally for him, and concerned in his immediate welfare; Art, on the other hand, liked the way the grass smelled, and the way the creek sides crowded closely against him, hiding him.

"My father," Art said finally, "might be over playing golf now."

"He isn't," Pat said, his voice muffled through his arm. "He's in the city working; today's Tuesday."

"If he wanted to he could play golf today," Art said.

"Mine couldn't." Pat rolled over on his stomach and began pulling small handfuls of grass and scattering them. "Mine couldn't do a darn thing except work and criticize other people."

"I'd rather have your father than mine," Art said. He put his chin down on his knees and regarded the trees sideways. "Bet those trees are fifty feet high," he went on.

"I'd rather have *your* father than *mine*," Pat said. "Yours just doesn't pay any attention to people."

"You *think* he doesn't," Art said. "He's *always* sounding off about something."

"Mine," Pat said carefully, "he just can't leave a person alone. He's always spying and prying and criticizing and pestering other people."

Art giggled. "My father's a windbag," he said.

Pat giggled. "My father's a pest," he said.

"My father's a bully," Art said.

"*My* father's a bully," Pat said.

"My father's a dope," Art said.

"*My* father's a dope," Pat said.

"My father's a big fat slob," Art said.

"My father's a *little* fat slob," Pat said. They both laughed again.

"My father's an old pig," Art said.

"*My* father's an old pig," Pat said.

"My father's a stinker," Art said.

"*My* father's a . . ." Pat hesitated. Then: "My father's a bastard," he said.

There was a pause, and then Art said, "*My* father's a bastard."

They were both quiet for a while, Pat with his face in the grass and Art looking at the trees. It was getting darker; over on the golf course the fairways were emptying, and men were changing their clothes in the locker-room, having a drink, talking cheerfully. The sky over the creek was changing from bright blue to pale green, and the trees were deepening. The wind, which seldom came far down into the creek bed, touched the grass along the sides lightly, and turned in the trees. Finally Pat raised his head. "Almost dinner time?" he asked.

"We better be going," Art said. They both got up and brushed the grass and dead leaves from their clothes; then, Art leading and Pat following, they climbed skillfully up the side of the creek and started across the vacant lot toward home.

"I understand the Williams girl is moving away," Mrs. Merriam said to Harriet at the dinner table.

Harriet looked up, surprised. "I didn't know that," she said. "Helen was always talking about it, though."

Mrs. Merriam nodded. "Miss Fielding told me today. They're moving in a week or so."

"I wonder where," Harriet said.

"As long as it's away from here," Mrs. Merriam said. "More potatoes, Harry?"

Mr. Merriam looked up from his plate blankly. "More what?"

"Potatoes," Mrs. Merriam said patiently. Lately, since she and Harriet had been seeing more of one another, she would look significantly at Harriet when Mr. Merriam did something indicating his personal coarseness; frequently, in the long talks which Mrs. Merriam and Harriet had so often now, Mrs. Merriam would say, "Never marry a man who is *inelegant*, Harriet; I can tell you it brings nothing but sorrow." If Harriet tried to press her on the subject she would shake her head and smile sadly; only when she was angry did Mrs. Merriam permit herself to sink so low as to reproach her husband for not being daintily bred. Now, saying, "More potatoes," she looked at Harriet and smiled, and Harriet smiled back confusedly.

Harriet had not told her mother about the Chinese man and the invitation to tea, and she was afraid. It was only two days until the appointment, and Harriet knew that Virginia was going to make her go. The subject preyed on her and made her uneasy. Several times her mother had said, putting a hand gently on Harriet's, "My dear, you're *worrying* about something. What is it?" and Harriet, moving nervously, had said each time, "Nothing." It was always easy to move Mrs. Merriam's mind from Harriet's troubles to her own; she was writing a poem, moreover, entitled "Death and Soft Music" (Harriet was writing a poem at the same time, called "To My Mother"), and any unseasonable disturbance in Harriet was readily attributed to the familiar and reasonable agonies of artistic creation.

"No more potatoes, thanks," Mr. Merriam said. "What's for dessert?"

"Pie." Mrs. Merriam rose and started into the kitchen with the plates. Harriet followed, and together they brought in the pie. Mrs. Merriam sat down and cut a single stately piece for Mr. Merriam.

"Apple pie," Mr. Merriam said. He looked around. "Am I the only one eating pie?"

"Harriet and I are not pie-eaters," Mrs. Merriam said delicately, and Harriet added virtuously, "I don't see how you can eat it." She would have eaten a piece of pie with enthusiasm, but artistic creation and delicate upbringing argued against it.

"I'll be very happy when the Williams girl is gone," Mrs.

Merriam said. "I have always felt that she was a bad influence on all the children in the neighborhood. Ever since. . . ." She coughed lightly, and looked at Harriet, who blinked her eyes miserably. "Not that I believe her influence on *you*, Harriet, was as bad as, say, some of the *other* girls." Her finger touched the edge of her coffee-cup lightly. "I think you know who I mean."

An idea came suddenly to Harriet, and before she had time to consider it carefully she found herself saying, "I heard something *awful* about Helen Williams the other day."

Mrs. Merriam looked up eagerly; Mr. Merriam went on eating his pie.

"Virginia Donald told me," Harriet said.

"Virginia is a very sweet girl," Mrs. Merriam said. "Don't misunderstand what I said before."

"It's about Helen. One day she and Virginia were walking down the street and they met a Chinaman who lives down on the corner in the apartment house." Harriet hesitated. It would be unwise to incriminate Virginia too deeply. "And Helen started talking to him."

"Of course she *would*." Mrs. Merriam sighed.

"And he ended up by asking them to come down and see him some day."

Mrs. Merriam widened her eyes and opened her mouth.

"He lives in the apartment house," Harriet went on, feeling relief carrying her away, "and he said they could come down some day and visit him in the apartment house."

"Did they go?" Mrs. Merriam asked. "What did he do to them?"

Harriet thought quickly. "I don't know whether *Helen* went or not. Virginia didn't say."

"I'm sorry about Virginia, of *course*," Mrs. Merriam said. "But it's just what I'd expect of that Helen Williams. Fooling around with Chinamen." She shivered violently. "I'm glad it wasn't *my* girl," she said.

"*I* wouldn't," Harriet was beginning enthusiastically, but Mrs. Merriam was saying, "Harry, did you hear that? Helen Williams is running around with Chinamen now."

"That so?" Harry Merriam looked up at his wife and then reached down for his cup. "More coffee, please."

Filling her husband's coffee-cup, Mrs. Merriam said to Harriet, "I'd like to hear what happened. You know,"—She dropped her voice slightly, glancing sideways at her husband—"they just *love* white girls." She smiled slightly in spite of herself, and said, even lower, so that Harriet had to lean forward to hear, "Their houses are made with heavy walls, extra heavy, so you can't get out and no one can hear you if you scream. Scream," she repeated with relish, and Harriet felt herself hot and embarrassed. "I've heard of cases," Mrs. Merriam said. She sighed again, leaning back. "Poor Helen," she said.

"But in the apartment house," Harriet said. "After all. . . ." She felt a need to protest; she believed everything her mother was saying, but that her mother should appear to enjoy it so much . . . "I'm *sure* nothing like that could happen," Harriet said.

Mrs. Merriam laughed shortly. "You wait and see," she said. Then her eyes opened wide, and she said, "Well, if that certainly isn't the reason Mrs. Williams is in such a hurry to move away!"

"No, Mother," Harriet said, but her mother was up from the table and moving toward the phone.

"I'm just going to call Mrs. Donald," she said.

Mr. Desmond put his book down and looked across the living-room at his son with tolerant fatherly amusement. "Been a long time since I had a chance to talk to you," he said.

Johnny looked up and smiled back. "We've both been pretty busy, I guess," he said. Although they were legally father and son, John Junior had not, as so many adopted children do, grown to resemble his father in small subtle ways; he had taken none of his father's mannerisms, none of his tricks of dressing, not even many of his father's words. In some ways he was a sorrow to Mr. Desmond; who believed, and said often, that adoption was a two-way process. "The children should adopt the parents," he would say soberly, "as surely as the parents adopt the children." So that, sitting on opposite sides of

the room, they were already two men—Johnny at nearly sixteen as large and broad-shouldered as his father—two men sitting of an evening talking. Mrs. Desmond stood in the
doorway looking at them. She was proud of them both, and
proud of small Caroline just put to bed for the night. When
she thought of her family, beyond meals and clothes and table
linen, she thought of them as a unit, the adopted son as permanent and beloved as the natural daughter, the father and
mother kindly, loving parents.

She came almost silently into the room and sat down to take
up her sewing. As she sat down, both her husband and her son
looked up and smiled at her, and she smiled back, the smile
still on her face as she bent over her needle-point, and they
went back to their conversation.

"I could get my license this winter when I'm sixteen,"
Johnny was saying.

Mr. Desmond still looked humorous and tolerant; it was an
old argument and he had every intention of giving in eventually, but first he must prove Johnny in a number of vehement
arguments over a period of months, must find the boy manly
and proud and strong-willed. Mr. Desmond admired strength
in any form, and finding it in his adopted son was a sort of
bonus to him, as though, beside the qualities of health and
bodily perfection he had originally specified in the child to be
adopted, he had been rewarded for his generosity to the child
by unexpected good qualities: this strength, a quiet humor,
Johnny's undefinable self-possession which sometimes awed
Mr. Desmond. Some day Johnny would play all-American
football, or great golf, or championship tennis; Mr. Desmond
saw him happily as beloved of women (perhaps even already;
there were the letters that had caused such a fuss recently, and
who knew what else?), admired of men, his hand on his father's
shoulder, his friends, broad-shouldered champion young men
all, toasting Johnny's father, his *adopted* father.

"I don't believe," Mr. Desmond said, following this train of
thought, "that any young man should have a car unless he has
proved himself adult."

"I can drive now," Johnny said mistakenly.

Mr. Desmond put his book on his knee (it was a mystery story, and Mr. Desmond read them lovingly; some day Johnny could read Homer and Chaucer for him; as Mr. Desmond said so often, "That's what we have children for"), and regarded his son cynically. "What about this girl who wrote you the letters?" he demanded. "You take her out riding all the time if you had a car?"

Johnny made a face, "*Not her,*" he said.

Mr. Desmond smiled at Mrs. Desmond, who smiled back. "Listen to him," he said.

"Of course," Mrs. Desmond said fondly. "And all the boys will be crazy about Caroline."

"I wish you'd just let me get a car," Johnny said. His eyes became far-away. "Allen has the nicest little car," he said.

Mr. Desmond frowned. "I've heard about nothing else, it seems," he said. "Remember, you're not a rich man's son yet. Allen's father can afford nice little cars; if I ever let you drive, you will be using the family car for a good many years before you have a car of your own."

"I could earn the money for a second-hand car," Johnny said. "I don't want anything but a car to go around in."

Mr. Desmond was mildly annoyed. "I will probably be able to afford some sort of a respectable car for you some day," he said, "without your going out and slaving for it. There is no need to think that at fifteen you can earn the money for a car which your father cannot afford at forty."

Johnny was stopped. "At least let me get my license," he said.

"We'll see." Mr. Desmond picked up his book. "What are you reading?"

Johnny tossed the comic book on to the couch beside him in sudden irritability. "Stuff," he said. He got up and moved restlessly around the room. "I'm going over to Allen's," he said.

"So late?" Mrs. Desmond looked up anxiously, but her husband said, "You boys. Out all night and never think how your parents worry."

"I'll be back early," Johnny said.

"Let us know if you're going to be late," his father said. He chuckled amiably. "Driving around in Allen's car, whistling at girls," he said.

Marilyn Perlman sat on her front porch, wearing slacks and drinking coke and reading *Pendennis*. Inside the house her mother was humming far away; she was in the kitchen making a cake for Mr. Perlman's birthday dinner that night. Marilyn had turned the porch chair so that she could see through the vines off down the street—Helen Williams was moving away. That morning, without any previous knowledge of the Williams's departure, Marilyn had come outside, and the moving van was there; incredulous, Marilyn checked it against the house—it was certainly the Williams house, the moving men were taking furniture *out*. There had been, for a minute, the bare possibility that the Williams family had bought new furniture, but the old furniture was definitely coming *out*, and after two hours it seemed beautifully certain that Helen Williams was leaving Pepper Street. Marilyn relayed the news to her mother, who came out on the porch for a minute, with flour on her hands, and nodded and said, "It's a good thing."

All the neighborhood children were gathered around the Williams house, and Helen Williams was holding her last court on the front lawn, sitting on one of her own living-room chairs while her grandmother sat indoors in her room holding Lotus and crying, and her mother moved nervously in and out, directing the movers, entreating them to be gentle with certain favored remnants. The Williams furniture was embarrassingly shabby, and Mrs. Williams was obviously conscious of the eyes of her neighbors and their children; they saw her seldom enough as it was, without getting their last look at her by daylight, surrounded by the pitiful implements she used to live and eat and dress and sleep and sit and hold and bring her children up with.

Mildred Williams, in authority for the first time in her life, was ordering people away from the furniture, bestowing favors on children she allowed to come near the moving van. Mrs. Desmond drove past with Caroline in the car, and stopped to say good-bye courteously to Mrs. Williams, and

Mildred ran up and pressed a grimy rag doll into Caroline's arms. "This is from my mommy and me," she cried, and Mrs. Desmond was able to say good-bye again, and thank you, before her repugnance hurried her home, to take the doll by an arm and drop it into the garbage can before she took Caroline into the house to wash.

Marilyn watched, thinking of life without Helen Williams— maybe they were moving far away, far enough so that Helen would never be in school again—and realizing, as she saw the threadbare, unmatched furniture, that it had not been necessary to be so afraid of Helen. If Helen dressed every morning for school in front of that grimy dresser, ate breakfast at that slatternly table, then Marilyn had no need to run from her; no one whose life was bounded by things like that was invulnerable.

By noon the truck was full and ready to drive off. Helen's grandmother was brought out of the house with Lotus in her arms, Mildred was forced into a coat, and wearily, desolately, Mrs. Williams prepared to lead her family to the bus that would take them to their new home, a place darker, perhaps, and poorer, but where Mildred would grow up for another year or so, where the old grandmother would sit in her room and perhaps die, where Helen would continue as before, surrounded by new friends, frightening a new Marilyn, and where Mrs. Williams would be able to come home every night after a shorter journey, sitting alone every evening in a new living-room, planning so that they would not have to move into another home eventually, another home still darker. Miss Fielding, on her front porch, stood up to lean forward and say good-bye to Mrs. Williams and bow to the old grandmother, Mildred danced along the street, calling back to the other children, "I'll come and see you some day," and Hallie Martin, holding her arms around Helen and sobbing, cried out "Write to me, Willie, write to me, *please*." Mrs. Merriam waved from her kitchen window, and the neighborhood children, secure and firm on Pepper Street, stood in a body watching until the Williams family had turned the corner to Cortez Road and the highway, and mothers began calling them home for lunch.

"I'll be back in a minute," Marilyn called into the front door, and without waiting for an answer she ran down the front steps and out on to the sidewalk of Pepper Street. The street was empty. The moving van was gone, the children had evaporated into their houses, the sun was coming down on the sidewalk and the street and the lawns and the houses—the pink flowers were gone by now—and on the unmistakable debris left at the Williams house. Marilyn ran quickly down the street, driven by a compelling urge to see Helen's house from the inside, to be in there and out again before anyone saw her.

She went through the half-open door without hesitation; even in moving away the Williams family had been as ramshackle as their furniture—Mrs. Williams had neglected to lock the doors in her haste to get to her new home; one window still had curtains. ("Sloppiest tenants I ever had," the landlord confided to Miss Fielding that afternoon, when he came to see if Mrs. Williams had stolen the light bulbs.) Inside, Marilyn stood in the dim echoing air of a house still ringing with complaint; she looked into the living-room and saw that the sun never came there, she went down the long hall and knew that there had never been a carpet on the floor, she saw the still-dirty bathroom and the old grandmother's room, which she supposed had been Helen's, from the fifth on the floor, a calendar still hung in the kitchen, with the moving date circled. Marilyn looked into the refrigerator and found it warm and empty. On her way back down the hall she discovered a small memorandum book dropped into a corner, and she took it out into the sunlit doorway and opened it and found items like "call furnace man" and "black dress at cleaners thurs." At the back of the book was a list of figures, identified occasionally, as "Helen spring coat $17.95." That must be the red coat Helen has been wearing, Marilyn thought in surprise, so cheap. She had only seen it vaguely; it had been a warning sign of Helen's approach, but now she remembered it, and it had *looked* cheap. The figures in the book totaled fifty-one dollars; Helen's coat was the biggest item. Marilyn dropped the book back into the doorway, and thought, Mildred was a nice little girl, *she* was always nice.

She came down to the sidewalk, and Tod Donald, riding his

bike past in the street, braked to a stop and said loudly, "What are *you* doing, in other people's houses?"

"Oh, shut up, dopey," Marilyn said, and walked on home.

The weather had to be very warm indeed before Mrs. Mack would venture outdoors. The children believed that she spent all day in her shack peering out at them through the boarded-up windows, putting spells on anyone who entered her yard or touched the battered apple trees. Mrs. Mack was allowed to continue on Pepper Street (although it would have been easy enough for Mr. Desmond or Mr. Roberts or even Mr. Perlman to get rid of her), because she had apparently always owned the little piece of land where she lived; and because she lived in a shack far back from the street, with the heavy apple trees in front and a hedge in front of these; and, finally, because she only ventured outdoors in the very warmest weather, and no one, as far as even rumor could discover, had ever been harmed by her spells, at least no one who lived on Pepper Street.

The children called her a witch, and the parents called her an unfortunate old woman, and she looked like either one, with her hair in strings and her shoulders bent, and her perpetual whimpering mutter. If anyone passed her house while she was outside and neglected to speak to her the mutter would rise to an audible criticism, but Mrs. Desmond had been known to observe, and the parents believed her, that Mrs. Mack actually loved the Pepper Street children, and was a harmless old woman, very unfortunate. The day after Helen Williams moved away, Mrs. Mack came out. Mary Byrne, out picking roses from the side of their house nearest Mrs. Mack's, came running into the kitchen to say to her mother that Mrs. Mack was on the front step of her shack in the sun, and Mrs. Byrne said absently, "Be nice to her, dear."

Peering through the line of rose bushed which were the boundary between the Byrne place and Mrs. Mack's, Mary called, tentatively, "Isn't it a lovely day, Mrs. Mack?" and the old woman, scowling around her, said, "Who's calling me?" before she saw Mary waving through the rose bushes. Then she waved back and said, "Sally, are you out in the sunshine too?"

It had been Helen Williams's great contribution to neighborhood lore, that a witch could not put spells on anyone if she didn't know their name, and Mary said, comfortable in the knowledge that some unfamiliar Sally would get her spell, "How are you feeling?"

"Better now," Mrs. Mack said. "Better now." No one knew any of Mrs. Mack's history except that a friend had given her her dog, and that she was always ailing in some way. "Where's your dog today?" Mary asked, to be as thorough and polite as she could, and Mrs. Mack nodded back, sage in the sunlight. "Indeed yes," Mrs. Mack said. "Not nice people at all."

"Of course not, Mrs. Mack," Mary said.

"Don't belong at all in a nice neighborhood," Mrs. Mack said. "Glad to see the last of them."

"You mean the Williamses?" Mary stopped in her rose-gathering to listen.

"This has always been a nice neighborhood," Mrs. Mack said. She lifted a stick from the ground beside the step and began to make figures in the dirt. "I always liked living here."

Mary crossed herself wildly, gasped, "I guess I've picked enough of these old roses," and fled indoors. "She was making charms in the dirt," she told her mother breathlessly, "I could see her writing names." For a minute the comfort of Mrs. Mack's not knowing anyone's name deserted her, and she said in terror, "She was looking right at me."

Tod Donald rarely did anything voluntarily, or with planning, or even with intent acknowledged to himself; he found himself doing one thing, and then he found himself doing another, and that, as he saw it, was the way one lived along, never deciding, never helping. When he found himself one afternoon walking down Pepper Street nearly at the Desmond driveway, and saw Mrs. Desmond backing the car out with Caroline beside her in the front seat, it never occurred to him to slip into the Desmond yard; and once there, when he saw the glass door from the Desmond terrace slightly open, his mind did not encompass the notion of stepping into the Desmond house, nor did it suggest to him, once in, that he had no right to be there.

The glass door took him directly into the Desmond dining-room, and, since he had never been inside the Desmond house before, he first regarded the walls, and the ceilings, and the floor, before going on to a more intimate investigation. With the glass doors at his back, he stood coolly surveying what he could see of the house, estimating it, weighing it in his hand. The walls, for instance, were painted, not papered as in the Donald house; the table in the dining-room was long and slim. Tod went to the painted wall and felt it with his finger, leaving an almost imperceptible touch on the light paint. He bent over the table and saw his face reflected dimly in the polished wood. He looked at the chairs; they had light leather seats and graceful rising backs; the rug on the floor, barely pressed by the legs of the chairs and the table, was pale and smooth. Tod took hold of one of the chairs; it was unexpectedly heavy, and he had to use both hands to tip it over backward and examine the under part. When he put the chair back into place he caught sight of his face reflected in the silver coffee service on a side table. As he came closer to the coffee-pot his face became more distorted, elastic in the long coffee-pot; he looked back into the table and found his face there, back to the coffee-pot and found his face again. He ran his hand caressingly down the side of the coffee-pot, his fingers lingering as he turned away, to the doorway beyond which lay the living-room.

Facing him as he entered the living-room was the wall of tall shrouded windows; because they were covered against the afternoon sunlight the great living-room was shadowy and cool. Far away, down the length of the room, the grand piano stood unvibrating, quiet. Tod, going past heavy armchairs and stiff embroidered chairs and small round tables with curved feet and large flat tables with lamps on them, stood finally next to the piano, where he saw his face reflected in the sleek blackness. He put one elbow on the piano and looked down on the piano bench, and said, barely aloud, "*She* plays this. It's their piano."

He thought of Mrs. Desmond, tall and pale in a long dress, sitting on the piano bench playing the piano, and he walked around and knelt one leg on the piano bench and pressed his fingers down on the keys, gently, but without sound. He kept his fingers down for a minute, looking at the way the keys slid smoothly together, the black keys fitting exactly into the white keys, each capable of independent movement, but tightly put together. Then he turned and went back down the living-room, stopping for a minute to look down at a chair which was dark red and big and comfortable, and had Mr. Desmond's pipe in the ashtray next to it.

He began to whistle softly and tonelessly as he went back through the dining-room into the kitchen, clean and breathtakingly white. He saw his face again in the toaster, but not on the kitchen table, although it was white and shone in the sunlight. Pretty dishes stood in a long row on a shelf along one side of the Desmond kitchen, yellow-trimmed dishtowels hung neatly on a rack. Tod took down one of the dishes, still whistling, and turned it over to see the back; the lettering there had been almost washed off, but he made out something that seemed to say "fine china."

There was a yellow square in the linoleum floor for every green one, a green one for every white one, a white one for every brown one. Caroline's high chair stood back against the wall; it was white like everything else, and lined with yellow oilcloth. Caroline eats here, too, Tod thought. He looked around and assigned the chair next to the toaster to Mrs. Desmond, the one across to Mr. Desmond, the third to Johnny Desmond. Mrs. Desmond has to make the toast, he thought, Mr. Desmond probably likes toast.

He came back again through the dining-room into the long hallway which ran through the whole house; he had realized vaguely that the Desmond house was all on one floor without any upstairs, but still it gave him a queer shock to open the first door past the dining-room and find it was Johnny Desmond's bedroom; he knew it was Johnny's because Johnny's clothes were on the chair and in the closet, and a bookcase in the room held schoolbooks and adventure stories labeled "John Desmond Jr." When he closed the door behind him he looked down at the doorway leading to the dining-room and said, "You can eat and then go to bed right next door."

The door across the hall took him into a handsome study, where there were deep red leather chairs and a long clear desk. "Old man Desmond," Tod said, and closed the door without going in. On his way down the hall he found two bathrooms; the Donalds had two bathrooms, but they were on different floors.

He was whistling again as he reached the last doors in the hall; his whistling was still very soft, but it had acquired a tune to which Tod knew the words: "There she goes, there she goes, all dressed up in her Sunday clothes."

There were three doors still unopened at the end of the hall; Tod opened the first door and then stood wide-eyed, his whistling checked for a minute before it began again. The room inside was Mrs. Desmond's bedroom, and it was so pretty that even the presence of Mrs. Desmond would have been superfluous. The pale green curtains were moving gently at the window, and the mirrors all over the room showed the movements over and over again, a faint green stirring, so that the stillness of the pale green bedspread was a surprise and the straight immaculate walls seemed all that held the room steady, as though without their firmness the room of movement and pale green would flow softly within itself, moving on to the sea, where it wanted to be. The floor here had a yellow rug, shadowed with the movement from the windows; on the pale dressing table stood bottles of perfume, many-colored and catching reflections which were in turn lost in the tenderly moving depths of the mirrors. Tod stood in the doorway watching, still whistling, until he found power to move across the room and look at himself in the mirror beyond the perfume bottles; there he was, tangled in the stirring mirror; he watched himself for a long time. Behind him, reflected in the mirror, he saw Mrs. Desmond's soft green bed, and Caroline's small bed beside it; there was a long soft yellow chair, and on the dressing table next to him Caroline's face was framed in gold. When he looked at the picture he saw his own face again, reflected sharply against Caroline's.

He picked up a perfume bottle and lifted out the top. The scent was overpoweringly sweet, and he poured some out into his hand before he stoppered the bottle and put it back. Then his hand smelled of the same overpowering sweetness, and with his hand up to his face he walked across the room and opened the door on one side of Mrs. Desmond's bed; rows of Mrs. Desmond's dresses hung there, pink and lavender and yellow and green and pale blue and grey; corresponding to them, on the other side of the closet, were Caroline's dresses, pink and blue and yellow, and shoes on the floor, Mrs. Desmond's narrow and arched, Caroline's tiny and white. The perfume was in the dresses, on his hand, and it made him blink his eyes. Half-shutting the closet door behind him, he wormed his way in through Mrs. Desmond's dresses and negligees until he reached the most hidden part of the closet, and he sat down on the floor, his perfumed hand over his face. There, far back in the closet in Mrs. Desmond's room, he said, quite loudly, all the dirtiest words he knew, all the words he had heard his brother James ever use, all the words George Martin taught the kids secretly and knowingly. Since there were only three or four words really bad enough, he said them over and over.

Finally, taking care not to disarrange the dresses, he came wearily out of the closet, smoothing the dresses down before he closed the door on them. The perfume still on his hand was beginning to make him sick, and he rubbed his hand against a dark coat of Caroline's, but the scent stayed. Holding his hand in back of him, he rapidly investigated the other doors; one was a third bathroom and the last was Caroline's playroom, with small clean toys put neatly around the walls; a tiny chair and table, a doll bed and doll dresser; the doll herself asleep in a doll carriage beneath a yellow coverlet. Mrs. Desmond's sewing-box was set prettily on a table in this room, next to a rocking chair, and Caroline's smaller sewing-box was set next to her mother's, with a smaller rocking chair alongside. Tod began to whistle again, and sat for a minute in the larger rocking chair.

He went out through the same dining-room door he had

used to come in, carefully not touching it, but slipping out sideways. In the garden, with the high Desmond hedge all around him, he crossed the driveway and went down to the end of the garden, where the lawn ended against flowering bushes and carefully trained lines of flowers in different colors. He sat down on the lawn and looked back at the Desmond house. He could see the glass doors, see into the dining-room, but not the hallway, not into the bedrooms.

He sat there for a long time, and then lay down. The grass, close to his face, interested him, and he pulled up a blade of grass and held it close to his face, trying to look deep into the rich green, letting his eye move up to the pale green at the tip and down again, trying to see into the heart of its tightly curled length. Against the sky it was long and straight, but it moved a little because his hand was shaking; it was hard to hold it still enough to see into it. He twisted it around his finger, and it moved back to its straight stand; he tied it in a loose knot, and it eased back straight again. Tying it he had bruised it; it turned a darker green where it was hurt, and he dropped it back on to the lawn again, although he could still see it limp and dark against its living brothers. He reached over his head and pulled a yellow blossom off a bush; this, too, interested him, and he looked at it as closely as he had the grass. Its petals were precise and neat, so soft he could hardly feel them against his fingers; annoyed at its soft pliability, he crushed it flat with his fingers and rolled the petals cruelly, until the flower was a little damp ball and he dropped it.

He must have fallen asleep; he was painfully aware suddenly of the perfume on his hand, under his face, when the realization of his face reflected in all those mirrors, shining distorted in the silver coffee-pot, superimposed on Caroline's picture, frightened him; and he sat up just as Mrs. Desmond's car turned into the driveway. Moving quickly, he went behind the garage, waiting there until the car was safely inside, pulsing tiredly in the building for a minute before it stopped. Then Mrs. Desmond and Caroline got out, and Mrs. Desmond said, "Do you have your teddy bear, darling?"

Tod heard them walking toward the house; he began to edge around the side of the garage, but did not dare put his head out to watch them go into the house. When he heard a door close he looked tentatively around the corner of the garage, saw no one, and fled down the driveway to the street, turned toward his home, and began walking slowly.

CHAPTER THREE

Mrs. Roberts put the toast down emphatically in front of her husband, not looking at him. She was still angry at him from the night before; she had sat up in bed, late, telling him how he looked to other men, how he disgusted other women, and had turned, finally, her hair over her eyes and her voice tired, ready to forgive him, and had found him asleep. Overnight (she had not slept, at last, but sat in the bedroom chair smoking all night and, watching the sky get lighter outside, had planned in detail how to pack the boys and their clothes and take them to New York, where she would find a job, anything, and Mike would never see them again), her anger had subsided into a cool watchfulness; as the sun came into the bedroom windows in the morning she realized for the hundredth time that she could never get the boys away, and if she did, could never get a job in New York or anywhere else, and if she did, would have to come back to Mike anyway. Mike could not be threatened, or frightened, but he could be driven somehow into a position so extreme that he must humiliate himself to get back. Mrs. Roberts was willing to wait.

A pounding upstairs indicated that the boys were up and quarreling. Mrs. Roberts went out to the foot of the stairs and called kindly (she was kinder to the boys at these times, waiting for her husband to enmesh himself, just as she was more impatient with them when she loved her husband best), "Listen, you silly kids, stop fighting and get dressed, or there won't be any breakfast for you."

There was a silence upstairs, and then Art said, "Well, he was kicking me."

"I was *not*," Jamie said with all the indignation of false innocence. "I never went near him."

"He was *so*," Art said. "I was lying here not doing anything. . . ."

"Never mind," Mrs. Roberts said. "Both of you get dressed."

She went back to her husband and sat down across the table from him. "I'll be glad," she said conversationally—it was a neutral topic—"to have that new girl here today."

"New girl?" Mr. Roberts was unable to read a paper at breakfast; until he had his coffee he existed in a sort of unpleasant stupor; it was the only thing, he maintained, which enabled him to shave and dress at all each day. Like anyone who possesses such a dubious gift, he was inordinately proud of it, and he delighted, later in the day, in anecdotes of how horrid he had been that morning, or, if he set off in the morning late without breakfast, driving with Mr. Desmond, how he had sat numbly in a corner of the car. Sometimes Mrs. Roberts felt in the morning that her husband was exaggerating his habits in order to make a better story at lunch. This morning seemed to be such a one; Mr. Roberts stared at her with glazed eyes, his hand shook when he lifted his coffee-cup, and when she spoke to him he turned his head slowly to look away from her. Mrs. Roberts, who was tired herself this morning, made her voice more sharp and her words more emphatic.

"We are," she said bitingly, "hiring a new servant this morning. Servant!" She laughed shortly. "A high-school girl. She is coming to help with the housework and the kids. Her name is Hester Lucas. Are you able to hear me?"

Mr. Roberts lifted his head, and then let it slump again.

"She's not a very pretty girl," Mrs. Roberts went on in her vicious voice, "but you may be able to find some charm in her."

Mr. Roberts closed his eyes once, briefly.

"But that is a subject," Mrs. Roberts said, pouring herself a third cup of coffee, "which I do not want to discuss any more with you."

She was not finished, and the arrival of Artie and Jamie in a wild shrieking chorus left her feeling cheated. Mr. Roberts stood up as the boys came in, put his napkin down, and went upstairs to finish dressing. With an effort Mrs. Roberts recalled her kindly feelings toward the children, and smiled down on them as they fought for the sugar.

"We're going to have a new servant," she said to the boys.

"Like Joan?" Jamie said.

"*Not* like Joan," Mrs. Roberts said shortly. Her eyes wandered to the stairs; Mr. Roberts would be down in a minute. "Not like Joan at all," Mrs. Roberts repeated. "This girl is named Hester. She is going to help me with the house."

"What will she do?" Artie was reading already; one hand brought cereal accurately to his mouth while the other hand held the book down on the table. Jamie ate slowly, babyishly, playing with his spoon and asking questions to keep his mother from seeing the untouched cereal. "What will she *do*?" he asked again.

Mrs. Roberts waved her hand vaguely. "All the things I don't want to do," she said. "Wash dishes, and keep an eye on you boys."

"She can't keep an eye on *me*," Jamie said. "I'll run away so fast."

"She's not much older than Artie," Mrs. Roberts said. "I hope she's a good worker."

"Like Harriet Merriam?" Jamie asked.

Mrs. Roberts was surprised. "Why like Harriet?" she asked. "Harriet doesn't have to work."

"Harriet's not much older than Artie," Jamie said.

"Harriet's *younger* than Artie," Mrs. Roberts said. "She's just bigger."

"Much bigger," Jamie said.

"Not like Harriet at all," Mrs. Roberts said. "Not like anyone. No one else in the neighborhood has a servant living with them."

Although Marguerite Desmond rarely smiled, she had never spoken a harsh word to or about anyone in her life. She had lived with Mr. Desmond for nineteen years, and in all that time had never raised her voice to him, or acted in any manner that was not genteel; she never treated her adopted son with anything less than perfect courtesy, and her attitude toward her neighbors was such as to set her apart in a lovely aristocratic isolation; she had never, to her knowledge, had a friend. In the few crises of her life, Mrs. Desmond had been collected and thoughtful; during the long uneventful years, serene. She was ungenerous because her family had been poor before she married Mr. Desmond, she was unsympathetic because no one had ever required any sensitivity of her, she was gracious because her mother before her had been gracious and because her daughter Caroline must in her turn learn to be womanly and lady like. Mrs. Desmond was neither intelligent nor unintelligent, because thinking and all its allied attributes were completely outside her schedule for life; her values did not include mind, and nothing that she intended ever required more than money. It must not be concluded, however, that with all these aspects Mrs. Desmond did not sleep and eat, cook and clean, comb her hair and drive her car, like the other mothers on the block. The only thing that set Mrs. Desmond apart was that she never knowingly said, or did, or thought, an unkind thing. Like Mrs. Merriam, Mrs. Desmond slept in her private room, away from her husband, only Mrs. Desmond had Caroline by her bed. Like Mrs. Roberts, Mrs. Desmond was fond of lobster; like Mrs. Byrne, she was excessively concerned about the cleanliness and general superiority of the food she served her family; like Mrs. Perlman, she did her own dusting and bedmaking, leaving the heavy scrubbing for a girl to do every morning; and, like Mrs. Ransom-Jones and Mrs. Merriam, Mrs. Desmond wore her long hair gathered in a knot at the back of her neck; Mrs. Merriam's hair was grey, Mrs. Ransom-Jones's hair was dark, but Mrs. Desmond's hair was pale yellow, almost white. Caroline's hair was the same color; together they made a pair of delicately shaded creatures, not quite colorful enough, without enough body, to mingle freely with the rest of the world.

It was a wrench to Mrs. Desmond, although not altogether a surprise, when, after four years of barrenness in his marriage, Mr. Desmond cautiously and tenderly approached the idea of adopting a son.

"You see," he told Mrs. Desmond gently, "this way we choose our own child—make sure he's healthy, and so on. It's not like—" Mr. Desmond stopped, and started again. "I mean," he said, "we'd take some poor unfortunate waif and give him a good home."

Mrs. Desmond felt that it was not her place to be lukewarm toward any of Mr. Desmond's enthusiasms, but she allowed herself to say, desolately, "I feel, somehow, that it's *my* fault."

Mr. Desmond took her hand and said very softly, "If you feel that way about it, Marguerite, we'll never mention the subject again." He dropped her hand and said, with a pathetic smile, "I would have called him John Desmond Junior."

The Desmonds did not entertain frequently, although the neighborhood ladies met at the Desmond house to sew as often as they met at the Merriams', or the Donalds'. When Mr. Desmond insisted that they invite people from the city for dinner, or for bridge, Mrs. Desmond, as cool and reserved as ever, sat at the head of her table speaking gently and competently, but the next morning she usually stayed in bed with a sick headache, allowing no one in to see her except Caroline.

With the neighborhood children, however, Mrs. Desmond was not shy, so that Mr. Desmond's plan for the children found her almost eager. "I've been thinking," he said one evening, abruptly setting aside his book. "I think these young hoodlums around here ought to be thinking of something else than roughhouse and foolishness." When his wife raised her eyebrows over her sewing to show that she was listening, Mr. Desmond went on, "What about all of them getting together and say, reading Shakespeare? Not *all* of the plays, of course," he added, before Mrs. Desmond could speak. "A few of the best, like *Romeo and Juliet,* and *Julius Caesar.* Then at the end of the summer, maybe, we could give a performance. Invite all the parents." He waited, beaming at Mrs. Desmond.

"I'm sure there's a good deal of talent in the children," Mrs. Desmond said, after thinking for a minute. "James Donald, for instance, is a very talented boy."

"James Donald," Mr. Desmond said, "and I think that older Roberts boy would do well with something like this to interest

him. Get him into the spirit of working with a group." He
stood up and walked over to the low bookcase beside the
fireplace, ran his finger along the books until he came to a
complete Shakespeare. "Here," he said, "now we can tell better." He sat down again in his chair, and began to turn the
pages over quickly. *"Midsummer Night's Dream,"* he said,
and smiled reminiscently. "Great stuff," he said affectionately
to the book. "Here's *The Merchant of Venice.* The quality of
mercy is not strained, and so on. Virginia Donald ought to do
that one," he said to his wife, and consulted the book. "Portia.
Virginia ought to do it very well."

"You'll have to have all the children, of course," Mrs. Desmond said.

"All of them," Mr. Desmond said. He closed the book on
his finger and said straightforwardly to his wife, "Now there's
something. It's absolutely up to people like us to lead the way.
A thing like this ought to include even—" He stopped, and
then said, "After all, Shakespeare's for *every*one."

"Let me see," Mrs. Desmond said. She was quite enthusiastic and put down her sewing. "We could make it once a week,
all the children here, and as soon as you finish one play you
could start another. And we could serve cookies and lemonade
afterward."

"Eighteen, nineteen," Mr. Desmond said, counting characters. "And that doesn't include all the servingmen and messen-
gers and so on. Someone will have to read two or three parts,"
he said. "How many children have we in the neighborhood?"

"Let me see," Mrs. Desmond said again. "There's Harriet
Merriam, and our Johnny."

"Like to hear old Johnny read Romeo," Mr. Desmond said,
and chuckled. "There's a part for our son." He took a pencil
from his vest pocket and wrote, "Harriet Merriam, John Desmond Junior—Romeo," in the back flyleaf of the book. "And
the Byrne children," he said, "Art and Jamie Roberts. I don't
know but what Jamie's too young," he said reflectively, looking at the names. "Might start a roughhouse."

"He's very well-behaved," Mrs. Desmond said. "I was wondering," she began tentatively.

"Wondering what?" Mr. Desmond said. He was writing down, "Virginia Donald—Juliet."

"The Perlman girl," Mrs. Desmond said. "Marilyn."

"What about her?" Mr. Desmond asked. "We're going to have everybody, you know."

"I wouldn't want to see her left out," Mrs. Desmond said. "She seems to be a very sweet girl. But if you read something like *The Merchant of Venice*, isn't there . . . wouldn't it be apt to embarrass her?"

Mr. Desmond stared for a minute, and then he said with some discomfort, "I see what you mean, yes." He turned the pages of the book quickly, read a few lines, turned a page and read a few lines again. "You're absolutely right," he said. "I'm glad you thought of it in time. And I think there's one in *Romeo and Juliet,* too."

"Could you read some other writer?" Mrs. Desmond asked. "Marilyn is such a nice girl."

"No sense in it unless we read Shakespeare," Mr. Desmond said. "Parents would probably think we just asked her down to insult her. They're so touchy, you know." He looked at his list, and said, "I haven't put her down yet."

"Perhaps after things are going well, and the children are enjoying it," Mrs. Desmond suggested, "you might invite her down for an evening when you know they won't be reading anything—anything unkind."

"I'll put her in a special list," Mr. Desmond said. He drew a line and wrote "Special Reasons" over it, and under it he wrote Marilyn's name. "Suppose old Steve Donald would like to join in?" he asked cheerfully.

"He's such a pleasant person," Mrs. Desmond said. "I'm sure he'll be pleased to know his children are enjoying themselves."

"Desmond, Merriam, two Donald, two Byrne, two Roberts—eight," Mr. Desmond said. "Who else?"

"Well." Mrs. Desmond thought. "There are the Martin children," she suggested.

"Well, now—that little Martin girl," Mr. Desmond said.

"Hallie," Mrs. Desmond said.

"I don't know as I can quite see her reading Shakespeare," Mr. Desmond went on cautiously. "Most of these kids, you can tell that even though they're young, there's stuff in Shakespeare they can *get*. Mean something to them. But I can't see Hallie."

"She's quite young," Mrs. Desmond said.

"Really too young, I think." Mr. Desmond drew another line, wrote "Too young," over it and "Hallie Martin" underneath. "And her brother," he said. "I can't see inviting one and not the other of them, can you?"

"Perhaps their family wants them to be together," Mrs. Desmond said. "It would be rude to invite George and not Hallie."

"Special reasons," Mr. Desmond said. He wrote George's name under Special Reasons, and leaned back. "That's everyone, isn't it?" he asked.

"Unless you want to include that girl the Roberts got today," Mrs. Desmond said humorously.

"*She* doesn't live in the neighborhood," Mr. Desmond said. "This is just for the children around here. I won't ever put her down." He began to count.

"I can't think of anyone else," Mrs. Desmond said. "Caroline can sit here with me, and watch."

"Still eight," Mr. Desmond said, frowning, "I don't know if there's a play with only eight characters." He began to leaf through the book again.

"They could each read two parts," Mrs. Desmond said.

"They all need so many people," Mr. Desmond said. "I don't even know as there's a play with only eight *principal* characters, even."

"You could read some parts, too, you know," Mrs. Desmond said. "The children would probably feel much better if you did, anyway."

"I don't know," Mr. Desmond said. His enthusiasm was evaporating, and he held the book idly on his lap. "If we ever wanted to *give* a play—"

"Perhaps the parents?" Mrs. Desmond suggested.

"But this was for the kids," Mr. Desmond said petulantly.

Disappointed, he put the book down on the table next to him. "I'll see what Johnny thinks," he said.

"Well, for heaven's sake," Virginia said, "we can *walk* down the *street*, can't we?"

"We might meet him or something," Harriet said. "Please, Ginnie. Let's go the long way around."

"It's too far," Virginia said. "Listen, if you're scared—"

"I'm not *scared*, exactly," Harriet said.

"He can't do anything to you," Virginia said. "You're silly, Harriet."

She began to walk deliberately down Cortez Road toward the highway, and after a minute Harriet followed. "It's just that my mother wouldn't like it, either," Harriet said.

Virginia stopped. "Listen, Harriet Merriam," she said, "if you're going to be scared all the time and always be wanting to go around the other way and afraid of your mother and everything I'll just go on down to the store by myself and not talk to you any more." She pulled her arm away from Harriet and stood, offended, looking away while Harriet hesitated.

"All *right*," Harriet said, "but if we get into trouble it's your fault."

"You're silly." Virginia put her arm through Harriet's again. "*Nothing* can happen."

Once decided, Harriet was persuaded to find arguments for Virginia's side. "After all, we're right where we can call for help from anyone," she said reasonably.

"And anyway my mother was as mad as yours was," Virginia said. When they were in front of the apartment house she slowed her steps down deliberately, and Harriet's anxious haste was retarded.

"Come *on*," she kept saying, caught by panic. "Ginnie, come *on*."

"I'd just as soon go right in and see him," Virginia said teasingly. "I'm not afraid. I sort of liked him."

"I didn't." Harriet let go of Virginia's arm abruptly as the door of the apartment house opened. "It's him," she said, "let's run," in a whisper; but when Virginia stood still Harriet waited, perhaps from loyalty, perhaps from terror.

"Hello, young ladies," he said. He was smiling, and Harriet recalled that they were right where they could call for help.

"Hello," Virginia said.

"I was sorry you could not come to tea on Tuesday," he said. He was not in a hurry today, and he looked very gay and pleasant, standing with his hat in his hand, his head bent courteously toward Virginia.

"We were busy that day," Virginia said easily. "We were sorry too."

"I was hoping to show you the apartment house."

"Perhaps we can come another time," Virginia said. For a minute Harriet was admiring Virginia's facility, her good manners, and then a sudden thought came to her: she wants to go, Virginia wants to go see that Chinaman, she was mad when she couldn't go, she really wants to go.

"I'll see you later, Ginnie," Harriet said. She started to walk away, but Virginia said, "Harriet, don't be silly," and Harriet stopped and turned. The Chinese man was looking at her, and he said, "I imagine I'm delaying you. You're in a hurry."

"No, of course not," Harriet said foolishly. "We were just going for a walk."

"Perhaps," he said, turning again to Virginia, "perhaps you would like to come in for a few minutes now?"

Trapped, Harriet heard Virginia saying, "Thank you, we'd love to," and realized that the Chinese man had turned back to the door and Virginia was following him. "Come on, Harriet," Virginia said, "we're going in."

Harriet was thinking of two things at once: she couldn't let Virginia go alone, not and ever be friends again afterward, but once inside they were no longer right where they could call for help. The two ideas merged stupidly. She ran after Virginia and whispered, while the man waited silently at the door, "We *can't* go in, Ginnie. My *mother.*"

"You're so silly," Virginia said. "And you're rude to whisper. Don't come if you don't want to." She spoke out loud and Harriet was aware of the Chinese man looking at her quietly, aware of her bad manners. She followed Virginia miserably through the doorway and over to the elevator. The foyer of the apartment house was brightly muraled; tropical fish pursued one another insanely over and around doorways, gilt—still unchipped—lay lavishly on the ceilings and floors, and on the elevator doors two more orange fish, goggle-eyed, solemnly regarded the unwary passenger. Harriet followed mutely while Virginia and the Chinese man got into the elevator. Virginia was saying, "I don't know why they paint fish all over everything."

"I suppose they feel that a dark building needs to have cheerful decorations," the Chinese man said. He pressed a button and the elevator began to move effortlessly upward; Harriet, crushed into a corner, watched the lines of floor slip by the little window in the elevator door; I can't get out till it stops, she was thinking.

"What floor do you live on?" Virginia asked.

"Five," he said. "The top."

The elevator door opened and he led them out and down a long dark carpeted hall. Now we're really far away, Harriet thought, probably there's no one else home in the whole house. They stopped at the last door, and the Chinese man said, "By the way, my name is Lee," and Virginia said, "I'm Virginia Donald and this is Harriet Merriam," and he opened the door and they went in. For a minute Harriet lingered in the doorway, wondering if this were her last chance to get help, wondering what horrible thing this man and Virginia were conspiring against her.

Inside they found a living-room that might have been in the Merriams' house, or the Donalds' house. The furniture was the same, the pictures were similar and similarly placed, and the small kitchen just visible beyond might have housed the Donald flowered plates or the Desmond pressure cooker. Harriet sat down in an overstuffed chair that looked comfortably familiar, while Virginia went over to the window and said, "Look, how far down. Harriet, come look."

The Chinese man disappeared into the kitchen, and Harriet whispered, "Ginnie, come here," and when Virginia came over, Harriet whispered again, "Look, how do we get out of here?"

"Look," Virginia said firmly, standing in front of Harriet with her hands on her hips, "look, this is lots of fun. You don't have to go spoiling it all the time."

She turned when the Chinese man came out of the kitchen carrying a tray. "I don't know," he said as he put the tray down on a coffee table in front of the couch and busied himself with glasses, "I don't know if you young ladies are allowed to drink wine?" He looked up inquiringly, and Virginia said, "I've never had any."

He gestured at the small bottle and the tiny thin glasses on the tray and said, "This is a very light wine, suitable for ladies." He laughed comfortably and went on, "I know that ladies as young as you are not in the habit of drinking wine, but perhaps just a taste." He poured a few drops into one of the tiny glasses and handed it to Virginia. When she took it she raised her eyes to him for a minute and then dropped them again, half-smiling. "I had tea ready for you on Tuesday," he went on, "but today I had no time, of course, to get anything special." He handed another small glass to Harriet, and she said, "Thank you," in a very small voice. Then, in a minute, still talking, he passed her a dish of candy, and she took a piece of that and set it on the ashstand next to her, along with the little glass of wine. Her mind was not functioning, but her mouth, well-trained, said "Thank you," automatically when someone handed her something.

Virginia tasted the wine and made a face, and Mr. Lee laughed and said, "This wine is made of rice; it is a Chinese wine."

"It's nice," Virginia said. She looked at Harriet and said cruelly, "My friend was afraid to come up here."

Mr. Lee was puzzled, and said, "I don't know why. I very often have guests for tea." He turned to Harriet and said very politely, "I hope you won't be afraid to come any more. I hope you'll come again."

Harriet said, "Thank you," again, almost inaudibly. After

waiting for a minute Mr. Lee turned back to Virginia and said, "Do you go to school?"

Virginia made a gesture of distaste. "I don't ever think about it in the summer," she said.

"I had to go to a school to learn English when I first came to this country," Mr. Lee said, as though he were beginning a story.

"You speak English *awfully* well," Virginia said. She sipped at her wine again and finished the little bit he had given her. "May I have some more?" she asked. "It's delicious."

Mr. Lee hesitated before reaching out for her glass. "I'm not sure—" he said, and then stopped. When Virginia continued to hold out her glass, with a bright smile on her face, he took it finally and filled it with wine.

Virginia, sitting back with her full glass, said dreamily, "It must be wonderful to have a nice place like this, so high up over the street, and you just sit up here and drink wine and eat candy."

Mr. Lee laughed and said, "I wish that were all I have to do."

Virginia looked at the pictures on the walls and said, "Are you an artist?" and Mr. Lee laughed again and said, "No, if I had my choice I would be a writer, but as it is I do what I have to and make it as comfortable as possible."

"What *do* you do?" Virginia asked.

Mr. Lee looked puzzled again. "I work here," he said.

"What sort of work?"

"Why," Mr. Lee turned his head to look at the kitchen. "I wash dishes, and mix drinks, and answer the door."

"But is that all—" Virginia was saying, but Harriet cut in, saying abruptly, "Do you mean you're the help here?" When Virginia looked sharply at her, Harriet said, "He's the help, the maid. This isn't his place at all."

"Did you think it was?" Mr. Lee looked at Virginia and then at Harriet. "I couldn't rent an apartment in this house," he said. "Not in this neighborhood. They wouldn't rent an apartment to me."

Virginia stood up. "Thank you very much," she said, "but we'd better be going." She put her full wine glass down very carefully on the tray.

With the realization that no harm was going to come to her, Harriet remembered her conscious manners. "You were very nice to ask us to come," she said. "I hope you won't get into trouble for having guests up here."

Perhaps Mr. Lee was angry with them, but he followed them politely to the door. "I am allowed to entertain my friends," he told Harriet drily, and said to Virginia, "I'm sorry you have to leave."

"Thank you very much," Virginia said, and Harriet echoed, "Thank you very much."

He closed the door after them as they went toward the elevator, and Harriet said, "I *told* you."

"I didn't know he *worked* there," Virginia said. "How could I know? He never told us."

"My mother will be furious," Harriet said. "So will yours." She thought for a minute and then said, "If they find out."

"Don't blame me," Virginia said. "It's not *my* fault."

When Tod Donald came across the street after lunch to see if he could get Art Roberts to go to the movies that afternoon, there was a strange girl sitting on the Roberts's front porch, and Tod stood for a minute at the foot of the walk before the girl looked up and saw him, and said, "Hi." As Tod came slowly up the walk she watched him, and when, he came close enough she said, "You looking for someone?"

She had a big head, big like a movie close-up, because her mouth and eyes and nose were all big, and her hair fell down straightly around her face, and the hair itself was almost orange. She seemed to be small and thin, otherwise, and Tod was not so much confused by her when he came close, and she spoke to him with her large mouth, and her voice was pleasant. "I'm looking for Art," he said. "Artie Roberts."

She jerked her head at the Roberts house in back of her. "You mean one of *them*?" she asked. "They've all gone out."

"Where did they go?" Whenever Tod had saved a little money

from his allowance he would ask Pat Byrne or Art Roberts to
go to the movies or down for a soda with him, his treat; that
way, although they never asked him in return, he had at least
their society for a while, and sometimes even overt friendly gestures from them. However, if Art and Pat were together, there
was no use in Tod's asking either or both of them to go with
him; he could have afforded, today, to take them both to the
movies, but he could not bear being the lonely third, the butt of
their laughter while he paid for their tickets.

"*He's* not home," the girl said, and after a minute Tod realized that she meant Mr. Roberts. "The boys have both gone
out somewhere to play, and *she* went to the store. Would I be
sitting out here," she demanded suddenly of the vacant air
beside her, "if *she* was around? No, I would not. I would be
inside working my ass off while I had to listen to her troubles."
She looked fiercely at Tod and continued, "Do you know what
happened to her fat little hand this morning? She burned it on
the stove, that's what she did. It nearly ruined the rest of her
life. So now she stands over me while *I* burn my damfool arms
off and all the time she's talking about how there's so much
work she just can't do it all herself and she's unhappy with her
husband and I'm to be very careful about not offending him.
Me *offend* him!"

It became somehow clear to Tod that this last sentiment was
admirable to the girl, and he smiled reassuringly. "Of course
not," he said feebly.

"I saw him down at school one night," the girl said. "One
night he came down when his lousy son was in that lousy play
they had. *I* saw him." She stopped meaningfully.

Her hair is dyed, Tod thought, appalled. Emphatically dyed.
It was positively black close to her head, and then it became
suddenly, dreadfully orange. Dyed. He wanted to touch it.

"Who are you?" the girl said suddenly.

Trying to remember, Tod could only think about her hair.

"You're Jim Donald's kid brother," she decided. "*I*
know Jim."

"Why do you dye your hair?" Tod asked unexpectedly. He
would never have asked if she had not identified him with Jim.

She frowned at him, bringing her big eyebrows together over her big eyes, and twisting her big mouth with contempt. "It's not dyed," she said. "That's a hell of a thing to say. It's natural." She touched it affectionately and then stood up suddenly.

Tod felt an arm around his shoulders, an unfamiliar, possessive arm. It was tight and did not belong around him, and he turned around to find Mrs. Roberts's head above him, her arm determinedly around him.

"Did you finish the dishes, Hester?" Mrs. Roberts asked icily. "Is the living-room dusted? If I neglected to give you enough work to keep you occupied—" Mrs. Roberts's fury took her breath away, and she stopped.

Hester said meekly, "I didn't quite finish. I came outside for a minute."

"This little boy," Mrs. Roberts said, "is the son of one of my friends. He is not one of your charges. I introduced you to my sons this morning."

"Yes, Mrs. Roberts," Hester said. She turned and went back into the house, and Mrs. Roberts took her arm away from Tod and followed, without speaking to him.

Tod moved back across the street disconsolately. He could still feel the taut pressure of Mrs. Roberts's arm across his shoulders; it was the first time Mrs. Roberts had ever put her arm around him.

"Back at last, are you?" Mrs. Mack said. She held the door open wider and her dog Lady trotted in with a guilty sideways look at her; Lady was big and slow-moving, and his usually clean brown fur was, tonight, streaked and daubed with mud, the white spot at his throat almost hidden. "Back at last," Mrs. Mack said. "Well, sit down, then, I've kept your dinner."

The dog, still guilty, leaped as unostentatiously as possible into a chair by the table, and Mrs. Mack went on, as she put the plates down, "Nothing's got cold, because I kept it warming for you, but if it's dried out you've got yourself to blame." She looked severely down at the dog for a minute, and the dog, not touching the food, only looked back at her until Mrs.

Mack smiled involuntarily and said, "Well, then, I'm not angry. Go, eat your dinner." She patted the dog on the head, and the dog, with signs of infinite relief, licked her hand, wagged his tail, and began to eat greedily from the plate. When the dog put a paw on the table Mrs. Mack slapped the paw and said, "Will you never remember?" and the dog took the paw down again hastily.

Although no one had been inside Mrs. Mack's house in the years since her husband's death, the two rooms in which she and the dog lived were kept clean and swept. The grey little house, so rotten and tottering outside, held, inside, a faded set of overstuffed chairs and sofa, a polished wood-burning stove, and, in the bedroom where Mrs. Mack and Lady slept, an old-fashioned mahogany bedroom set, with a glass of fresh dandelions in front of Mr. Mack's picture on the dresser. Lady sat in a plain kitchen chair at the table, and while he ate his dinner Mrs. Mack resumed work on the crocheted rag rug of astronomic proportions which was to go on the bedroom floor.

"Look," Mrs. Mack said to Lady, "not far to go now." She spread the rag rug over her lap on to the floor, and Lady regarded it with interest.

"It *is* pretty," Mrs. Mack said, as though agreeing with the dog's opinion. "I'll be glad when it's finished and we have a warm floor."

"Are you finished?" Mrs. Mack asked the dog, leaning over to look at the plate. "Aren't you going to have your tomato? I picked it only this afternoon." When the dog made no move, Mrs. Mack said, "Well, then, if you won't there's no making you," and she rose and carried the plate over to a low shelf where her dishpan stood, next to the small cabinet in which were the flowered dishes she and Lady used. She poured hot water into the dishpan from the kettle on the stove, and washed and dried the dog's plate while she said, conversationally, "I don't know as there's any use, really, in growing tomatoes if you won't learn to like them. They don't please me enough to eat them all alone, and even one tomato plant brings more than I can eat in a summer." The dog slipped down from his chair to move to one of the upholstered chairs, where he curled up comfortably, watching Mrs. Mack while she worked. "I suppose there's no use asking you where you've been?" Mrs. Mack said. She looked anxiously at the dog, but the dog turned his face away from her, and she said, "Well, when you're ready you'll tell me. I won't be angry, I promise you."

When the dish was washed and put away—all Mrs. Mack's movements were slow and cautious, and it took her almost a minute to set the plate down correctly, so that it would not jar its fellows—Mrs. Mack picked up the kerosene lamp from the dinner table and brought it over to set it on a small table next to the sofa. The weak light from the lamp could be seen only dimly from the Desmond house or the Byrne house, on either side of Mrs. Mack's house, because, although Mrs. Mack's windows were neatly curtained on the inside, they were covered with newspaper outside. Mrs. Mack turned the lamp up a little higher, and settled down with a sigh in the corner of the sofa. "It's a nice quiet night," she said. "No wind." Then she sighed again, and said, "Well."

She took a book from the table where the lamp stood, and said, "I want to go to bed soon, so we'll have an early lesson tonight." She opened the book to the place where the bookmark lay, and, running her finger down the page as she read, she began, "'Therefore is judgment far from us, neither doth justice overtake us; we wait for light, but behold obscurity; for brightness, but we walk in darkness. We grope for the wall like the blind, and we grope as if we had no eyes: we stumble at noonday as in the night; we are in desolate places as dead men. We roar all like bears, and mourn sore like doves: we look for judgment, but there is none; for salvation, but it is far off from us.' That means," she said to the watching dog, letting the book lie open in her lap, "that means, let me see. Obscurity, that's when it gets dark. Desolate, that means there's nothing there. You see," she went on eagerly to the dog, "we are all evil blind people. Salvation means some way out. You see," she said again, "the Lord is watching us all the time, and watching for every thing we do that is bad, because the Lord won't stand for anything that's bad." With the book still open on her lap she fell into brooding thought, her fingers moving slowly up and down the edge of the book's cover. The dog waited patiently for a little while and then dropped his head on his paws and closed his eyes.

Marguerite Desmond was tired by the end of an ordinary day, and she was shy and formal with guests at the best of times. Tonight, more than ever before, she felt that her husband was imposing on her, living happily far away in his distant softly colored world, while his wife labored and sometimes cried unnoticed. Tonight, with an appreciative smile on her face for Mrs. Montez, Mrs. Desmond was thinking darkly of her husband, who stood by the piano, his face rich with moving emotion while his hands moved softly in time to Mr. Montez' playing. Mr. Montez at least spoke English; he even spoke English through his piano playing, but he was blind. Mrs. Montez could see, but she spoke only Spanish, which neither Mr. nor Mrs. Desmond understood.

When Mr. Desmond looked around to his wife with poignant emotion on his face, Mrs. Desmond managed a slight smile, which she turned to include Mrs. Montez, who sat unattractively in a great chair and smiled steadily back.

Mr. Desmond had invited them in from San Francisco, without introducing them first to his wife, because he obviously felt that a man who could play the piano and was blind did not need an introduction anywhere but carried his calling card in his hands and his value in his face. Johnny, who had been pressed into service for the evening, sat on the other side of the piano with his hands folded in his lap. Mrs. Desmond sat at the other end of the living-room with Mrs. Montez, smiling brightly occasionally, and now and then nodding enthusiastically. Mrs. Montez smiled back, nodded, and watched her husband helplessly as though soon, somehow, he would turn to her and explain, in a language she could understand, the meaning of the evening, the long trip out on the bus, this polite blank woman who sat with her.

Johnny moved suddenly with a sigh, and Mrs. Desmond

and Mrs. Montez smiled again at one another. Then Mrs. Montez, still smiling, gestured at Johnny and looked inquiringly.

"Oh, yes," Mrs. Desmond said, and nodded more forcefully.

Mrs. Montez nodded back, complacently. Then, as though she had only just thought of it, she pointed to herself, her ample bosom, and held up three fingers.

Mrs. Desmond put her head on one side and looked extravagantly surprised. "Three?" she said, holding up three fingers, and Mrs. Montez nodded.

Mrs. Desmond pointed to herself and held up two fingers, and Mrs. Montez, nodding, held out her hand, palm down, in three step gestures, each one lower than the last.

Mrs. Desmond pointed at Johnny and then held out her hand, very low, and Mrs. Montez laughed and then so did Mrs. Desmond. Mrs. Desmond waved toward the back of the house and said, very distinctly, "Caroline."

"Caroline," Mrs. Montez said, making it sound different. She held out her hand to indicate the smallest of her three steps, and then, watching to see if Mrs. Desmond was following, put her hand on her stomach and made a face of great pain.

"So did I," Mrs. Desmond said. "Thirty hours, really, and the doctor said—" She stopped, and made her gesture for Caroline and a painful face such as Mrs. Montez has made. "Terrible," she said. Mrs. Montez nodded, made her largest step gesture, put her hand on her stomach, smiled pleasantly, and then spread her hands in surprise.

Mrs. Desmond looked incredulous, and Mrs. Montez shrugged, made her second largest step gesture, another pleased expression and then surprise. Then she made her smallest step gesture, put her hand on her stomach again, and looked agonized.

Mrs. Desmond said, "Sometimes it just happens that way," and when Mrs. Montez frowned, Mrs. Desmond shrugged and spread her hands. "I'm never going to have any more," Mrs. Desmond said. Then she put her hand on her stomach, shook her head violently, and made a pushing-away gesture.

Mrs. Montez laughed again, and nodded, repeating Mrs. Desmond's steps as emphatically.

Mr. Montez was still playing the piano; he played very softly, with large movements of his hands, a great deal of going up and down the keyboard. He had, as far as Mrs. Desmond could see, an expression of rapture on his face. Mr. Desmond looked just the same. Mr. Montez was thin and ethereal, and Mrs. Desmond realized suddenly that his playing was very inferior. Johnny caught her eye across the room and winked, and Mr. Desmond looked around at his wife with a confused blend of two emotions, his eyes sharp with annoyance, his mouth still trembling with fervor over Mr. Montez.

Mrs. Desmond, looking around to see Mrs. Montez, saw that she was still laughing. "You know," Mrs. Desmond said without thinking, "sometimes it *does* get a little on my nerves."

Mrs. Montez answered her quickly in Spanish, words that sounded in agreement, and Mrs. Desmond said quickly, "Of course, I think the *world* of my husband," and Mrs. Montez nodded, and said something again in Spanish, and Mrs. Desmond smiled reluctantly, and said, "I suppose they all have their faults, but sometimes it *does* really seem . . ."

Harriet stopped in the living-room doorway, dumfounded, her mouth open and her great feet stilled. "What are you doing, Daddy?" she asked. "What are you doing here?"

Mr. Merriam looked up at her from his armchair and smiled. "Can't I come home early for a change?" he asked.

"But it's *so* early," Harriet said. "Not anywhere near dinnertime."

"Thought I'd like to see my family for a change," Mr. Merriam said. "Spend a little time at home."

"Mother's not here," Harriet said. She moved back against the doorway and said, "She went out quite a while ago. You should have told her or something."

Mr. Merriam moved his newspaper against the arm of the chair. "Suppose you come sit down and talk to Daddy, Harriet. Been a long time since you and I spent a day together."

Harriet looked helplessly over her shoulder. "I was going

out," she said. "I just came back for my paper dolls." She looked over her shoulder again at the front door and said, again, "I thought I'd go out."

Mr. Merriam's smile faded, and he took up his newspaper. "You run along if you want to," he said.

Harriet was embarrassed, and she said hastily, "I don't *have* to go. I can stay here for a while."

"That's all right, you go ahead and play," her father said.

"I'll stay here for a while," Harriet said. She moved her feet uneasily and said solicitously, "Can I get you a cup of tea, Daddy?"

"No, thank you," Mr. Merriam said. "You go ahead and play," he said insistently.

"I don't want to now." Harriet came over cautiously and sat down on a stool near her father's chair. She was still embarrassed and uncertain what to say, but finally she remarked brightly, "Have a hard day at the office today?"

"No," Mr. Merriam said solemnly, "as a matter of fact, I thought it was such a nice day I wouldn't work at all, so I came on home."

"You're not sick, are you?" Harriet said suddenly, struck with suspicion.

"No," Mr. Merriam said. He shook his head. "I'm not even sick," he said.

"Mother should be back very soon," Harriet said. "She went to sew at Mrs. Donald's house. They sew every week at someone's house and this week it was Mrs. Donald's turn."

"What do they sew?" Mr. Merriam asked.

"They take their own sewing," Harriet explained. "They all sew. Next week they go to Mrs. Ransom-Jones's, I think."

"They do that *every* week?" Mr. Merriam said.

"Unless they're sick or busy or something," Harriet said. "They always go to a different house each week. They come here, even."

"Can you sew?" Mr. Merriam asked with interest.

"Not very well," Harriet said. "Mostly I'm a writer."

"I see," Mr. Merriam said. "What do you do with yourself all the time, Harriet?"

"I write," Harriet said, "and I play with the kids, and Mother is teaching me to cook."

"When are you going to make me a cake?" Mr. Merriam asked cheerfully.

"I can't make *cakes* yet," Harriet said. "Mostly Mother lets me help her with things like the sandwiches for tea, when the sewing ladies come here, you know, and I make the salad every day for lunch."

"I have a salad for lunch sometimes in town," Mr. Merriam said. "Isn't it a lot of bother to make?"

"We're on a diet," Harriet said, her face red. "I lost two pounds."

"Yes," Mr. Merriam said. He waited a minute and then said, "Be glad when school starts again?"

"No," Harriet said. She listened intently and then stood up. "Here's Mother coming," she said. "I guess I can go along now."

After the morning he had come peacefully across the street and found Hester Lucas sitting on the Roberts's front porch, Tod Donald began hanging around the Roberts house more and more; when Art was away, or busy, Tod cultivated Jamie. His most earnest desire was to be in the same house as Hester, to be where he might hear her voice, or find her suddenly, or talk about her to people who saw her constantly. Both the Roberts boys loathed her, and before long the neighborhood knew that she was leaving their house—after a bare two weeks, not quite so long as Mrs. Roberts's maids usually stayed—so that Tod was forced to do his investigating quickly. He had no idea what he was looking for, or why it seemed that he might find it through Hester, but she had come with a good omen, Mrs. Roberts's arm around him, and her larger-than-life eyes and mouth brought Tod back to her again and again with the conviction that here, somehow, he might gain back what he had lost by being born at all.

One evening, coming across the lawn to the Roberts's—he meant to borrow a book from Art, or ask if Jamie was home, or any idiot purpose that might bring him around Hester—he saw Hester sitting on the porch steps, almost the way he had found her first, and in the darkness he was able to distinguish only vaguely that it was his brother who sat with her. Sudden suspicion silenced his steps, and he went roundabout past the Byrne house and into the bushes by the porch, where they sat without ever having noticed him. From the bushes he could watch and hear everything, and see, most particularly, Hester's big head against the faint light from the doorway.

Hester was saying, "And so she tells me I have to go, as though I ever wanted to stay. That old goat."

Tod pressed closer behind the bushes, felt the cold rough stone of the porch against his shoulder. "*And* I didn't say a word," Hester went on. "The things I could of told her."

"No sense making trouble," James said. His voice sounded disturbed, reluctant. The night air, and the cold stone, and his brother's voice, made Tod shiver.

"I wouldn't make any trouble," Hester said. "I've had enough trouble, thanks." She snorted. "I know enough so's I can handle some old guy in the kitchen, thanks."

"Are you going to get back into high school?" James asked. Then, as though to cover up what must have been a private train of thought, he added quickly, "I mean, if you lost this job—"

"*I* don't care."

"I figure you must of gotten a bad deal," James said. "You didn't do anything."

Hester laughed. "I did so do something," she said. "I did plenty. *They* don't know what it's all about."

"I mean—" James seemed to be speaking very carefully; he sounded as though he were avid for detail and yet not anxious to ask directly, "I mean, they said they brought you right back and all."

"My father said he'd fix me if I didn't get an annulment," Hester said. "You see, an annulment, that means you didn't do anything, but a divorce—well." She laughed again. "If I got an annulment that meant I didn't do anything," she explained, and then added, significantly, "but we'd been *married* two *weeks* before my father even caught us."

James laughed too, falsely. "That must have been something," he said.

"I can get back in high school if I want to," Hester said. "They can't keep me out of high school if my father says I can go."

There was a long silence; Tod, craning his neck until the bushes rattled suspiciously, could only see Hester and his brother sitting far apart on the steps. Finally Hester said, softly, "I bet *you* wouldn't mind it either."

"What?" James said, startled.

"Being married to me for maybe two weeks," Hester said insinuatingly. "It was fun."

"I don't know," James said deprecatingly. "I mean, I never thought much about it."

"I *bet* you didn't," Hester said. She leaned toward James; Tod could see her. "It's *fun*," she repeated.

"I'm not ever going to get married," James said. "Not till I'm thirty-five, at least, and earning a lot of money; a wife wants a man who can take care of her." He moved uneasily, and then stood up. "Ought to be in bed," he said. "Training."

"Training?" Hester said.

"Football," James said, surprised. "Good night, Hester." He started across the street, and Hester watched him go from the steps and Tod watched him go from the bushes. Tod had no idea what his brother should have done, but he knew it was wrong for Hester to be sitting there alone right now. Forgetting that he revealed his eavesdropping, Tod pushed out of the bushes and came up onto the steps.

Hester watched him without curiosity. "What are *you* doing?" she asked.

Tod walked manfully up the steps and sat down next to her, where his brother had been sitting, and she looked at him tolerantly.

"I was listening to what you said," he told her.

"I saw you come out of the bushes," Hester said. "Your brother and his football."

"He really does play football," Tod said earnestly. "I'm going to play football too when I'm in high school."

Hester was quiet, looking at the Donald house across the street. "That his room?" she asked, gesturing at the upstairs window where a light had been turned on.

"His and mine," Tod said. "It's funny, he goes to bed earlier than I do sometimes and he's older."

"That's because of the football," Hester said.

Tod waited for a minute and then said, "Was that really true about you? About being married?"

"Sure," Hester said. She touched her dyed hair lightly with one hand. "I ran away from school and got married. *Everyone* knew about it."

"What did you do?" Tod asked, and knew suddenly that the question was a mistake; Hester was looking at him oddly, he had been too blunt, had pushed his need for information too far.

"You run along," Hester said. "You go on home to bed."

Desperately, trying to make it up, Tod said, "*I'd* like to be married to you."

"For God's sakes," Hester said. "The very idea." She stood up and went to the door of the Roberts house and said over her shoulder, "What do you think I am, anyway?"

Harriet Merriam sat by herself on the curb in front of the house-for-rent. All day the painters had been there, and apparently plumbers, and strange heavy men in dark business suits, and the children had pressed around them, saying, "Is someone going to move in here?" and, "Mister, are you fixing it up for someone to live in?" One of the painters said genially to Virginia Donald that he thought "there wouldn't be all this work going on if they was going to tear it down," and so, finally, it was confirmed: there were to be new people on Pepper Street, perhaps new children.

Everyone else was down at the vacant lot playing baseball, but Harriet seldom joined in, at baseball or tag or hide-and-seek, actually because she was fat and the other children made fun of her, ostensibly because her mother had forbidden her to play. "I have a sort of weak heart," Harriet confided once to Virginia and Virginia told everyone else, "my mother thinks and the doctor thinks I shouldn't do much running around like the other kids."

Harriet was wondering if there would be any girls moving into the house-for-rent, and if so, if one of them might not be a good kind of friend for her; since the affair at the apartment house she had been suspicious of Virginia, afraid that some silly word from Virginia might lead Mrs. Merriam to the traces which would bring her inevitably, and inexorably, to Harriet's part in the affair. Perhaps one of the new girls who would live in the house—they would be like in *Little Women*, and Harriet's friend would be Jo (or just possibly Beth, and they could die together, patiently)—would love and esteem Harriet, and some day their friendship would be a literary legend, and their letters—

Marilyn Perlman walked past, slowly, and then stopped and turned back. "Hello," she said.

"Hello," Harriet said. Marilyn came over and stood beside Harriet, looking back at the house-for-rent.

"I guess someone's going to move in," she said.

"Sure," Harriet said. She was bewildered; she had never spoken particularly to Marilyn; why should Marilyn stop and speak to her? She had no idea what to say or where to look; whenever she saw Marilyn she was embarrassed about remembering the ugly look on Marilyn's face that day in school when Helen Williams had made some sort of a meaningless fuss about Christmas. Marilyn sat down, suddenly, next to Harriet on the curb. "Listen," she said in an honest voice, "I wanted to talk to you for a long time."

"What about?" Harriet said.

Marilyn put her chin on her hands and stared straight ahead. "Just about everything," she said. "You like to read, don't you?" When Harriet moved her head solemnly Marilyn said, "So do I," and then stopped to think. "Do you get library books?" she asked.

"No," Harriet said. "I've never been to the library yet."

"Me neither," Marilyn said. "We could get library cards, you know."

"Have you read *Little Women?*" Harriet asked.

Marilyn shook her head and asked, "Have you read *Vanity Fair*?"

"I haven't read that yet," Harriet said. "I liked *Little Women*, though."

"Is it at the library?" Marilyn asked. "I want to get books at the library. They give you a card and you go in and take any books you want and then you bring them back when you've read them. Of course you've got to take very good care of them."

"I liked *Jo's Boys* too," Harriet said.

"You want to go down to the library sometime?" Marilyn asked.

"I could probably go some day," Harriet said.

"Tomorrow," Marilyn said. "It opens at two in the afternoon, I'm pretty sure. And I know where it is."

"All right," Harriet said; it was settled, and they sat quietly together in a silence now companionable. "I was just thinking," Harriet said finally, "what kind of people are going to live in this house."

Marilyn looked over her shoulder at the house. "Couldn't be any worse than Helen Williams," she said.

Sitting easily beside Marilyn, Harriet said, "I hear she's in San Francisco now and she goes around with any man." It was not true, and Marilyn knew that as well as Harriet, but it seemed to both of them a completely justifiable (although almost meaningless) assumption.

"I didn't like her much," Marilyn said. She added carefully, "You know who else I don't like much?"

"Who?" Harriet said, becoming at that moment an accomplice.

"Virginia Donald," Marilyn said with finality. "I don't like her at all."

"She's not much," Harriet admitted. As a final recognition of bond with Marilyn she said, "I know something about *her*."

"What?" Marilyn said.

"Promise?" Harriet asked, and Marilyn nodded expectantly. "She goes around with Chinks," Harriet said.

Marilyn opened her mouth in horror, and for a minute Harriet was frightened. "You promised not to tell," she said.

"I won't," Marilyn said. "I promise *again*."

It was the night before Hester was to leave; she was to get breakfast in the morning and then pack and go home and because there seemed to be no possible harm she could do, Mrs. Roberts let her come outdoors and join the neighborhood children at their nightly games. After strenuous prisoner's base and wild tap-the-finger, they had settled down on the Donalds' lawn to play some quieter game. When they saw Hester coming across the street to them, Pat Byrne said, "Let's make Hester play," and they all laughed, and someone—probably Tod Donald—shouted, "Come on over and play, Hester."

"That's just what I'm doing," Hester said. With the children she was usually good-natured and amiable; it was only when she met adults, those mysterious creatures whose world she had invaded too soon, that Hester became menacing and ugly, as though it were necessary to her to establish, immediately, her status as an invader by right of superior ability. "What you kids playing?" she asked as she came on the lawn.

"You know how to play Tin-Tin?" Virginia, as hostess, asked her, and when Hester shook her head they explained raucously. Tin-Tin is probably as old as children; Hester recognized it as a game she had played under another name. Wherever children congregate they will probably have their own version of Tin-Tin, its elaborate ritual determined by the children and their fathers and their grandfathers operating individually on an immutable theme. Pepper Street's Tin-Tin was as nonsensical as most; the entire introductory ritual had lost its meaning and probably its accompanying dance:

It: (starting at the head of a line of children sitting on the curb) Tin-Tin.

Victim: Come in.

It: How much tin do you want today? (In a sing-song pattern, as fast as possible.)

Victim: Ten pounds (or) As much as will fit on the head of a pin (or) A hundred-and-fifty tons (or any idiot sum coming to mind).

After questioning every person in the line, and receiving an answer, "It" began again at the head, whispered some familiar word or name or nonsense syllable into the victim's ear, and began the new ritual:

It: Tin-Tin.

Victim: Come in.

It: Where will I get the money for my tin?

To which the victim must answer with his secret name, and "It" might then continue questioning, asking any personal or outrageous or hilarious question, to all of which the victim must answer with his idiot name. The object was, of course, to make the victim laugh; as soon as he did, he yielded a forfeit, and the whole procedure filled some deep undefined need in neighborhood life never exactly equaled by prisoner's base or tag.

If "It" spent a reasonable length of time on one victim, with the rest clamoring for service, he abandoned the persecution, and the first resisting victim in each game became the next "It." Virginia Donald was "It" at the moment, by virtue of an almost impregnable solemnity under the name of "Clark Gable." When Hester came over and sat down at the end of the line Virginia had already begun with Harriet, who was first, and Hester said quietly to Tod, who sat next to her, "Where's your brother tonight?"

Tod had turned eagerly to Hester when she sat down, had waited shyly for her to speak to him, and now he said miserably, "He's out somewhere."

"With some girl?" Hester asked. "He ever go out with girls much?"

"I guess so," Tod said. He turned away from Hester to watch Virginia moving down the line to him, and Hester said kindly, "He's pretty lucky to have a kid brother like you."

"Tin-Tin," Virginia said indifferently to her brother.

"Come in," Tod said, and Virginia said, "How much tin you want?"

"Four-hundred-million-billion-quadrillion pounds," Tod said, and no one heard him.

"Tin-Tin," Virginia was saying to Hester.

"Come in," Hester said.

"How much tin do you want today?" Virginia asked, giving the words her fullest singsong.

Hester hesitated, and Tod began "Million-billion . . ."

"Shut *up*," Virginia said to Tod, and Hester said, "Enough to make a hat."

Everyone laughed, and Virginia went back to the head of the line. She named Harriet "Crazy Cat," and Harriet laughed on her first question. She named Art Roberts "Popeye," and Art survived so long on "Popeye" that Virginia gave him up and went on, establishing him as "It" for the next game. She went along down the line, whispering, laughing herself to make others laugh, making desperately funny questions. There was a debate as to whether a grimace Mary Byrne was unable to control constituted a laugh. When Virginia came to Tod she named him perfunctorily "Hallie Martin," and when Tod did not laugh, but only repeated his frightful name in a whisper, she gave him up after two or three questions and went on to Hester; everyone was waiting for this, and Virginia had been puzzling all down the line for a good name, excruciating questions. Perhaps the fact that Art Roberts's mother was on her front steps across the street, listening, and had heard Art win on "Popeye," suggested the final name to Virginia; at any rate, she named Hester, secretly and with malice, "Art Roberts."

Hester drew back and stared. She knew, as well as everyone in the neighborhood, that Art detested her, that he had begged his mother to send her away, that he called her, killingly, "Filthy Lucas." Virginia knew, too, what Hester probably did not, Art Roberts's neighborhood boast that he had told his mother the story of Hester's runaway marriage, gleaned and enlarged from neighborhood gossip, was thus immediately instrumental in her dismissal.

"Where will I get the money for my tin?" Virginia asked slowly.

Hester was silent. Somehow, as she sat on the curb with the

children around her and Mr. Desmond sauntering up the block on his evening walk and Mrs. Roberts on her front porch, it came to Hester that the evening was focusing on her; tomorrow night she would not be here, last night she had not been allowed to play, and in ten years, wherever she was, whatever she was doing to keep alive, these children would still be quietly growing, protected and sheltered with the strong houses of their parents and the quiet assumption that streets were made for them to sit on. It occurred, certainly, to Hester for the first time, that regardless of what she and Mrs. Roberts thought of one another, and whatever cruel vengeance operated between the Hesters and the Mrs. Robertses, Virginia Donald definitely and automatically thought of herself as superior. Mr. Desmond might be diplomatic and tolerant, Mrs. Ransom-Jones indifferent, James Donald awed and reluctant, although somehow accessible, but Virginia Donald stood calmly looking down on Hester, as she always had and always could.

Hester put her head back and said to Virginia Donald, and loud enough so Mrs. Roberts—who, after all, lived on Pepper Street with the rest of them—could hear, "Mike Roberts."

It was against the rules of the game for "It" or anyone else to remind the victim of his true name; by changing her name Hester was definitely out, but Virginia knew that everyone in the game, and Mrs. Roberts, who was staring across the street, thought that she had given Hester that name. "*That's* not the name I gave you," Virginia said emphatically.

"Mike Roberts," Hester said.

"I didn't give her that name," Virginia said to the other children in the quiet line, "I gave her another name than that."

"Mike Roberts," Hester said.

"Listen," Virginia said, and Hester said, "Mike Roberts," and began to laugh.

"Arthur. James," Mrs. Roberts said clearly across the street. "Come home at once."

There was no need for her to speak again. Art and Jamie were halfway across the street already, and as the other children rose and started quietly up or down the block, across the street, into their houses, anywhere away from Hester and the unmentionable thing she had said, the only voice was Tod Donald's, chanting insistently, "You lost, Hester, you laughed. Hey, everyone, she laughed."

CHAPTER FOUR

It was dreadful; they moved in during a hot morning and everyone was there. Harriet Merriam and Marilyn Perlman walked arm in arm up and down the block, pretending not to watch; Virginia Donald, who associated pointedly with Mary Byrne of late, sat with Mary on the Byrnes' front lawn, and they giggled; most of the boys played a haphazard baseball game in the street, far enough away to be out of the way of the moving van—if you could call it that—close enough to see everything. Tod, alone, came near in order to say "Hello" to the driver, and got a glare and a "Get away from there, kid," for his pains. Everyone was careful to seem unaware of the whole thing; until it had been assimilated and talked over with parents and finally decided upon in neighborhood grapevine conclave, no one dared say anything definite, even smile too broadly. It *might* be acceptable, after all.

The moving van was a truck, with open slatted sides and furniture heaped on it, not stowed carefully inside, as Pepper Street furniture tended to be in transit, but piled, as though careless people had gone through a previous home room by room, carrying out the furniture as they came to it, throwing it into the truck, and going back for more. Besides the driver, who sat sullenly in the front of the truck without moving, there was only a thin uneasy young man to help the girl who was carrying in most of the furniture. She was perhaps no older than Harriet or Virginia or Marilyn or Mary, she was certainly no taller than Art Roberts, she was busy and worried and seemed not to know that she was being watched by eyes her own age.

"*Please* try to hurry," she said once to the thin young man. "They'll be here soon."

The young man growled something, and the girl stopped for a minute and looked at him and then shrugged and went on tugging a table up the steps. She was not strong, apparently, but she was nearly as strong as the young man, and the furniture seemed to be mostly lightweight wicker chairs and tables; the beds were cots which came up in one folded piece, and such things as lamps and dressers and desks and bookcases seemed not to be there at all. All the furniture that went into the house-for-rent came out of the small truck, and most of it the girl carried in alone. Much of it was in bundles, apparently of clothes or tablecloths or curtains or tapestries, tied roughly together, which the girl hauled along the sidewalk, dragging dirt with them.

When all the furniture was out of the truck and inside the house, the driver got heavily down from the cab of the truck, and he and the young man stood on the sidewalk talking with the girl. They argued, the driver waved his big arms, and the young man stamped his foot, and the girl looked from one of them to the other, and finally, her shoulders tired, counted her money out to them. They went back together and got into the truck while the girl stood on the sidewalk looking from the truck to the house. As the truck started away, the young man leaned out and yelled something at the girl, which no one but her was able to hear, although she blushed darkly and turned away. Then, as the truck pulled off down the street, she looked up and for the first time seemed to realize that Harriet and Marilyn were close to her on the sidewalk, Virginia and Mary across the street, the boys quiet for a minute in their ball game, and Tod Donald at the curb. She looked at Harriet and Marilyn, who were closest, and ran her tongue over her lips nervously.

"They made me pay them nearly twice what they said they would," she said. Harriet was embarrassed and looked away, but Marilyn said immediately, "That's a real dirty trick."

"It certainly is," the girl said. "It was too much in the first place." She was, seen close up, definitely not a pretty girl; she wore heavy glasses and balancing heavy bands on her teeth, and her hair was cut across her forehead in an uneven over-grown bang. She was wearing a man's shirt and a pair of blue dungarees, and she looked very much as though she had been working hard all morning, at dusty, unrewarded work. When she spoke to Marilyn she blinked earnestly through her glasses.

"Is that *all* your furniture?" Tod said from the curb, and the girl turned around and looked at him for a minute; it was, everyone discovered eventually, one of her many nervous habits. She looked for a long time at everyone who spoke to her, recognizing and estimating the words and their source before daring to reply.

"What do you mean by that?" she asked finally, and Tod said insistently, "Do you live all by yourself?"—the question everyone wanted answered.

"My mother," she said, "and my sister. They're coming in a little while."

"Like Helen Williams," Tod said, but Marilyn was asking, "Why did you have to move in all alone, then?"

"My mother had to bring my sister," the girl said. "I always do all these things." She stopped for a minute and looked at Marilyn, and then at the other children, one by one. "I never moved before, though," she said. "I don't remember what happened the last time we moved."

"I stayed with my aunt when we moved," Marilyn said.

"I don't have any aunt," the girl said.

Virginia Donald was coming across the street, with Mary following timidly. Gradually the whole group of children was drawing in, the boys abandoning any pretense of a game and coming slowly closer, and the girl standing in the center with Marilyn and Harriet next to her.

"What's your name?" asked Virginia from the middle of the street.

"Frederica Helena Terrel," the girl said. "Frederica Helena Terrel," she said it again, and then a third time, "Frederica Helena Terrel."

"Frederica Helena Terrel," Virginia said. She came close to the girl and looked her up and down insolently. "Fred-er-ic-a Hel-en-a Ter-rel."

The girl began to blush again, as she had when the truck driver yelled at her, and Virginia said, "What's your sister's name?"

"Beverley Jean Terrel," Frederica said. She looked at Marilyn, and Marilyn started to say something and then closed her mouth when Virginia went on, "And what's your mother's name?"

"*Mrs.* Terrel," Frederica said.

Virginia laughed shortly; it was because she had nothing else to say, but it sounded menacing and unkind.

Suddenly, appallingly, Marilyn said what she had to say. She had never spoken to Virginia before, or to either Roberts boy, or to the Byrne children. Since she and Harriet had been friends they had talked to each other, but suddenly Marilyn, in the group of children for the first time in her life, found herself outside of a familiar situation; she was one of a group of spectators, watching and participating tacitly in the torment of an outsider by a Virginia Donald or a Helen Williams.

"You shut your fat mouth," Marilyn said to Virginia. "You just shut up for once in your life and try to act decent."

Pat Byrne made motions of fainting on the sidewalk, but the look on his face was pleased. Virginia opened her mouth and then obviously could not remember the words she wanted to use, looked at Mary Byrne, who looked away, and then at Harriet, who said weakly, "Marilyn, don't start a fight."

"You can go ahead and fight if you want to," Frederica said unexpectedly. "I've got to go indoors and get the furniture arranged before they come."

She went in through the door of her house before anyone could speak. Then Virginia gave Marilyn a cold look that swept up and down, gestured to Mary Byrne, and walked back across the street. The boys melted away, and Tod chased after one or another of them, calling frantically, "Hey, wait."

Harriet and Marilyn, arm in arm, started off toward Marilyn's house.

"I'm glad," Marilyn said as they walked.

"That Virginia's a *terribly* mean girl," Harriet said. "Did I tell you what she does?"

When Harriet and Marilyn went to the creek they went to a different spot than the one the boys favored; instead of climbing down to the old creek bed and sitting in the faintly damp grass at the bottom they went a few hundred feet past the fallen log to a place on the bank where the trees lining the creek circled out to make a little clearing. Here the grass was always dry, and mossy, and, since they were across the creek from the golf course, and far away from any houses on the Pepper Street side, Marilyn and Harriet could sit quietly and secretly, safe even from their friends. They had dug a hole in the center of this clearing, marked by a small stone at each corner, and lined it with rocks, spending a pleasant co-operative afternoon doing it, reverting to the completely informal mud-pie state of mind. Neither had been thinking particularly as they dug and grimied themselves, neither had worried about what she said or how she looked, and finally the hole in the ground was so special a symbol of their new and enduring friendship that they could not decide what to put in it. When one has created a thing exactly necessary; when a hiding place so accurate exists, the difficulty which arises is that the thing, containing itself, has room for nothing else. Even in a new friendship between maidens, there may be nothing worth hiding in a secret place.

Harriet wanted to make the hole a time-capsule site. "A tin box," she said, "and we each of us put in whatever we like best, that is, of just what *we* think and write and all that. Not even other people's poems we like," Harriet added, thinking of what her mother would say if she knew about the secret hiding place. "We don't *have* to put stuff in, of course," she went on, "but maybe things like—" she stopped helplessly.

"We could put in things like pictures of people," Marilyn said dreamily, "and souvenirs, and . . . like memories, and things."

"I don't have any pictures of people," Harriet said reluctantly. "Except my family, that is."

"I don't really have many pictures either," Marilyn said.

The hole in the ground stayed empty for nearly a week, a long time in a fast-moving summer. Several times Harriet and

Marilyn came to their secret place, with their library books
and the notebook each had taken to carrying, and their candy
bars and ice cream cones, and they sat for long afternoons on
the grass, talking deeply, and opening the grass cover of the
secret hiding place to make sure that no one had disturbed it,
and that the sides hadn't fallen in. Hidden by the trees, and certain they had not been followed, they told one another about
their pasts, their futures, and their talents. One afternoon
Marilyn said, lying with her head on her arms, looking off into
the grass by her face, "Do you believe in reincarnation?" and
Harriet said, looking up from *The Girl Scouts at Rocky Ledge*,
"You mean, like turning into wolves?" and when Marilyn said
scornfully, "Wolves!" Harriet fumbled with her book and then
said pettishly, "You and your big ideas!"

"Honest," Marilyn said after a short silence. "You know,
reincarnation is where you used to be someone else once,
before you were born this time."

Harriet listened, interested. "Like what?" she asked.

Marilyn had something she wanted to say, something burning in her mind to be told; perhaps the only reason she needed
Harriet, or any friend, was to get this said, finally. "Lots of
people," she began, "think that maybe once they were like
Julius Caesar or Jo March before they were . . . well, born,
this time. And then when those people died they turned into
the ones they are now. Like for instance you might have
been—" Looking at Harriet, Marilyn sought for a word.
"—Becky Sharp, before you were Harriet Merriam."

"Or Jo March," Harriet supplied, fascinated.

"Maybe we both knew each other once before," Marilyn
said. "See? That's why we're friends now."

"Maybe you were Amy," Harriet said.

Marilyn frowned slightly. "I *know* who I was," she
announced dramatically. Then, suddenly shy, as though Harriet were after all not the person to tell, as though she had
come, unwilling and driven, too close to what she wanted to
say, she turned quiet and sat looking down at the grass again,
her wide ugly face pressed close against the fresh green.

"You mean," Harriet said slowly, considering, "you mean, I

could be *anything*?" The sound of the wind moving through the trees, a distant shout from the golf course, seemed to bring her an echo of barbaric rites, clashing temple bells, perhaps from the distant, only-just-remembered past; "I bet I was Egyptian," she said, carried away, "I *always* wanted to go to Egypt."

"I know," Marilyn whispered softly to the grass, "I remembered a long time ago."

Harriet was silent, smiling faintly, lost in her dim pagan temple. "I think about it all the time now," Marilyn said, "I remember lots." Uneasy and reluctant, she stopped again, and then said, "I remember all the time, I lie in bed and think about it."

"Well, *what*, for heaven's sake?" Harriet said. "I told *you*."

"I *remember*," Marilyn said emphatically. "I really do." Her voice became softer, as though she were describing a scene familiar and lovely. "There's a very very *very* blue sky, and the hills and grass are so green they almost hurt your eyes and the road is white and it curves around the hill and there are flowers and trees and everything is so *soft-looking*, and far away beyond the hill you can see where the road leads into a little town. . . . I can see the town, too," she added, never looking at Harriet. "It has little houses with low roofs and a bridge over a little river and all the houses are white and they have brown wood trimmings and there's a village green in the center of the town. . . ." She was quiet, and Harriet waited breathlessly. "Then," Marilyn said, her voice stronger and filled with longing, "there's a little covered wagon that comes down the road and inside they're all talking and laughing and singing. . . . There's Pantaloon, and Rhodomont, and Scaramouche, and Pierrot, and—" She stopped again. "And Harlequin," she said into the grass, and then began to speak very fast. "And I'm standing on top of the hill waiting for them and when I see them coming and he is standing in front beside the man who is driving—I forgot to tell you, they have an old white donkey pulling the wagon—and he is waving and calling me, and I run down the hill as fast as anything, I can feel how fast I'm running and my feet just touching the ground and the wind in my face blowing my hair back and I'm running. . . ." She stopped again; her words patently had no more power to carry her meaning.

When Harriet saw that Marilyn was tearful she was embarrassed. "Where *is* all this?" she said harshly. "It doesn't make any sense to *me*."

"No place," Marilyn said. "Forget it." She sat up, her ugly face angry. "It's silly," she said. "I'll tell you all about it sometime."

"I think," Harriet said, trying to look inspired, "that I was one of those people who had to take care of an idol or something. In a long white dress with jewels in my hair. And chanting."

"I know what let's put in the box," Marilyn said suddenly.

"What we remember?"

"That's all over with," Marilyn said. "Let's put down what we think we'll be this time. I mean, like in this reincarnation. See, in maybe ten years we'll be grown-up and then we'll know. What we're going to be this time, I mean."

"No," said Harriet, meaning she could not understand.

"What I mean is," Marilyn said carefully, "let's both write down what we're going to be like in maybe ten years from now."

"What we'll be in ten years," Harriet said reflectively. "I'll be twenty-four."

"We'll write it down, and we won't look at each other's," Marilyn said, "and then in ten years when we meet here again we can look at it."

"We have to promise, though," Harriet said; they were building it together now. "We have to promise never to look at them until ten years."

"Let's write it now," Marilyn said.

A mystic raptness seized them. Solemnly they tore identical pages out of their notebooks, and, taking their pencils, sat down to write. Harriet wrote half a page, Marilyn only a few lines, but it took them both a long time. Then, as solemnly, each folded her own, and they opened the secret hiding place and put the papers in.

"Rest here, all my hopes and dreams," Marilyn said, and

Harriet, a little embarrassed, said, "A curse be on whoever touches these papers."

Then the hiding place was covered and all traces of it effaced. Marilyn held her hand out over the hiding place and Harriet took it, and Marilyn said, "Now you're my closest and dearest friend, Harriet."

"We'll always be true friends," Harriet said. "We'll never separate. We will always be able to communicate in our thoughts."

"I'll always know where you are and what you're doing," Marilyn said.

"And each other's most secret thoughts," Harriet said.

There seemed to be no way to end it. Finally Marilyn drew her hand back and Harriet dropped her hand to pick up her book. They were quiet for a while, and then Marilyn said in her normal voice,

"Golly, if Virginia Donald ever finds this place."

"She wouldn't know it was us," Harriet said. *"Probably."*

Frederica Terrel's family came so quietly that no one knew they were there; perhaps they stole in through a back door, or walked quickly up the street unobserved; at any rate, they came softly and invisibly, and the first anyone knew they were there was when Frederica came hesitantly down the front steps, looked up and down the street and, after standing on the sidewalk for a minute, noticed Miss Fielding sitting on her front porch and came to the foot of Miss Fielding's walk.

"Excuse me," Frederica said. She blinked nervously through her glasses. "Where would I find a grocery store near here? I want to get some food and things."

Miss Fielding leaned forward to look over the stone railing of her porch. "A grocery store?" she asked. She went to the nearby grocery almost daily, had done so ever since moving to Pepper Street, but the fact of someone's asking her a direct question frightened her. She thought deeply, and Frederica fidgeted nervously, blinking through her glasses. "I guess," Miss Fielding said, "at least—do you want just plain things? Like potatoes, for instance, and bread?"

"And canned goods," Frederica said. "And my sister has to have milk."

"Well," Miss Fielding said. She thought again. Perhaps Frederica would not be favorably impressed with Miss Fielding's regular grocery, and then Miss Fielding would be blamed; worse still, the man in the grocery (Mr. Jowett, that would be) might find Frederica, coming with Miss Fielding's recommendation, insolent, or demanding, or extravagant, or even, just possibly, someone who wanted to open a charge account—to buy, in other words, without paying—and the thought, in Miss Fielding's mind, of herself facing Mr. Jowett tomorrow after having sent him such an unreliable customer. . . . "Well," Miss Fielding said. Her face brightened and she looked beyond Frederica. "There comes Mrs. Ransom-Jones," she said with relief. "I'm very sure she knows the *best* place to go."

Frederica turned around slowly, planting her feet one beside the other in little steps so as to pivot without losing her balance. She regarded Mrs. Ransom-Jones heavily as Mrs. Ransom-Jones came down the street, and Miss Fielding, leaning even farther forward, called out delicately, in her shrill old woman's voice, "Mrs. Ransom-Jones? *Will* you come here for a moment, please?"

Mrs. Ransom-Jones, just passing the house-for-rent, brought her eyes back guiltily from the frank stare with which she was watching the lower windows; she had, most patently, been trying to see inside, and her tone was sharp as she said, "Miss Fielding! Good afternoon." Miss Fielding waved her hand to bring Mrs. Ransom-Jones closer and said, "This is our new neighbor, I believe. She is in trouble, and I think you can help her better than I."

"I want a store," Frederica said abruptly. "I want to buy some groceries."

Mrs. Ransom-Jones considered prettily, trying with over-courtesy and every conceivable air of good breeding to persuade Miss Fielding and this lumpy girl that the Ransom-Joneses did not peer in windows. "There's Delamar's, of course," she said. "But of *course*." She laughed lightly, good breeding and all. "It's a little *expensive*," she went on. "He has things like *paté de fois gras* and all sorts of elaborate things like that. I really only shop there when I want something special. For dinner parties or something."

"I want to get some baloney," Frederica said. "And some milk and some bread and a can of peas and a dozen eggs and probably a bag of potato chips."

"There's Mr. Jowett," Miss Fielding said. Mrs. Ransom-Jones's recommendation would be above reproach.

"Mr. Jowett," Mrs. Ransom-Jones said. "Yes, Mr. Jowett would do."

"And I ought to get light bulbs," Frederica said. She turned around again to Miss Fielding, quickly, with the first emotion she had shown; it seemed to be anger. "You know those damn people they took away every single light bulb?" she demanded.

"Isn't that nice," Miss Fielding said, flustered, and Frederica turned back to Mrs. Ransom-Jones. "*That's* cheap, isn't it?" she said. "We'll be in the dark."

Mrs. Ransom-Jones, whose good face depended on a complete lack of interest in Frederica's family, said, "If you turn right at this corner and then left at the highway and go straight down for about three blocks you'll find Mr. Jowett's. In a little block of stores."

Frederica opened her mouth slightly to listen better, and when Mrs. Ransom-Jones had finished Frederica repeated the directions in her usual dull voice, and turned in response to Mrs. Ransom-Jones's daintily pointing finger and trudged off down the street.

"Not even 'Thank you,'" Miss Fielding said in the tone of one who was not at all surprised.

"Well. . . ." Mrs. Ransom-Jones said, in the tone of one who was used to it. She and Miss Fielding smiled at each other, and then Miss Fielding said, "You've got a nice day for your walk, Mrs. Ransom-Jones."

"I thought I'd get some air," Mrs. Ransom-Jones said. "Lillian was asleep, so I thought I'd run out for a few minutes."

"How *is* your sister?" Miss Fielding asked immediately.

Mrs. Ransom-Jones smiled sadly, and waved one hand. "Not very much better," she said.

"I *am* sorry," Miss Fielding said.

"But of course. . . ." Mrs. Ransom-Jones said.

"You never can tell," Miss Fielding said. "I've known people, people who were just like that. . . ."

"Nothing seems to help much, one way or the other," Mrs. Ransom-Jones said. She put one foot forward, and nodded brightly. "Such an *odd* girl," she said.

Miss Fielding stayed leaning forward for a minute and then sat back, resigned. "I imagine the whole family must be odd," she said.

"Indeed, yes." Mrs. Ransom-Jones, her walk apparently over, turned to go back up the street. She waved good-bye to Miss Fielding, and, keeping her face carefully averted, started past the house-for-rent. Because Mrs. Ransom-Jones was looking steadfastly across the street at the Byrne house, and because the girl, apparently Frederica's sister, was tiptoeing down the walk looking backward at her own house, they collided square in front of the house-for-rent, and Mrs. Ransom-Jones said, "Good heavens!" and tried to recover her balance, while the girl, with a solidness and lumpy stolidity reminiscent of Frederica, stood gaping.

"Don't you know how to apologize?" Mrs. Ransom-Jones said with annoyance. "Do you just stand there like an ape?"

The girl grinned; unlike Frederica, she had strong white teeth and a great heavy unthinking face; when she grinned at Mrs. Ransom-Jones it seemed to be partly apologetic, partly complete uncomprehending bewilderment; perhaps she was dazzled by Mrs. Ransom-Jones's smooth hair, her smartly planned linen dress, the clean white shoes. Mrs. Ransom-Jones, thinking of this in order to recover her poise, noticed that the girl was barefoot. She was a tall stout girl, taller perhaps than Frederica, and certainly barefoot. Mrs. Ransom-Jones said, "Barefoot? A girl your age?"

The girl grinned again, but Mrs. Ransom-Jones seemed to have communicated with her, because she looked down at her feet and then back at Mrs. Ransom-Jones. It seemed to be an effort of mental enthusiasm for her to move; in order for her to hold out her hand to Mrs. Ransom-Jones she first had to think of it, then think of the hand, then send some kind of slow deliberate message down the arm to the hand, all the time regarding her hand with rapt concentration. When the hand moved and went out to Mrs. Ransom-Jones the girl was pleased; she smiled again, and Mrs. Ransom-Jones, moving back a step, said, "What—?"

"Money," the girl said slowly. Her voice was thick and again reminiscent of Frederica's dull tones. "I've money." Speaking seemed to be less of an effort than anything else except smiling; perhaps the girl was accustomed to sitting quietly while people took care of her when she voiced her wants. "Plenty of money."

"Really," Mrs. Ransom-Jones said helplessly. She was acutely conscious that Miss Fielding, somewhere behind her, was leaning forward again—leaning forward and perhaps even standing up—and that what Miss Fielding was seeing did not lend any appreciable dignity to Mrs. Ransom-Jones's poise and graciousness. For Miss Fielding's benefit Mrs. Ransom-Jones straightened her back, put her shoulders steady, and said carefully and emphatically, "I don't think you ought to be out with all that money, my dear. Your mother should be with you. Now you turn right around and go back inside your house and tell your mother I—" Mrs. Ransom-Jones emphasized the "I" slightly—"said that you should not be out alone. Do you understand me?" Mrs. Ransom-Jones rested and then added, for Miss Fielding, "My dear."

The girl stared blankly, looking from Mrs. Ransom-Jones to the money in her hand, and, once, down at her feet again. Mrs. Ransom-Jones took a breath and said, sharpening her voice a little, "You *must* turn right around and go back into the house. I'm *sure* your mother doesn't know you're out here." Finally Mrs. Ransom-Jones said, "How *old* are you?"

The girl smiled again. "Twelve-and-a-half," she said.

Mrs. Ransom-Jones gasped. Certainly the girl was *big* enough. . . . "Twelve-and-a-half," she said, without any change in her voice, which she imagined was soothing and yet forceful. "Now you turn right around and go back in—"

"How old are you?" the girl said. "I'm twelve-and-a-half."

Certainly the girl had no trouble talking; Mrs. Ransom-Jones estimated anxiously that the real problem seemed to be elsewhere, perhaps *very* slow reactions, Mrs. Ransom-Jones thought; it was difficult to imagine, on Pepper Street, in broad daylight, that a new tenant, and unfortunate girl, could be—

"Dear," Mrs. Ransom-Jones said, "suppose we go in together and see your nice mother. I'll just go up to the door with you and we can tell your nice mother that you met me outside and I made you come home again. I'm sure she'll be happier to know that you're back in the house, and safe." For one swift minute Mrs. Ransom-Jones allowed herself to look down at the money again. She retained in her mind, from the first glimpse, a vision of (was it possible?) a twenty-dollar bill, among others. Her second glance confirmed this. A twenty, and several ones. "A girl twelve years old!" Mrs. Ransom-Jones said involuntarily. She took the girl's arm with determination and faced toward the house. For a minute the girl resisted, and Mrs. Ransom-Jones, with a renewal of the feeling of how she must look to Miss Fielding, had the sensation of tugging against a battleship heavily moored, which gives slightly to a tug, but ultimately remains where it is. Then the girl, leaning against Mrs. Ransom-Jones, began to move along beside her, and Mrs. Ransom-Jones guided her up the walk to the front door. She rang the doorbell and the girl chuckled affectionately. After waiting for a few minutes Mrs. Ransom-Jones said excusingly to the girl, "Just so you're safe inside," and tried the door-handle gently. The door opened, and Mrs. Ransom-Jones put her head inside and said, "Hello?" There was no answer, and Mrs. Ransom-Jones said, her voice a little anxious, "Where *is* your nice mother, dear?"

"Asleep," the girl said.

Mrs. Ransom-Jones put her head inside again. The furniture was still pushed roughly against the walls, but someone had been trying to arrange it. The table had chairs around it, the chairs were all facing correctly—that is, none of them were facing the walls—and there was a path between them and around the room. "Hello?" Mrs. Ransom-Jones said. Then she took the girl by the arm and swung her inside. "You just go in and stay there," she said, with an irritation that deepened when she again noticed the money in the girl's hand. Must be thirty dollars there, Mrs. Ransom-Jones thought; she saw the girl well inside the door and closed her in. Then, coming down the walk, Mrs. Ransom-Jones refused to look at Miss Fielding, but turned doggedly up the street to her own house.

Miss Fielding, relaxing into her chair again, watched indifferently while Mrs. Ransom-Jones tripped up the street. Miss Fielding was old and sensed constantly, rather than knew sometimes with sharp clarity, the decay of her body around her, the gradual easing of tensions that had once been vital. Miss Fielding was interested in anything for a little while, would rise from her chair to watch a cat crossing the road, but after the little while was over, Miss Fielding, in her chair, went back to searching the face of death.

Consequently Miss Fielding watched unregarding the back of Mrs. Ransom-Jones going rigidly up the street, the face of the odd girl's sister looking out the front door. When the heavy girl Mrs. Ransom-Jones had put so firmly inside her own house came out of the house again, no more warily than before—like an animal that persistently and dumbly walks against the bars of its cage expecting each time around that they will have ceased to restrict it—Miss Fielding raised her eyes and let them follow the girl down the street. Miss Fielding's eyes were not good any more; she had not seen the money in the girl's hand while the girl was talking to Mrs. Ransom-Jones, but when the girl passed Miss Fielding's porch Miss Fielding's dim eyes registered vaguely that there was money about the girl: some spot of unmistakable green. It was past Miss Fielding's usual hour for retiring indoors; she rose uncomfortably and went inside.

In her neat little house she was able to move comfortably with the steady pull of her body toward death; for more years than she could remember Miss Fielding had been following herself along a well-defined path, around the circle of hours that made a day, around the circle of days that made a year, around the circle of years that made Miss Fielding older and nearer to lying down for good. When she was forty-odd and had finally resigned any thoughts of new ways of life (perhaps at one time Miss Fielding had regarded marriage as she now regarded death, perhaps she had thought of a somewhat larger, more involved life), Miss Fielding had set out to make her world as clean and uneventful as a convalescent room; sometimes it seemed, even, that Miss Fielding's long convalescence from birth would culminate in sufficient strength for her to die without effort. The tiny house on Pepper Street was Miss Fielding's only home; there was no other room on earth where she could go and be recognized. She had no relatives, no friends except those people who passed her front door. A slight reliable flow of money, from a bank Miss Fielding had never seen, fed her and clothed her and kept her housed. Her little home was dark and well-fitted; Miss Fielding had gradually sold (not given away; there was no one she knew well enough to give things to) most of the furniture she had been encumbered with at the death of whoever had preceded Miss Fielding in this quiet life; and now, with her chair by a neat table, her narrow bed, her dresser where her clothes lay, her two-burner stove, and her brush and comb, Miss Fielding waited for her time to be up. "Passing on," she called it.

When she died her things would dissolve neatly; the little money from the bank would stop automatically when its purpose was ended, her small residue of furniture would be sold and the money neatly applied to Miss Fielding's passing, the Pepper Street house would snap back to its original purpose as a dwelling for the living, and the pinpoint of consciousness of Miss Fielding which would be left would be in the minds of children and busy people, and would grow tinier and vanish in a reasonably short time. Some lives, ending as Miss Fielding's would, leave a grain of memory, like a grain of sand, in the depths of another mind, a grain of sand which is like the constant irritation under an oyster's shell, eventually to grow with coating after coating of disguising beauty into a pearl. Sometime this memory would be pried loose, in its rounded beauty, to stand by itself as an object of delight. Miss Fielding had no fears of ultimate survival, even in beauty. When she passed on, she would draw after her every trailing mist of herself, effacing herself so completely that even after her death, even after her bones, which she could not help, were gone, she would be a bother to no one, would intrude on no mind.

She rocked slowly in her familiar chair while her supper eggs were boiling; the toast was made and the teapot steeping. When the doorbell rang she was frightened; she ran first to cover the toast, and then had to come back from across the room to lift the pan of eggs from the stove—they could coddle in the hot water—and hover apprehensively over the teapot. She had never been interrupted making her tea before; the wise thing was to plan to throw it out, but that would be wasteful. Unreasonably Miss Fielding took the lid off the pot and set it aside—perhaps the rising fumes. . . .

When she answered the door Frederica Terrel was standing solidly outside. "Yes?" Miss Fielding said, the door open an inch.

"My sister?" Frederica said. "Have you seen my sister, please?"

"Your sister?" Miss Fielding wondered. If she entered into explanations of Mrs. Ransom-Jones and Frederica's sister, she would have to be here, standing, and with her tea growing too strong. The girl had no right. "Ask Mrs. Ransom-Jones," Miss Fielding said, and started to close the door.

"Why?" Frederica frowned and put her hand out to stop the door. "Did you see my sister? What does Mrs. Ransom-Jones know about her?"

Miss Fielding sighed. "I don't know," she said. "Please go away."

"But I've got to find my sister," Frederica said. She made her heavy voice begging. "You see, she runs away sometimes, and it isn't safe. So I've got to find her."

Miss Fielding was in panic. By refusing to discuss the events of the afternoon she had tangled herself in a worse problem. She felt time running away behind her, the tea spending itself, the eggs solidifying. "I really don't *know*," she said.

"Please," Frederica said. "Where does Mrs. Ransom-Jones live?"

"Up the street, up the street," Miss Fielding said. She waved her hand toward up-the-street.

"Don't you even know which way she went?" Frederica was urgent, hoping that some question might provoke an answer with information.

A horrible thought found Miss Fielding. Her eggs would be too hard, she would have to do them over, she would be late finishing her dinner, it would be dark by the time she got to her porch, with nothing to watch she would be bored and go in before she had had enough air, and then sleep badly and wake up with a headache tomorrow. "I don't *know*," she said. "Go and ask Mrs. Ransom-Jones, won't you?"

This time she closed the door. She heard Frederica breathing noisily outside for a minute or two and then the sound of the heavy shoes going down the steps. Miss Fielding flew back to her teapot.

"If you're not going to pay attention," Mrs. Mack said severely to her dog, looking at him over the top of the book, "we won't have any lesson tonight at all." When the dog pulled his gaze hastily back to her, Mrs. Mack looked down at the book and began to read: "'So will I break down the wall that ye have daubed with untempered mortar, and bring it down to the ground, so that the foundation thereof shall be discovered, and it shall fall and ye shall be consumed in the midst thereof: and ye shall know that I am the Lord. Thus will I accomplish my wrath upon the wall, and upon them that have daubed it with untempered mortar, and will say unto you, The wall is no more, neither they that daubed it.'" She let the book fall to her lap, and said to the dog, "You remember about how the Lord destroys evil people?"

The ladies were sewing at the Roberts house; there was a bowl of salted nuts between Mrs. Merriam and Mrs. Donald, a dish of chocolates between Mrs. Ransom-Jones, who was making herself a blouse, and her sister, who did not sew, but sat with her hands folded, turning her eager eyes from one lady to another. A bowl of fruit stood on the round table in the center of the room, and Mrs. Roberts, with frequent mysterious trips to the kitchen, and numerous secret smiles and hints, had managed to convey the fact that there was to be something exceedingly special for tea.

"How well you do that, dear," Miss Tyler said to Mrs. Donald, leaning forward to look at the sweater Mrs. Donald was knitting. "Your fingers go so fast, it makes me dizzy." She looked at her sister and laughed apologetically. "We never learned to knit, did we, sweetie?"

"I never learned any useful arts at all," Mrs. Ransom-Jones said cheerfully.

"I'm trying to teach poor Harriet to sew," Mrs. Merriam confided, "but she's actually *clumsy* at it."

"You know," Mrs. Donald said, "it seems funny not to see little Caroline Desmond sitting there so quiet, sewing away on her little embroidery."

"I missed her today," Mrs. Ransom-Jones said. "I like to watch little Caroline, always so busy."

"Harriet just won't *apply* herself," Mrs. Merriam said. "She's intelligent, of course, but she will *not* apply herself."

"Oh, Lord," Mrs. Roberts said, from the midst of the complicated business of sitting down after one of her trips to the kitchen. "Don't try to make the child work, Josephine. This is summer—vacation."

"Anyway," Miss Tyler said, leaning toward Mrs. Merriam, her eyes wide, "your little girl will have servants to do everything for her when she grows up." She looked around at her sister. "Servants still do all those things?" she asked hopefully.

"Not *my* daughter," Mrs. Merriam said, and tightened her lips. "Harriet will be a lady, I hope, but I don't want her growing up to expect service from others. Not *my* daughter."

"I could use a little service from others," Mrs. Donald said, and sighed. "I don't know why the men don't have to do the housework for a change."

Mrs. Roberts giggled. "I can see Mike," she said, and Mrs. Ransom-Jones said, "Or Brad," and they both laughed, looking at each other.

"Brad would do it, Dinah," Miss Tyler said. "You shouldn't say things like that. Brad would do anything *you* asked him."

"Mike Roberts," Mrs. Roberts said. She spread her hands

wide in a gesture of hopelessness. "He can't even boil water," she said.

Mrs. Merriam said casually, "Your Hester is gone now, isn't she, Dorothy?"

Mrs. Roberts hesitated, looking down at her sewing, and Mrs. Ransom-Jones said smoothly, "None of those high-school girls can really do housework."

"They are *terribly* inefficient," Mrs. Donald said, nodding profoundly.

"*I* had a high-school girl once, for about two weeks," Mrs. Ransom-Jones said. "It was awful."

"It was *awful*," Miss Tyler said to Mrs. Donald, in a loud whisper. "She was always making eyes at Brad—Mr. Ransom-Jones."

"Hester seemed like a nice quiet girl," Mrs. Merriam said.

"I smell something burning," Mrs. Ransom-Jones said emphatically, and Mrs. Roberts, still clutching the sock she was mending, rose and fled to the kitchen, scattering spools of thread as she went. "I think," Mrs. Ransom-Jones went on, addressing herself to the sewing on her lap, "I really think, girls, about Hester, you know, that we only make matters worse talking about it. *You* know."

"Let bygones be bygones," Mrs. Donald said earnestly.

"I'll *never* forget this girl of ours," Miss Tyler said to Mrs. Donald.

"Please let's talk about something else, Lillian," Mrs. Ransom-Jones said, and Miss Tyler turned around to stare at her sister for a minute. Then she said, her lip trembling. "Of *course*, Dinah, if you'd rather I went on home. . . ."

Mrs. Roberts came back into the room, and Mrs. Ransom-Jones said loudly, "Everything all right?"

"Fine," Mrs. Roberts said. She looked archly around the room. "I nearly ate it *myself*," she said.

"I'd never *forgive* you," Mrs. Donald declared.

"I realize," Miss Tyler said softly to her sister, "that you think I disgrace you whenever you take me out."

"You know," Mrs. Donald said to Mrs. Ransom-Jones, across Miss Tyler, "Virginia is driving me crazy to get her a yellow print evening dress like that one of yours—she's *wild* about it."

"It's much too old," Mrs. Ransom-Jones said, shocked. "She'd be *lost* in a style like that."

"She thinks she may be asked to some college dance or other this fall," Mrs. Donald said, "and she wants to look older."

All the ladies laughed, and Miss Tyler said softly to Mrs. Ransom-Jones, "I can get across the street by myself, all right."

"Tell her to keep on looking fifteen while she can," Mrs. Roberts said jovially. "They never realize."

"Having a pretty daughter," Mrs. Donald said despairingly.

"I *do* think you're wise," Mrs. Merriam said smilingly to Mrs. Donald, "not to try to *teach* Virginia anything. Anything useful, that is," she added, turning her smile on Mrs. Ransom-Jones.

Tod Donald, seated at his family dinner table, knew already that he hated every part of it more than anything else in the world. He had time, every night at dinner, to hate things individually: the blue-patterned plates, always seemingly set the same, although the chipped one was not always Tod's, but sometimes went to James or Mr. Donald; the cup by his mother's plate and the cup by his father's plate, and the straight glasses with daisies on them that sat by Tod and James and Virginia, full of milk. Tod even hated milk, when it was served in those glasses.

He hated the blue platter his mother served from, and the salt and pepper shakers, which were glass with red tops, and he hated the silverware designed in flowers, some pieces scratched almost beyond recognition. He even hated the round table and the succession of tablecloths, one pale blue with yellow leaves, one white with red and orange squares. He hated the uncomfortable chairs, particularly his own, where he sat squirming, and he hated his family and the way they talked.

Mrs. Donald, who was gracious and youthful at almost forty, and regarded herself as something more than a housewife, chose, like her daughter, to save her ingratiating side for worthy adherents; at home she was vague and discontented,

although she never forgot to dress prettily for her family and
herself and to put on fresh lipstick before sitting down at table.
She looked irresistibly like Virginia; a little older, her hair
short and curly instead of long and straight, her whole naïve
childishness a deliberate denial of the years of experience she
had had and Virginia was still entitled to; they might, under
some circumstances, be taken for sisters.

James and Virginia, with their mother, did most of the talking at dinner; Mr. Donald dined doggedly, as though com-
pelled to sit down with his jailors but not to be courteous to
them; Tod moved softly and constantly, eating quickly, trying
not to be noticed. Virginia and James spoke boldly in their
own house, soothingly to their mother, and James, who was in
unceasing training, permitted himself a delicacy of appetite
lovingly administered to by his mother and sister.

It was one of Tod's duties to appear regularly at the dinner
table, since a place was set for him and a potato cooked in
his name. He was expected to receive food, participate in
Christmas, sleep, and keep his clothes under his family roof;
his mother's bright head at the top of the table would turn
inquiringly to either side before she started carving, counting
her family in a small gesture of grace which assured her that
the food so energetically cooked would be used. If Tod were
absent he would be punished.

The night that Hester Lucas left, the Donalds dined on baked
beans and brown bread; the night that Frederica Terrel was out
begging her sister from Miss Fielding and Mrs. Ransom-Jones,
the Donalds ate ham and sweet potatoes. It was one of Mrs.
Donald's housekeeping shortcuts to plan solely in terms of
foods traditionally associated: she never served bacon without
eggs, corned beef without cabbage, pork chops without apple-
sauce; if she had had occasion to serve ambrosia she would
have made a point of getting nectar to go with it. Consequently,
meals at the Donald house occurred with a sort of unerring
accuracy, and inevitably the family conversation followed in
the same vein, helped out by the fact that Mrs. Donald carried
over her singleness of association into one adjective constant
for one person ("poor Miss Fielding, dreadful Mrs. Byrne")

and one state of mind for one situation. Mrs. Merriam's phone call about the horrid letters Virginia was writing to boys had caught Mrs. Donald in a mood of weary boredom, and dull stuff the letters had seemed ever since; the Williamses had moved while Mrs. Donald was washing her hair, and her recollection of that family remained in a state of wet, off-balance agitation, not unmixed with a hint of grey.

James inherited this sober single-mindedness, but in him it was transformed into a vast restriction of his life to two or three plain ideas, the principal one being his position as a football player and his consequent value, one of the lesser his future as an architect or just possibly a great dramatic actor. And Virginia, who might have inherited something from her father, sat nightly at the dinner table estimating the balance of power as it shifted back and forth between her mother and her older brother, flattering herself secretly with the thought that she was the cleverest person in the house.

As the summer drew on, roast lamb and mint sauce had come up again on the Donald menu. Mr. Donald, who stared at the blue plates in front of him because they were as familiar as the faces of his family, but more serene, was lost somewhere in thought, and Mrs. Donald was in a condition of unusual suspense.

"I declare," she said insistently, "I don't know what they're *thinking* about, those people."

"Not up to us," James said. "None of our business."

"It will positively ruin the neighborhood," Mrs. Donald said. She craned her neck to see down the table, and then said to Virginia beside her, "Get Father's plate, dear. He needs more lamb."

Virginia rose and walked to the other end of the table, giving Tod a spiteful poke as she walked by. He raised his head to look at her, his mouth full, and followed her with his eyes as she went to her mother again.

"I *wish* you'd make Toddie eat like a human being," she said.

"Toddie," Mrs. Donald said automatically, without turning her head.

"If you don't eat nicely you can leave the table." Virginia returned her father's full plate, circled wide around Tod to avoid the kick he had waiting for her, and sat down at her own place again, smoothing her skirt complacently.

"We won't be here forever anyway," James said. He looked at his father significantly and added, "I *hope*."

"Father does the best he can, dear." Mrs. Donald's adjective for her husband was "helpless." "If he can do anything about it we'll be able to move soon enough."

"I'd like to live past the gates," Virginia said.

"Past the gates," James mimicked in a falsetto. "Listen to the movie actress with a million dollars."

"What's the matter?" Virginia said viciously. "Would it hurt your training to live decently?"

"Children," Mrs. Donald said. She rested her chin gracefully on her hand and smiled at Virginia. "I wouldn't mind a big house with a couple of maids to do all the work."

"And a swimming pool and a tennis court," Virginia said.

"Anyway," James said positively, "about the wall, it's only a rumor, and they're probably not going to do anything at all."

"*Toddie*," Virginia said.

"What?" Toddie spoke defensively, without looking up.

"*Must* you smear your food all over your face?" Virginia made an elaborate display of disgust and said urgently, to her mother, "I just can't *eat* with him, honestly."

"I don't see how they could do it, anyway," James went on reasonably, "it would cost too much, for one thing, without making the neighborhood any better."

"It would certainly ruin the neighborhood," Mrs. Donald said. She raised her voice slightly with the inflection that meant she was talking to her husband, and said, "We're wondering about the new road they say they're putting in."

Mr. Donald looked at her and then down at his plate again, and Mrs. Donald said to Virginia, "We've got to think about clothes for you before school starts."

"I want a suit," Virginia said. "I want a perfectly plain suit with a couple of ruffled blouses."

"And you really ought to have shoes," Mrs. Donald said.

"Toddie," James said sternly across the table, "if you don't stop playing with your food you can just leave the table."

Life on Pepper Street was peaceful and easy because its responsibilities lay elsewhere; its very paving had been laid down by men now far away, planned by someone in an office building even Mr. Desmond had not seen. Like those who live directly in contact with the ground, like the people who had, more or less long ago, been ancestors to everyone on Pepper Street, their lives were quietly governed for them by a mysterious faraway force. The sky, which was close but uncontrollable, had been an immediate power to the forefathers of Mr. Desmond or Mr. Byrne, as had the wind or the earthworm, which might or might not belong to them, and then, finally, the other unseen governors: the prices in a distant town, regulated by minds and hungers in a town even farther away, all the possessions which depended on someone in another place, someone who controlled words and paper and ink, who could by the changing of a word on paper influence the very texture of the ground.

On Pepper Street, inhabitated by descendants of farmers, people were accustomed to thinking of themselves as owners, but even the very chair on which Mr. Desmond sat in the evenings belonged to him only on sufferance; it had belonged first to someone who made it, in turn governed by someone who planned it, and Mr. Desmond, although he did not know it, had chosen it because it had been presented to him as completely choosable. He might have taken one of several others, differing in style or color, he might have done without a chair, but ultimately the one chair he bought was completely controlled because Mr. Desmond wanted a chair, and if he wanted a chair, had to buy one, and if he were going to buy one, had to buy one that existed, and if it existed at all . . . and so on.

It was on the same principle that Mr. Desmond had a house, that he had a street in front of his house. Mr. Desmond would not have bought or built a house in a site where it was impossible to have electricity, but then someone he did not know had declared that electricity was possible in the first place. Mr. Desmond lived on the patience of all the people who did not kill him. He ate what foods he was allowed to buy. He regarded himself as an owner, as a taxpayer, as a responsible citizen, and so did Mr. Byrne and Mr. Roberts and Mr. Perlman and Mr. Ransom-Jones, and they sent their children to schools dictated and run by people they had never seen, and they slept at night between sheets made by hands they would never shake. They had nothing to say about how soon their houses would begin to rot, when the sheets might tear.

When they could do so without embarrassment they called themselves upright American citizens, and they looked around Pepper Street with its neatness and the highway beyond and the gates and the wall, and they possessed it with statements like "good place to live," and "when I decide to move." Consequently any change made on Pepper Street was beyond their control, and it was not even thought necessary to notify them in advance, although such a change might affect them more intimately than anyone else in the world. One morning a severely thoughtful man, a business man like Mr. Desmond, and a cross old lady in a paneled living-room, from the depths of their own private unowned lives, made a decision with the words and paper so necessary for momentous decisions, and never consulted Mr. Desmond or Mr. Ransom-Jones, never thought of asking Tod Donald, who was the one most terribly changed by it all.

Part of the wall was to come down. A breach was to be made in the northern boundary of the world. Barbarian hordes were to be unleashed on Pepper Street. A change was going to come about without anyone's consent. In ten years the people now living on Pepper Street could come back and not know the old place, it would be so changed. The plans of the man, whoever he was, were to extend Pepper Street through the estate hidden behind the wall, and run it directly across to meet the corresponding street on the other side of the estate. The old lady who owned the estate, who sat in the paneled living-room, chose to sell the little pocket of land thus excluded to another man, unknown to the first, for a new apartment building. Thus, instead of the wall running from the gates to the highway, there would be a wall running to Pepper Street and then along the new street on the estate side to meet the wall which ran down the other side, a smaller square than before, and, in the end so cut off, new houses. And the people who lived on the corresponding street, who saw their own familiar wall going down? Probably they felt the same way, and were apprehensive of the barbarian hordes from Pepper Street. The really comfortable people would be the ones who moved into the new apartment house which was to go up in the empty space; to them nothing was different.

Eventually a third man broadened Pepper Street by taking down the locust trees, and a fourth man changed its name to Something Avenue, but this was much later, late enough to astound the people in the new apartment house, who came back in their turn and found it hard to recognize the old neighborhood. Eventually, of course, it was more and more degraded, and the Desmond house became an old home, cut up into apartments and then into rooms, with the garden overgrown or built up; but by then the apartment house was out of date and not fashionable, and Pepper Street or Something Avenue had gone down in the world, too far to be revisited.

At any rate, one morning Pepper Street was stupefied into submission, as though it had a choice, by the arrival of a tractor, a gang of men in blue workshirts, and the sudden sound of physical work on the wall. The children were there, of course, standing as close as possible around the inviting tractor, asking questions, estimating among themselves the probable aim of the workmen, the age of the tractor, what they would find inside the wall. Mrs. Merriam on her front porch, which offered the best view of the work, paused in her aimless housework to wonder at the men's broad shoulders; Mrs. Desmond drew the shades on that side of the house and kept Caroline indoors that afternoon.

It was the destruction of the wall which put the first wedge into the Pepper Street security, and that security was so fragile that, once jarred, it shivered into fragments in a matter of weeks. That night for the first time Mr. Desmond thought practically of moving; careful examination of his bank account assured him that he was not ready to go beyond the gates at present without a cautious economy of home and life that would almost nullify the good effects of moving. Borrowing money was an aversion of Mr. Desmond's, but any removal not beyond the gates would be a step backwards.

Mr. and Mrs. Ransom-Jones discussed the advisability of a high and firm hedge around their garden, and Mr. Byrne found serious fault with the planning of the unknown man whom he might criticize although he would never influence or meet him. The most outrageous estimates in the neighborhood would have the road finished by the end of summer.

It may be a matter of some importance to note that on the other side, the corresponding street, a Mr. Honeywell was driven by seeing his side of the wall come down into committing himself on paper to the purchase of a modest estate beyond the gates; he had been debating for so long that his wife and children had begun to despair. His children subsequently met Johnny Desmond at a country-club dance and discovered that for years they had been near neighbors. Also on that other street a new family, recently moved in, complained to the family which had sold them the house that they had not been warned of the new road coming; the son of this new family later on walked to high school every morning with Mary Byrne. Mrs. Mack's old dog was generally supposed to be the father of eventual puppies on the other street. The workmen, who made all this possible, were family men and earned their money by their work just as Mr. Desmond did.

CHAPTER FIVE

The sounds of the wall coming down stayed on Pepper Street for almost a week, and it seemed that dust from the old bricks filled every living-room on the block, even as far as the Ransom-Joneses. Mrs. Desmond and Mrs. Merriam were the principal sufferers, since Pepper Street ended between their two houses; after two days of changing Caroline into clean clothes three or four times a day and brushing visible dust off the toys, Mrs. Desmond admitted defeat and went with her daughter to a nearby summer resort to stay a week. The Merriams endured the dust but not the noise; Mrs. Merriam twice called the construction company whose name was on the "Men Working" sign, and was twice politely told to mind her own business. Mrs. Merriam's temper was tarter than usual until the bricks were down and neatly stacked at the curb, and Mr. Merriam was kept posted by a nightly bulletin on the state of Mrs. Merriam's headache. Farther down the block, toward the Donald and Byrne and Roberts houses, the complaints were less physical and more aesthetic; the idea that placid Pepper Street was being deformed by workmen and dirt and great foul machines was almost as bad as the prospect of being shortly on a direct road with the rest of the world.

The children, of course, knew little of the discomfort of strange men and big machines; every morning while the bricks were coming down, they crowded together on the corner by the Merriam house—none of them allowed to cross Cortez Road for fear of falling bricks—and watched and commented eagerly on the process of the work; at one point it seemed that the wall itself was tottering all up and down Cortez Road, and Tod Donald called out across the street approximately at a man in tight corduroy pants, "Hey, looka that, the whole wall's going to fall on you," and the man turned and looked at the children and laughed.

In the Martin house there was dismal foreboding. It seemed likely that tearing down the wall might mean disaster for old Mr. Martin. First of all, perhaps the dust would reach as far as his flowers, penetrate the sealed greenhouses, dirty the roses. Secondly, once the wall was broken into, the fields of the estate, the sacred enclosed place which harbored the main house, the garages, the tennis court and the terraced gardens as well as Mr. Martin's greenhouses, would be exposed to intrusions from the outside world, perhaps small boys with stones, perhaps curious trespassers gathering flowers, perhaps all those people with large feet who trample down tiny growing things. More than that, even, came into Mr. Martin's old mind. Now, with this madness of destruction—the disregarding abandoned battering tearing-apart of things permanent because they had been standing so long—what with tearing down walls and selling land, who could tell what would follow? The tennis court might go to make room for an apartment house, perhaps the terraced gardens might be cut into front yards, perhaps even the greenhouses might vanish. Mr. Martin sat apprehensively, in the evenings, thinking on flowers, the blossoms of which were not his preoccupation, seeing in his dreams the broken glass, the crushed roots. Mrs. Martin shook her head and kept the children away; her daughter-in-law, mother of George and Hallie, was more silent than usual, and avoided the room where the old man sat. George and Hallie went quietly around the old house, washing when they had to, coming to table when they were called; and the old people knew brick by brick as the wall was going.

The wall began to bore the children after a few days. There was not much fun in standing across the street by the hour, daring an occasional comment, guessing which way the bricks were going to fall, knowing the watchful eyes from windows above to prevent their putting one foot off the legal curb. By about the third day they were back at their games, always ready for news of the wall but tired of bricks.

Late one afternoon when all the children were playing in front of their usual place, the Donald house, Hallie Martin came softly out of her house and stood in front of it for a minute looking across the street. She had on her best dress—it was velveteen plaid, and too small for her—and she had put on her mother's lipstick. She looked at the men working across the street and then back at her house. Her mother and grandfather were out, working at their respective jobs, and her grandmother was taking a nap; her brother George was with the other children. Daintily, Hallie put one foot into the street, and ran across. There were four or five men working on the wall; they were hot and irritable and covered with dust, and Hallie approached cautiously.

One of the men grunted; none of them looked up.

"Hello," Hallie said. "It's hot, isn't it?"

One of the men, brushing past Hallie, said with annoyance, "Get away from there, kid. Dangerous."

"I'm all right," Hallie said. She smoothed her hair with her hand and said, looking with great nonchalance off into the distance, "Bet you sure wish you were having a nice cold soda right now."

One of the men, the one with the tight corduroy pants, looked at another and laughed. "Glass of beer," he said.

"Or a glass of beer," Hallie said. "Bet you sure wish you had a nice cold glass of beer right now."

"You drink beer, kid?" the man in the tight corduroy pants asked Hallie.

"Sometimes," Hallie said carelessly. "I never touch much of it, though."

"Run along now," another of the men commanded. "You're going to be in the way."

Hallie tossed her head as Helen Williams used to. "You can't tell *me* what to do," she said.

"*Run* along," the man said.

Hallie moved a step or so and said defiantly, "I'm going to

the city, and I'm going to go in a store and get a nice big cold glass of beer."

"Go on," the man said, "get along." The man in the tight corduroy pants called to Hallie, "You better get over there across the street, kid." Hallie came nearer to him instead and said, "You come from the city?"

"Nope," the man said.

"I got lots of nice boy friends in the city," Hallie said.

The man said, "Out of the way there," and pushed past her to go with the heavy tool he had been using down to the place where the bricks were being stacked. "*He* doesn't know much," Hallie said to the man who had been working next to him.

"He knows you're gonna get killed if you don't get out of the way," was all the satisfaction she got.

Defeated, Hallie retired to the curb, where she stood for a few minutes, and then she said loudly, "Any one who wants a nice cold glass of beer can come along," and started down the street. When she had gone a little way she stopped and looked back at the men still working, yelled "Dirty bums!" and ran off toward the highway.

That evening Harriet was just putting away the last of the dinner dishes, and her mother was scouring the sink, when the doorbell rang. Mr. Merriam got up tiredly from his chair in the living-room and went to the door, opened it, and then called, "Harriet?"

When Harriet ran to the door she was first afraid and then embarrassed. "What are you doing *here*?" she said roughly, and then she saw Mrs. Perlman behind Marilyn, and at the same moment heard her mother's voice behind her. "Good evening," Mrs. Merriam said.

Marilyn was standing on the outside of the door as helplessly as Harriet on the inside. Mrs. Perlman said, over her daughter's head, "Mrs. Merriam? I'm Mrs. Perlman, Marilyn's mother. Marilyn wanted to see Harriet for a minute, and so we just stopped by."

Mrs. Merriam said, "Won't you come in?" and held the door open wider for Mrs. Perlman and Marilyn. Marilyn grabbed

Harriet's arm and said, "Listen, wait'll I *tell* you," and Harriet said, "What'd you *come* for?" and Mrs. Merriam called from the living-room, "No secrets, girls. Come in."

"I've been anxious to meet you and Mr. Merriam," Mrs. Perlman was saying when Harriet and Marilyn came in. "Marilyn has told me so much about Harriet."

"I don't think I've met Marilyn before," Mrs. Merriam said, looking Marilyn up and down. "Tell me, are you in Harriet's class at school?"

"She's a grade ahead of me, Mother," Harriet said, running her words together in her haste, "and we've been reading *Vanity Fair* together and I see her all the time in school."

"Harriet has been down to see us several times," Mrs. Perlman said.

"Indeed," Mrs. Merriam said. She waited, and there was a long silence.

"The girls do have such a good time together," Mrs. Perlman went on at last. She touched her lips with her tongue, and said, "I suppose you must know how much Marilyn has enjoyed being with Harriet. Such a charming girl. Although," she added with a false little laugh, "I shouldn't say it in front of her."

"Harriet tries to behave herself as well as possible," Mrs. Merriam said. There was another silence. Mrs. Merriam seemed to be content with it; she sat with her hands folded quietly, looking at the ashtray on the table next to the chair where Mrs. Perlman was sitting. There was a polite small smile on her face.

Mrs. Perlman was sitting on the edge of her chair, and she smiled widely whenever she met Mrs. Merriam's eye, or Harriet's, smiled blindly even at Marilyn, who sat next to Harriet on the couch and watched her mother eagerly.

"We were just passing by," Mrs. Perlman said. She seemed to have got back on the track of her planned remarks; her voice eased a little, and she said, "We took the little Martin girl home; she ran away, you know."

Mrs. Merriam lifted her eyes. She looked at Harriet and Marilyn, and hesitated. Finally she said, "What happened?"

Mrs. Perlman shook her head sadly. "I have no idea, really. My husband found her about a mile out of town, on the road to San Francisco. She was—" Mrs. Perlman looked at Harriet and Marilyn "—trying to beg a ride."

"Really?" Mrs. Merriam leaned forward a little. "All alone?"

"All alone," Mrs. Perlman said, and nodded. "All alone. She was just standing there with her—with her thumb, you know, and she was all dressed up, and she was wearing lipstick."

"Imagine," Mrs. Merriam said.

"Imagine," Mrs. Perlman agreed. "My husband stopped right away, of *course*. He was coming the other way, back home, you know, but he recognized her and made her get in the car and come home with him. A child like that."

"It's dreadful," Mrs. Merriam said. "Where was she going, did she say?"

"Just to San Francisco. She had begged rides from strangers that far, and she intended to go right into the city. Heaven only *knows* what she wanted to do there," Mrs. Perlman said.

"Did she have any money?" Mrs. Merriam asked. "I imagine her mother was frightened."

"Her mother isn't home yet," Mrs. Perlman said gently.

"Of course," Mrs. Merriam said. "She works until late at night." She gave the words an inexplicable emphasis, smiling a little.

Marilyn broke in eagerly: "Her grandmother said she was going to give Hallie the beating of her life, and I don't blame Hallie for not wanting to go home because they were sure mad at *her*."

Mrs. Merriam turned her head slightly to look at Harriet and Marilyn on the couch. "It was very lucky that Mr. Perlman came by at that moment."

"She might've been there all night," Marilyn said.

Mrs. Merriam was silent, and after a minute Mrs. Perlman said "Marilyn?" and started to get up. Mrs. Merriam stood up immediately, and when Harriet came over to her she moved a step away.

"I *am* happy to have met you at last," Mrs. Perlman said on her way to the door. "Marilyn, you can see Harriet tomorrow. It's late. I hope I'll see you again," she said to Mrs. Merriam.

"Thank you," Mrs. Merriam said. She stood with Harriet

by the door while Marilyn and her mother went down the walk. "Good night, Harriet," Marilyn called back, and Harriet heard her own voice answer strangely, "Good night."

When Mrs. Merriam shut the door she would not look at Harriet. She said quietly, "It's bedtime, Harriet. Go upstairs."

Harriet started upstairs without a word. Halfway up, she heard her mother's level voice saying, "I'll speak to you in the morning," and when she reached her own room she shut the door and thought, I could kill her for coming here tonight, why did she think she had any right to come?

Downstairs, after a minute, she heard her mother's steps going toward the phone.

Mrs. Roberts was restless; dinner was long over and yet it was too early to go to bed; Mrs. Roberts was quietly reading a mystery story in her chair by the fireplace, and the open windows on either side of the fireplace brought in the scent of flowers and the heavy hot night air. Mr. Roberts paced the living-room, went into the kitchen for a drink of water, debated having a highball but refrained when he thought about Mrs. Roberts, and came back into the living-room to wander aimlessly about.

"What on earth is the matter with you?" Mrs. Roberts asked amiably, looking up from her book; the Robertses were on good terms tonight, and she smiled when she spoke. "You got the jitters or something?"

"Just don't know what to do with myself," Mr. Roberts said. He struck an aimless note on the piano; he would have liked to sit down and play soft soothing music, long rippling chords that would blend with the night air and his mood, but the only tune that he could play was "Yankee Doodle," and he turned irritably away from the piano.

"Turn on the radio," Mrs. Roberts said. "Or go to bed or something." She went back to her book.

Mr. Roberts went to the window and stood looking out. The street outside was partially visible between the bushes on the lawn, but there was nothing there except the sidewalk and the trees sleeping quietly in the moonlight.

"Don't know what to do with myself," Mr. Roberts said.

"Um-hm," Mrs. Roberts said into her book. Mr. Roberts frowned down at her, changed his mind about the highball, and went out to the kitchen; but then he thought again of Mrs. Roberts and changed his mind back. He went quickly down the hall, said at the front door, "Going out for a walk," and had closed the door by the time Mrs. Roberts looked up, surprised.

Outside on the porch he breathed deeply of the night air, so gentle, so tender in its touch, and then the thought of Mrs. Roberts leaning forward in her chair to look out of the window drove him down the steps and along the sidewalk. By the time he reached the Desmond house he was carrying on a conversation in his mind with an imaginary companion. "Just living on the same, day after day," he was saying with infinite weariness, "a man gets tired of it all. What's it *worth*?"

He shook his head sadly, and his imaginary companion, touching his arm lightly, big eyes turned up to him worshipfully, said, "But *you—you're* more important than that, really you are."

"Perhaps I am, little girl," Mr. Roberts told her pityingly, "but perhaps you only think so, *now*."

Turning his head to look down on her, he tripped over the curb and nearly fell into Cortez Road. Recovering himself, he looked quickly back over his shoulder to see if anyone had been watching from the Desmond house. "Think I was drunk," he muttered, and crossed the road hurriedly. He stopped by the piles of bricks and looked at them; they were almost blue in the moonlight. The heavy machinery used for obscure purposes by the workmen at the wall—something Mr. Roberts recognized as a tractor, another thing he thought might be a cement mixer—stood, silent and sleeping, like everything else on the block. In a few hours this spot would again be the busiest in the neighborhood, enveloped in noise and dust and the swift conversation of men who knew what they were doing. Now, the machinery and the wall and even the bricks were unco-operative and still, as though recognizing that Mr. Roberts was unauthorized to call them into activity. Irritated anew to find that nothing moved, Mr. Roberts was about to start back across Cortez Road when the sound of quick footsteps held him. Someone was coming up from the highway, along his side of Cortez, and Mr. Roberts lingered by the pile of bricks, trying not to seem too obviously watching.

After a minute or so he recognized young Mrs. Martin, mother of George and Hallie; at the same minute she saw him, but did not appear to recognize him, since her footsteps slowed and she slanted her path toward the street, as though intending to cross. Mr. Roberts hurried down to meet her, saying, as he went, although softly, "Good evening, Mrs. Martin. You out for a walk, too?"

"Who is it?" Mrs. Martin said, but she hesitated in her walk.

"Roberts," Mr. Roberts said. "Mike Roberts." By this time he had reached her, and she stared at him for a minute and then smiled.

"Of course," she said. "I didn't recognize you, Mr. Roberts." She started to walk again, and Mr. Roberts walked along beside her.

"You out for a walk, too?" he asked again.

"I'm just coming home from work," she said, and laughed. She wore her hair long and fastened back at the nape of her neck; although her face was inclined to be rabbitty, like Hallie's, with a sharp nose and pulled-back chin, in the moonlight she looked soft and fragile, her black sports coat more expensive, her legs longer. "I always get home this time," she said. "You just out walking?"

"Couldn't stay indoors, night like this," Mr. Roberts said. For a minute it crossed his mind that Mrs. Roberts might have finished her book, might be standing, even, on the front porch looking for him, and he said, almost harshly, "I thought for a minute I scared you, standing there like that."

"You did," she admitted. "I never expect to see anyone up around here when I come home." She waved at the Merriams' house, across the street, dark and brooding under its overhigh roof. Next to it the Martin house was dark except for one light on the porch. "That's for me," Mrs. Martin said unnecessarily. She paused on the sidewalk across the street from the Martin house. "Well, good night," she said.

Mr. Roberts cleared his throat. "Stay out for a while," he said. "Night like this."

Mrs. Martin put her head on one side and considered. "I shouldn't," she said, and laughed again.

Mr. Roberts took her arm, and they began to walk lingeringly down the sidewalk again.

"Such a beautiful night," Mrs. Martin said, as though starting the conversation on a new basis.

"Beautiful night," Mr. Roberts said. He squeezed her arm gently, looking down at her. "Nice night," he said.

Mrs. Martin looked up at him, her eyebrows raised. "It certainly is," she said, and laughed.

Mr. Roberts squeezed her arm again, a little harder, and said, "Sure glad I met you. Needed someone to talk to."

"I'm glad I met *you*, too," Mrs. Martin said. "Too nice a night to go in." They stopped by the pile of bricks, and Mrs. Martin said, "I wonder if they'll ever get this thing finished."

"Sure," Mr. Roberts said. He waved knowingly at the machine he thought was a tractor. "Won't take them long now," he said.

"I certainly wish they'd finish it," Mrs. Martin said. They began to walk again up toward the Martin house.

"Doesn't take them long once they get started," Mr. Roberts said.

"The wall's been here so long," Mrs. Martin said. "I suppose it was built long before any of the homes around here."

Mr. Roberts squeezed her arm again. "Guess it was," he said.

Mrs. Martin stopped again, across the street from the Martin house. "Well," she said.

"You don't want to go in," Mr. Roberts said. "Stay out awhile longer."

Mrs. Martin laughed again. "I really shouldn't," she said.

They began to walk again. "Beautiful night," Mr. Roberts said.

"Have you lived here long, Mr. Roberts?" Mrs. Martin said.

"Quite a while," Mr. Roberts said.

"I know I've seen you sometimes out in front of your house. And Mrs. Roberts." She dropped her voice to an affectionate, longing tone. "I know you've got two pretty nice boys," she said.

"You know my boys?" Mr. Roberts sounded surprised.

"They play with my George sometimes," Mrs. Martin said.

"Yes?" Mr. Roberts said. They were back beside the pile of bricks, and Mr. Roberts kicked aimlessly at the top brick. It fell and rolled down to the ground. "All this stuff," Mr. Roberts said. He let go of Mrs. Martin's arm, and leaned over to pick up the brick and put it back. "All this junk," he said. He moved casually around the pile of bricks and past it to where the break in the wall ended and the wall was clear of rubbish.

From the inside of the wall Mr. Roberts said softly, "Not so bad in here," and Mrs. Martin, after one quick look over her shoulder at the Martin house, gathered her skirt tightly against her legs and edged around the pile of bricks to join him.

Frederica Terrel sat at a round table in the room where Mrs. Williams had at one time sat night after night in the darkness, the room which was now the Terrels' "big room." It was in this room—Frederica had found that with such an arrangement it was necessary to use and furnish only four rooms in a house— that the Terrels mainly occupied themselves; it was inadequately furnished even so, with the table, four straight kitchen chairs, a wicker couch and two matching rockers, and a rug which was actually an excellent affair of some value belonging to Mrs. Terrel; there were occasional pieces of this sort scattered among the Terrel furniture, pieces such as the great translucent blue bowl Frederica kept fruit in, and some of the tiny lovely jewels mixed in with the rhinestones kept in a shoebox on Frederica's closet shelf. The other three rooms Frederica used were the kitchen, where she kept the food; the bedroom where Mrs. Terrel slept; and the bedroom which Frederica and Beverley shared. In the big room, while Frederica worked at the round table, Beverley sat in one of the

wicker chairs, rocking and crooning over a book which she
was coloring with crayon.

Frederica was rereading an advertisement she had clipped
from a magazine the Williamses had left behind in the garage.
"Art Fotos," it began. "Six alluring fotos for only a dollar,"
and as she studied it Frederica chewed her finger and frowned.
The art fotos lay beside her; they had come in a determinedly
plain wrapper, and Frederica had them spread out on the table
while she considered them. The one nearest her hand was a
sepia print of a young lady lying in a field of leaves; her face
was in shadow but her naked body lay most chastely in the
sunlight. "I don't know," Frederica said as she took it up, and
Beverley paused in her song to say, "Don't know what?"

"Look at this," Frederica said, holding it out at arm's length.
"I just don't know about it."

Beverley put her head on one side and said tentatively, "Is it
Mommy?"

"Don't be silly." Frederica put the picture back on the table
and fell to considering it from that angle. "I wanted *some*thing
to go on the walls, it looks so bare here. But I thought they
would be pictures of trees and dogs and things."

Beverley looked around the room as though she had never
seen it before, and Frederica held up another picture and said,
"What do you think of this?" This one was a similar print of a
young lady lying, in the same professional nudity, on the edge
of a swimming pool. Beverley looked at it and shook her head.

"The other one looked like Mommy," she said.

Frederica took up the first picture and regarded it again.
"I'll put this in Mommy's room, then," she decided.

"In the bathroom," Beverly said. "One in the bathroom."

Frederica giggled. "Silly," she said. "*No* one puts pictures in
bathrooms. One in Mommy's room and one in our room and
the rest in here."

"Can I have one?" Beverley asked pleadingly. "Just to color?"

Frederica looked at her sister affectionately. "I suppose you
can," she said. "If you promise."

"Promise?" Beverley said innocently.

Frederica got up and went over to stand in front of her

sister. "I'm going in the kitchen to hunt for thumbtacks," she said. "I won't be gone more than a minute. Now *promise*." She put one finger under Beverley's chin and turned Beverley's face up. "Promise," she said again.

Beverley grinned and said, "Promise."

"Then you can have this one." Frederica selected a young lady leaning against a marble pillar and gave it to Beverley. "Color it all over, but stay inside the lines."

Beverley nodded, intent on the picture, and Frederica went to the doorway and stopped to say once more over her shoulder, "Remember now, you *promised*."

"Anyway I don't have any money at all," Beverley said, and began to rock and croon again as her sister left the room.

In the quiet late evening, the sun long gone and the stars shining correctly outside the window, Miss Fielding rocked slowly back and forth in her chair. She was inclined to be cold in her hands and feet these evenings of late summer, and so she had lighted the little oil stove which sat cleanly in the corner of the room, and the slight red glow from the holes in the sides and top of the stove, combined with the soft light from the lamp on the table beside Miss Fielding, made the little room seem homely and snug. When Mr. Donald knocked on the door Miss Fielding got up and walked over with her short old woman's steps to open the door and smile and say, "Come in, it's nice and warm."

When he was sitting down on the other side of the table, in a pleasant colorless old chair with a lace antimacassar on the back, Miss Fielding said, "Will you have a cup of tea?" and Mr. Donald said, as he always did, "No, thank you. Just thought I'd step in for a few minutes."

It was probable that everyone on Pepper Street knew that Miss Fielding and Mr. Donald were, oddly, friends, but it is certain that no one was particularly interested in it. Both Miss Fielding and Mr. Donald were so exactly the sort of people who want to hide, that the neighborhood was only thankful to have them hiding together, instead of intruding their modesty on busier people. Every so often one or another of the Pepper Street inhabitants, glancing out of a window in the late evening, or a child coming home later than usual, would notice Mr. Donald walking toward Miss Fielding's little house, and possibly even, see him, a half-hour or so later, coming back home, the lights in Miss Fielding's house out behind him, his own house completely incurious about his absence.

Miss Fielding and Mr. Donald were obviously two of a kind. When they sat in Miss Fielding's little room Miss Fielding sat with her hands on the arms of her rocking chair, rocking back and forth, as though she were alone; Mr. Donald sat back in the old-fashioned chair with his head against the antimacassar, his eyes closed as though he were asleep. When they talked it was because both of them were given to talking to themselves.

Tonight Miss Fielding said almost immediately, in her gentle careful voice, "I don't call those Terrel girls really highbred." The subject had been troubling her since Frederica had spoiled her pot of tea, and there was almost a harsh tone in her voice. "Those girls are not of the best breeding. I don't know the mother."

"I haven't seen them," Mr. Donald said. He sighed deeply.

"Not of the very best," Miss Fielding went on. "I can't say that they are the best-bred girls around here."

"There seem to be a lot of new people all the time," Mr. Donald said. "First the Williams people and then these."

"Take Harriet Merriam, for instance," Miss Fielding went on. "Or Virginia Donald. Even Mary Byrne, I can't say I hold religion against anybody. Take any of them."

"The Desmonds were first," Mr. Donald said. "Or the Merriams. I think the Merriams. After all, that house has been in his family. Yes, first the Merriams and then the Desmonds."

They were both quiet for a while. Miss Fielding rocked peacefully, as though in a cradle, and Mr. Donald, his eyes shut, let his fingers unclench and lie easily against the arms of his chair.

"You never can tell," Mr. Donald said finally, barely making words from the murmur of his voice. "You never can tell, never know, father knows best."

"There's a lot to be said for religion in any case," Miss Fielding said. "Not that I was ever very much of a religious. It's cruel not to give a child a chance."

"Spare the rod and spoil the church," Mr. Donald said suddenly. They frequently interrupted one another, or talked both at once, as though all that were necessary was to make a companionable noise. "Everybody worrying, everybody moving so fast, all going to church, all hitting each other, all worrying."

Perhaps Miss Fielding thought she had been talking right along since her last statement, for she went on, "and never asked him again. Not that he would have allowed it, of course."

"They ask me to watch," Mr. Donald said. "They just sit there and expect people to watch them and be interested. They expect people to think everything is important and necessary. That's the word, necessary. Necessary is the word."

"You take young people today," Miss Fielding said. "They're not as high-bred as they used to be. The Terrel girls, for instance. I don't know the mother, but the girls are really not first-class."

"Necessary is really the word." The light on Mr. Donald's face made him seem much younger, and he smiled shyly. "It's hard to remember sometimes," he confessed, "but sometimes I can think without trying. I remember the way the sun shone on my sister and me. She had a doll named Julia."

"You can always tell about people," Miss Fielding said.

"It used to be much warmer then," Mr. Donald went on. "Sometimes it's so cold now in the summer I wonder about it. Even in the summer."

"I expect to be very cool to them," Miss Fielding said. "I haven't met the mother yet, but when I do I shall be very cool indeed."

"I wish I knew why it happens," Mr. Donald said. He leaned forward, preparatory to standing up. "Why it's so much colder now in the summer." He looked directly at Miss Fielding, who turned her wrinkled old eyes to look at him.

"Why yes," Miss Fielding said. "I expect we're all older than we were."

When he stood up she rose and followed him to the door. "I'm very glad you came," she said formally. "Come again."

"Thank you," Mr. Donald said as formally. "Thank you for letting me come."

He went down the narrow flight of steps outside, and Miss

Fielding held the door open to give him light until he reached
the sidewalk. Then he called "Good night," and she said,
"Good night," and closed her door and turned the key.

Back in her little room she turned out the oil stove and
straightened the antimacassar on Mr. Donald's chair. "Not
really first-class," she was saying tunefully as she worked.
"We're all *much* older now."

Mrs. Merriam was sitting on the foot of Harriet's bed, leaning
forward eagerly, and her eyes were light and earnest. While
she talked she continually stretched her long hands out to her
daughter, as though to grasp Harriet's mind and force it to
accept her intent, as though to hold Harriet from running
away. "I know you are the most generous and tolerant girl
around here," she was saying, "but remember, what is *most*
important is not to let yourself get carried *away*."

Harriet sat dully on her desk chair. She had been writing
when her mother came in to talk to her; it was her regular
writing time her mother had assigned, the two hours after
lunch, and Harriet had been dutifully forcing metrical rhymed
lines down on paper. The greater part of her writing time had
been lost in her mother's talking; mostly Harriet was wondering if the lost time might still be required of her or if she would
be allowed to go outdoors at her usual time.

"We must expect to set a standard," her mother said. It was
perhaps the third time she had said it, and it registered mud-
dily on Harriet's mind. "We must expect to set a standard.
Actually, however much we may want to find new friends
whom we may value, people who are exciting to us because of
new ideas, or because they are *different*, we have to do what is
expected of us."

"What is expected of me?" Harriet said suddenly, without
intention.

"To do what you're told," her mother said sharply.

"But what am I supposed to do?"

"You may," her mother said, "in fact, I *insist*," she added
with relish, "that you see her once more, in order to tell her
exactly why you are not to be friends any longer. After all,"

Mrs. Merriam went on dreamily, "she ought to know why she can't hope to be your friend any longer."

"Yes, Mother," Harriet said. "I'd have to give her back her books anyway." She waited for a minute and then, when her mother showed signs of leaving, she said, "May I go out now?"

"Of course, dear," her mother said. She looked back at Harriet as she was leaving the room. "I can trust you, of course?"

"Yes, Mother," Harriet said.

"You remember, dear," her mother said lightly, "that little matter of those dirty letters. After all, I trusted you *then*."

"But I didn't—" Harriet began, and her mother went on quickly, "I have never been *so* disappointed in my girl. It will take a long time, Harriet, before I forget the *filth* that went into those letters. The filthy words, the filthy thoughts."

"I won't do it again," Harriet said helplessly.

"Of course you won't," her mother said gently. "We won't bring the subject up any more."

Mary Byrne was standing lonesomely on the sidewalk in front of her house, shredding a leaf she had pulled off the bushes and looking at it trying to think of what to do, when she heard someone saying, "Hello, lady." She looked up. She had, along with the rest of the neighborhood, encountered Beverley Terrel, had seen Frederica taking her up and down the block for careful walks; and she had, with the other children, laughed at her when Frederica was not around, imitating her clumsy walk and her thick speech. No one was afraid of Beverley, because she was always smiling, so Mary looked up and smiled back and said, "Hello, Beverley." She was mildly surprised for a minute because Frederica did not seem to be around, but she forgot to be surprised immediately when Beverley held out a hand full of money.

"I've money," Beverley said.

Mary leaned forward and touched it and then looked up at Beverley. "Where'd you get it all?" she asked, awed.

"Let's spend it," Beverley said. She gestured back and forth rapidly with her hand, so that a dollar bill dropped to the ground. Mary picked it up respectfully and tried to hand it back, but Beverley clenched her hand so tight around the money that after a minute Mary gave up trying to force in the dollar bill and put it instead into her own pocket. She kept her hand on it ready to give back to Frederica when she came.

"Come on," Beverley said. She gave Mary a push. "Come on, let's spend it," she said.

Mary looked up and down the street quickly. No one was in sight, and yet by taking the dollar bill into her own pocket, even knowing she would not keep it, she had become an accessory, a participant with Beverley in something exciting and dishonest. "What'll we do with it?" Mary asked, dropping her voice to a whisper.

"Candy," Beverley said immediately, "candy and hot butterscotch sundaes, and we can go to the movies if we want to, and we can buy lots of candy."

Mary's mind dwelt on a chocolate bar with almonds, and then she realized that even the dollar bill in her pocket would buy many of them, and Beverley had so much money in her hand that it was impossible to count it.

"I'd have a marshmallow sundae too," Beverley said. "And a butterscotch sundae and lots of candy."

"We better run," Mary said, as Beverley started toward Cortez Road. "My mother might not like it if she saw me." Beverley began obediently to move faster and Mary followed, frightened already at the prospect of going all the way down the street without being seen. She had a feeling of warm friendship with Beverley which overwhelmed and disgusted the faint nausea she felt at the thought of doing anything or going anywhere with this great awkward girl who talked like a six-year-old child.

"We better not go to any of the usual places," she said to Beverley. "We wouldn't want anyone to tell on us."

"Take a taxi," Beverley said. "We'll go far away. I've money." She gestured forward with the money-filled hand.

"Do you want me to carry it for you?" Mary asked considerately. She wanted to know how it felt to hold that much money, instead of the paltry dollar bill in her pocket, but Beverley snatched her hand away and glared suspiciously. *"Mine,"* she said.

"You don't have to be mean," Mary said. "*I* don't want your old money." She drew away from Beverley, indignant that Beverley should think she wanted to steal. "I won't even go with you," she said crossly.

"We'll have a marshmallow sundae," Beverley said appealingly, "and lots of candy."

"All right." No one saw them, after all. They hurried down the street side by side, almost the same height. Beverley had a handful of money and Mary had a dollar bill in her pocket, which she had already resolved not to spend, since Beverley had so much more, but to save and return virtuously when they came back.

"We wouldn't turn you out," old Mrs. Martin said down through the living-room filled with big vases and glassed-in flowers. She looked at her husband and he nodded heavily, his frightened old eyes blinking back at his wife. It was not the first time in his life, by any means, that old Mr. Martin had been frightened of his wife: there was the day they were married, young Mrs. Martin, as she was then, looking him over after the ceremony with narrow critical eyes, estimating accurately her future life with him; there was their son, storming out of the house against his mother's will, to go dancing with the girl he had set his heart on, and Mrs. Martin tight-lipped and threatening in the doorway; there was the night Hallie came home with Mr. Perlman. Mr. Martin, afraid of speaking for fear he should say something wrong, longing to be back in his greenhouses where things were steadily, quietly growing, looked at his wife and nodded, and then at his daughter-in-law with her bright pretty face, and nodded again.

"We wouldn't ever turn anybody out of our house, no one ever gets turned out of our house ever. Papa would never forgive me," old Mrs. Martin said, "if I tried to turn his own son's wife out of our house."

In the Martins' living-room there were great pink and blue pots holding plants Mr. Martin had brought home from the greenhouses, there were dark undistinguishable pieces of furniture, lined up soberly against the walls; the carpet was unfaded by the sun, because old Mrs. Martin drew the shades every afternoon to keep out the light. The family only sat here all together on Sundays, because then young Mrs. Martin did not work, but when they sat all together in the big echoing room it still seemed empty, because the ferns and the great furniture and the straight hanging curtains were made for an empty room, had sustained their purpose even against the voices, or the laughter and shouting of George and Hallie.

"But you've got to leave," old Mrs. Martin said. "You must leave here."

"I won't go," young Mrs. Martin said. She sat daintily in a chair much too large, George and Hallie on either side of her, looking back and forth with wide incurious eyes. "I just simply will not go."

"These changes," old Mrs. Martin said, "all these changes in the estate, are not good for Papa. They are making all kinds of changes in the estate, perhaps soon in the greenhouses even."

"May I point out just once more," young Mrs. Martin said precisely, "that I am your own son's wife? When my George died—" She hesitated for a minute, and allowed her lip to tremble. "—when my *dear* George died, he promised me that I would always find a home for my children with his parents. And now. . . . Your own son's wife." Young Mrs. Martin allowed her voice to catch and shake.

Mrs. Martin nodded this time, and her husband, looking at her, nodded afterward. "We would not turn out our own son's wife," old Mrs. Martin said. "But you must leave."

"And your grandchildren?" young Mrs. Martin said. "Your own son's own children. Who's going to take care of them?"

Old Mrs. Martin looked at George and then at Hallie, and for a minute her eye was cynical. "My own son's children," she said, and they looked back stolidly at her. "But the little one runs away, to beg from strangers, and the great one does nothing. And when the little one runs away," old Mrs. Martin said, with tremendous deliberation, "she is doing like her mother."

For a minute old Mrs. Martin met young Mrs. Martin's eyes, and then the younger said with anger, "You don't need to talk nasty like that. I never did anything I'm ashamed of."

"You must take my son's children and leave," old Mrs. Martin said. "Papa and I are old and now we are worried about the changes in the estate. You must not live here any more."

She looked at her husband, and this time he looked up and said, "Yes, yes, what Mama says." Then she looked triumphantly at her daughter-in-law and said, "You hear?"

From her position in the largest chair she could look down the length of the room at her daughter-in-law perched inconsistently in a leather armchair, and when a minute or two had passed and young Mrs. Martin still did not answer, old Mrs. Martin was satisfied and said, "So now that's settled." She smiled at George and Hallie and said, "Sometimes you will come and visit your old grandmother, no?" Young Mrs. Martin smiled too.

"'—And the fowls of the heaven,'" Mrs. Mack was reading, "'and the beasts of the field, and all creeping things that creep upon the earth, and all the men that are upon the face of the earth, shall shake at my presence, and the mountains shall be thrown down, and the steep places shall fall, and every wall shall fall to the ground. And I will call for a sword against him throughout all my mountains, saith the Lord God: every man's sword shall be against his brother.'" She smiled eagerly on the dog, and said, "You know what that makes me think of? You remember Micah?"

"Well, of course, dear," Lillian Tyler said to her sister, "of course it's your house, but I do think you're making a very serious mistake."

"What possible harm is there in being kind to an unfortunate girl?" Mrs. Ransom-Jones demanded, although kindly. "What's wrong with showing her some affection when the poor girl's probably never had an ounce of attention in her life?"

"She should be in an institution," Miss Tyler said emphatically. "The kindest thing you could do is get her locked up."

Mrs. Ransom-Jones stared open-mouthed. "What an *awful* thing to say!"

"It's true," Miss Tyler said doggedly. "A great big animal like that ought to be in a cage. And you bring her here!" She made a pushing gesture with both hands, her mouth turning in disgust. "You bring her into this house, that great big dirty animal, right in here with me."

"But, sweetie," Mrs. Ransom-Jones said soothingly, "I didn't know you were going to mind."

"And Brad," Miss Tyler cried, "didn't you see how Brad looked at her? It made him sick, just to think of having her in this house with me."

"Brad didn't mind," Mrs. Ransom-Jones began reasonably, but her sister interrupted her:

"Don't tell *me* what Brad minds," she screamed. "I know all about Brad, and you and I know what he minds, and he was *sick* to think of you bringing that *thing* in here with me, and I just wish you could see how he looked at *you*."

She stopped, breathing wildly, and Mrs. Ransom-Jones dropped her eyes and put on an air of quiet patience and looked steadily at the carpet.

After a minute Miss Tyler's breathing quieted, and she said softly, "After all, dear, Brad's *your* husband and this is *your* house." When Mrs. Ransom-Jones still did not look up, she went on, "I wouldn't have said anything for the world, except that I thought you ought to know what Brad was thinking when that girl was here."

"Don't tell *me* what Brad was thinking," Mrs. Ransom-Jones said, in a desperately calm voice. "After all, he's *my* husband."

"Of *course* he is, dear," Miss Tyler said. "He's your husband." She closed her mouth firmly on a little smile and sat back with gracious resignation. Her eyes wandered to the window, and she sat up for a minute and then relaxed. "Here's Frederica," she said.

Mrs. Ransom-Jones got up without looking at her sister and went to the door. She talked to Frederica for a minute and then came back to her sister, Frederica moving uneasily behind her. "She says Beverley's lost again," Mrs. Ransom-Jones said accusingly to her sister. "She's gone off somewhere."

"Come in, dear," Miss Tyler said to Frederica, leaning forward again to watch the girl. "Come in and tell us about it."

Frederica stood solemnly in the exact center of the room,

facing Miss Tyler. After a minute she said in her slow voice, "She's just gone. Like always."

"Did she have any money?" Miss Tyler asked.

"I guess so," Frederica said. She looked at Mrs. Ransom-Jones for confirmation. "She never goes unless she has money."

"You shouldn't let her have money, then," Miss Tyler said gently.

"I *don't* let her have it." Frederica almost wailed. "I can't watch her every *minute*."

"And your mother?" Miss Tyler asked.

"She was asleep," Frederica said. She moved uncomfortably. "Please," she said, "if you know anything about her . . . ?"

"Does your mother always sleep?" Miss Tyler asked. With her quiet voice, and the soft touch she gave the words, they sounded sympathetic.

"She sleeps a lot," Frederica said. "I don't know what she does."

"Where does the money come from?" Miss Tyler asked. "Where does your sister get it?"

"I guess she takes it," Frederica said.

"Takes it?"

"From Mommy's pocketbook."

"I see," Miss Tyler said. She looked Frederica up and down steadily. Mrs. Ransom-Jones moved forward abruptly, but Miss Tyler stopped her with a motion of one hand. "Do a lot of . . . men . . . come to see your mother?" she asked delicately.

"No," Frederica said, surprised. "No one ever comes to see us."

"Are you *sure*?" Miss Tyler said even more delicately. "Perhaps after you're asleep at night?"

Frederica shook her head, staring at Miss Tyler dumbly, and after giving her a minute Miss Tyler said, letting the words almost drift away from her, as though they were being spoken for her, "Then where does the money come from?"

"I don't know," Frederica said. "I don't *know*. From Mommy's pocketbook."

Miss Tyler leaned back again, and Mrs. Ransom-Jones came up to Frederica and said, "Maybe she's just at that same place, having a soda." She tried to speak lightly, as though it were a friendly joke, but Miss Tyler cut in sharply, "She ought to be locked up, you know."

"Who?" Frederica demanded, startled.

"Your sister, dear," Miss Tyler said. "She ought to be put in a home for feeble-minded people."

"That's not true," Frederica said. It took a minute for her slow-moving mind to bring forth the emotion to go with the words, but finally an expression of anger came on to her face.

"She's apt to become dangerous," Miss Tyler said, accenting the last word just enough to make it terrifying. "I was in a home for a while, you know," she went on idly, "my sister has probably told you."

"Lillian!" Mrs. Ransom-Jones said urgently.

"I was ill, of course," Miss Tyler said. "Not feeble-minded, like your sister."

"There's nothing wrong with my sister," Frederica said.

"You know, I think sometimes they'd like to put me *back*," Miss Tyler said, and laughed lightly. "Three's a crowd," she said.

"Frederica," Mrs. Ransom-Jones said levelly, "we don't know where your sister is, we haven't seen her. Run along, please, dear."

Taking Frederica by the arm, she led her to the door and put her outside. When she came back to her sister, Miss Tyler was lying back with her eyes shut.

"Do you mind if I lie down for a while?" Miss Tyler said. "I feel quite worn out."

"I just want you to know," Mrs. Ransom-Jones said, her voice weak with indignation, "I just want you to know that I'm going to tell Brad every word of this when he comes home."

Walking up the street, Harriet was acutely conscious of the workmen at the wall; she was mortally afraid that they were looking at her, and that perhaps her skirt was caught up in back or torn, or that there was a hole in her stocking. She was so horribly frightened of the men that she walked more quickly, to be a few steps ahead of Marilyn, so that Marilyn would shield her from the staring eyes of the men, but Marilyn walked quickly too, so that they were together, and Harriet said irritably, "What on earth are you running for?"

"*You* were running," Marilyn said amiably.

Harriet thought she could hear the men laughing behind her; for the first time she had dared to walk with Marilyn past the Merriam house, to the short-cut beyond the Martins' to the creek, and she was oppressed with the dreadful thought that perhaps her mother would hear the men laughing at her, look out of the window, perhaps come down into the street. She was sure she could hear loud shouting laughter behind her, and she thought hotly that they had no right to laugh at her, they were *hoi polloi*; then she thought that perhaps all the truth about Marilyn was obvious, maybe anyone who looked at her could tell, as Mrs. Merriam had been able to tell, maybe everyone but Harriet knew right away, and *that* was what the men were laughing at, Harriet walking along with Marilyn as though it were perfectly all right. Maybe the men were laughing, Harriet thought madly, because she was so fat, and Marilyn looked so small beside her.

Looking at Marilyn walking along placidly, Harriet realized how absolutely atrociously ugly Marilyn was, neither more or less safe from the laughter of the *hoi polloi* than Harriet; they were both ugly.

"Come *on*," Harriet said. "Do you have to be so *slow*?"

Marilyn hurried obediently. She was eating an apple, and the sight of it offended Harriet; it was difficult for Marilyn to hurry and eat the apple at the same time, and she stumbled.

"Clumsy," Harriet said, and Marilyn looked up at her over the apple, frowning. "What's eating you?" she asked around the apple, and Harriet shrugged impatiently and hurried on ahead. With Marilyn almost running along behind her, Harriet reached the creek and sat down with determination in their special secret place. By the time Marilyn had dropped down breathlessly beside her, Harriet had her first words ready.

"I can't play with you any more, is all," she said.

"Why not?" Marilyn was puzzled, and she screwed her face

up so that Harriet could not bear to look at her, but looked instead loftily into space.

"My mother says it's not suitable," Harriet said. "My mother says to tell you that people of my class are always nice to everybody in spite of their religion or their background but that we have to set standards. Standards," Harriet repeated; it was a solid word in the midst of confusion. "So," Harriet went on rapidly, "I can't talk to you any more or play with you or come up here or go to the library. My mother says so."

Marilyn still had the apple, and looking at it in her hand, Harriet said, "And *furthermore* my mother hopes you won't ever try to tell anyone I was your *friend*."

"I see," Marilyn said. She swallowed the bite of apple in her mouth and asked meekly, "Is that all your mother said?"

Suddenly Harriet realized that she had no words to use to go any further, whatever she tried to say now would only be the same words over again. She had used up, so quickly, all that her mother had spread over so long a time, so Harriet finished icily, "Isn't that enough?"

"Sure," Marilyn said. She put the apple down on the ground and began pulling out handfuls of grass to drop on it.

When the apple was covered Harriet thought miserably that she had not done any of it right. She would have liked to start over again from the beginning, make it mean more. "Listen," she said.

"I don't want to listen any more," Marilyn said wearily. "You big fat slob." She got up suddenly and ran as fast as she could toward the road that led to her home. Harriet sat dumbfounded for a minute, thinking: she didn't need to get so mad, I was going to say all of it again, right. Then she remembered what Marilyn had said, and she wanted to cry. That's mean, she thought, that was a mean thing to say, and she shouldn't have said that. After a little while she stood up and began to walk home slowly. I'll tell my mother, she was thinking.

Virginia Donald and Mary Byrne walked lazily up Cortez Road with Beverley Terrel between them. Virginia had a wrapped box of candy under her arm, and she was chewing gum. Mary was chewing gum, too, and she had, in the big pockets of her linen beerjacket, three or four bags of candy stuffed in one on top of another. Occasionally she stopped walking to take out a bag and offer it to Virginia and Beverley before taking a piece herself. Beverley, walking happily in the middle, was carrying a pint package of ice cream. "I wanted to ride all the way home in the taxi," she said for about the twentieth time.

"We never take taxis *all* the way home," Virginia said. "Do we, Mary?"

"We *never* do," Mary said. "We always get them to leave us off at the highway."

"I *like* to ride all the way home," Beverley said obstinately.

"Look." Virginia poked Beverley's shoulder. "You want us to go with you again tomorrow?"

"Yes," Mary echoed. "You want us to go again tomorrow?" Beverley nodded, looking from one to the other.

"Then you let us do what we want to," Virginia said. "If you don't let us do it the way we want to we won't go with you."

"I just wanted to ride all the way home in the taxi," Beverley said.

"Well, you *can't*." Virginia tossed her head emphatically. She reached into her pocket and took out a paper bag, handling it tenderly, and leaned back to say to Mary behind Beverley, "I'm so pleased I got my pretty pearls."

"I should of gotten pearls too," Mary said. She held out her hand. "Let me look."

Virginia shook her head. She reached into the bag and took her hand out with the pearls dramatically draped around her fingers, entwined in what seemed to both Virginia and Mary to be the pose of a beautiful hand in an advertisement, holding priceless jewelry.

"They *look* real," Mary said admiringly. "From here you really couldn't tell."

"They're almost real," Virginia said with the patronizing air of an owner. "They're not bad pearls at all, for the price."

"What do you want that stuff for?" Beverley asked suddenly. She held her pint of ice cream tighter and said, "That stuff's no good."

"I don't like five-and-ten jewelry as a rule," Virginia said to Mary behind Beverley's back, "but sometimes you can find something really good."

"There's Frederica," Beverley said. They had turned the corner into Pepper Street, and Beverley pointed ahead. "Frederica," she said.

Frederica saw them from in front of her own house, where she had been standing looking anxiously up and down the street, and she started to run toward them.

"If you want us to go again tomorrow," Virginia said roughly to Beverley, "don't you tell her we bought anything."

She slipped the bag with the pearls hurriedly into her pocket and tried to slide the candy box behind her arm inconspicuously.

"Frederica," Beverley called. "Here I am." She stood smiling and pleased as her sister ran up to her, and when Frederica came close enough Beverley held out the box of ice cream and said, "This is for you and Mommy."

"Where have you been?" Frederica demanded. She spent one glance up and down on Virginia and Mary, and then said to her sister, "Where's all that money? Tell me where you've been."

Beverley's face began to twist unhappily. "Ice cream," she said.

"We just met her on the corner," Virginia cut in brightly, "and we were bringing her home."

"We knew you'd be looking for her," Mary chimed in, "so we told her she had to come right home with us."

Frederica took her sister's arm and said, "You come with me. You've been very bad."

Beverley began to cry quietly, her face contorted like a baby's, and Frederica shook her and said again, "You're a bad, bad girl."

"I'm sorry we didn't find her sooner," Virginia said insistently. "We could of brought her right home for you."

Frederica looked at Virginia and Mary again. Her eyes stopped briefly at the candy box under Virginia's arm and Mary's bulging pockets, and she said, "Come on, Bev." Pulling her crying sister along beside her, she started down the block.

When she was out of hearing, Virginia nudged Mary and they both began to giggle, covering their mouths with their hands. Once, almost in front of her own house, Frederica looked back again, and they were both sober instantly, faces dead and straight, and then when she looked away they began to giggle again.

James Donald honored the games with his presence that night. They were all playing prisoner's base, and after standing for a little while on the sidewalk he said suddenly to Pat Byrne, who was near him, "Think I could join in?"

"No one's stopping you," Pat said, but Mary Byrne heard and began shouting that James was going to play, demanding that new sides be chosen and the game started again. Very conscious of his own dignity, James allowed himself to be disputed over; Pat Byrne declared ostentatiously that he was too tired to play again; and the game got under way shortly before it was time for Mr. Desmond to start his evening walk. Mr. Roberts, standing on his own sidewalk, observed to Pat, who was lying on the grass, "There's a fine fellow, that Donald boy," and Pat said, "You mean Tod?"

Mr. Roberts looked at him and said genially, "Nose a little bit out of joint, old man?" Pat rolled over in disgust, burying his face in the grass, and Mr. Roberts laughed shortly and walked down the street a ways. He stood there for a few minutes before Mr. Desmond came out of his house and, when he saw Mr. Desmond, turned in a leisurely manner and walked to meet him. Johnny Desmond was with his father, and he was saying earnestly as they came up to Mr. Roberts, his face turned toward his father, and his voice pleading, "I'll *never* be able to do anything without a car, all the fellows—"

Mr. Roberts held out a hand and said loudly, "Glad to see you again there, Johnny. Been away?"

"Pretty busy," Johnny said, turning his face reluctantly away from his father.

"Quite a fellow, your son," Mr. Roberts said to Mr. Desmond, and Mr. Desmond said proudly, "Quite a fellow."

"You know," Mr. Roberts said, dropping his voice as they began to walk up the street, "that's a funny fellow, that Byrne boy. Seems very envious and bitter."

"Well. . . ." Mr. Desmond said consideringly.

"Frankly," Mr. Roberts said, "I don't altogether like seeing him with my boy so much of the time."

"Can't say I blame you," Mr. Desmond said. Johnny had stopped to watch the game in the street, and the two men stopped a few steps farther on. "They usually grow up all right, though," Mr. Desmond said, looking fondly at Johnny.

"Oh, well," Mr. Roberts said. "You've got a fine fellow there."

Johnny walked down to the curb and was watching the game when Virginia Donald came up to him. "Want to play?" she said daringly.

"Not for *me*." Johnny laughed loudly, so his father could hear him. "That sort of stuff is for babies," he said, and looking at James Donald, added sourly, "and football players."

Mr. Desmond and Mr. Roberts had begun to walk on again slowly. Mr. Desmond was saying, "You want to treat them like *men*, not children; give them responsibility."

Virginia looked over her shoulder at her brother in the middle of the game and called jeeringly, "Did you hear that, James?"

James stopped running and looked around wonderingly. "Who's that?" he asked. He came over slowly and said, "Johnny Desmond? What's going on?"

"He was just admiring your running," Virginia said. She looked up at Johnny for approval, and said, "He thinks only a football player could run like that."

"Listen," James said, hurt.

"Don't let it bother you," Johnny said wearily. He started to move along after his father and was stopped when Tod Donald ran furiously against him, yelling, "Don't you talk to my brother like that!"

"Get out of here," Johnny said, shoving him away, and James said crossly, "Oh, Toddie, leave him alone."

"But the way he was talking," Toddie insisted tearfully. "He can't go talking like that."

"Mind your own business, Toddie," Virginia said sharply. She smiled brightly at Johnny, and said to James, "He was only kidding."

"I just wondered," Johnny said to James, "how you could spend your time on kid stuff like these games."

"What's wrong with football?" James demanded, perplexed. "You trying to say something about our football team?"

Johnny laughed weakly and started off again after his father, but James said commandingly, "You just tell me what you mean," and Johnny shrugged his shoulders despairingly and stood still. The children, without James, had stopped their game and were standing silently about in the street, faces all turned to the spot under the street light where James and Johnny were standing, with Virginia nearby wearing a self-conscious smile.

"I'm on that football team, you know that?" James said, his ferocity only modified by a faint anxiety. "You *know* that?"

"What's going on?" Mr. Roberts said. "Artie?"

"Yes?" Artie's voice came thinly from among the crowd of children. Mr. Roberts snorted, and came up to Johnny and James, putting one hand on each. "Break it up, fellows," he said. "What's going on?"

"Johnny?" Mr. Desmond said anxiously from where he had turned and was hurrying back. "What's wrong, Johnny?"

"Nothing, nothing," Johnny said.

"This is disgraceful," Mr. Roberts said. "Artie, what are you doing out there?"

"Nothing," Artie said.

James Donald's face was working angrily and he shoved against Mr. Roberts's hand. "Let me *alone*," he said.

"You better apologize," Mr. Roberts said to James.

"I didn't do anything," James said weakly.

"That's right," Johnny said. He shook off Mr. Roberts's hand. "I don't want anyone apologizing to me."

Mr. Desmond, now beside his son, said severely, "*Naturally* you would be satisfied with an apology, Johnny. James?"

There was a long silence, and then James said miserably, "I'm sorry."

"There," Mr. Desmond said. "You boys don't really want to fight. You two just shake hands."

"For *God's* sake, Dad," Johnny said violently. He looked at James. "Listen," he began.

"You all go to hell," James said, with vast adolescent contempt, and turned and walked away through the silent group of children.

Text of two manuscripts found at the creek, late in the summer, by Tod Donald:

In ten years I will be a beautiful charming lovely lady writer without any husband or children but lots of lovers and everyone will read the books I write and want to marry me but I will never marry any of them. I will have lots of money and jewels too.

I will be a famous actress or maybe a painter and everyone will be afraid of me and do what I say.

CHAPTER SIX

Mrs. Ransom-Jones was wearing pale blue linen, with her dark hair piled up on top of her head. She looked exactly like a finely trained hostess receiving her garden-party guests. "How *nice* to see you," she was saying in her high sweet voice, and, "So *glad* you could come."

Miss Tyler, somewhat in back of her sister, but wearing pale pink and a wide hat, bowed and fluttered and murmured little incoherent emphases while her sister spoke, and then, in her turn, said to each guest, "It's been so *long*," and handed them one by one on to Brad Ransom-Jones, who was far too small for two wives, but red-faced and genial.

"Indeed, indeed," he shouted at each new guest, "imagine living here all this time and not meeting *you!*" And he shook hands enthusiastically and led guests out to the Ransom-Jones garden, which many of the guests had not seen before, and which all of them admired extravagantly.

"It's a neighborhood party," Mrs. Ransom-Jones said beautifully to Mrs. Desmond. "We thought it was a shame that all of us had never gotten together in a really *neighborhood* party before." Johnny, tall and white-jacketed behind his mother and father, got an especially warm handclasp from Mrs. Ransom-Jones and a "But you're so *big!*" with a little laugh over her shoulder at his mother. "And little Caroline!" without words to express her delight at seeing even little Caroline. Mrs. Desmond smiled maternally down at Caroline and started to speak to Mrs. Ransom-Jones, but Mrs. Ransom-Jones was already saying, "Mrs. Roberts! How nice to see *you*."

Out in the garden the neighbors gathered uneasily, standing for the most part with the people who lived next door to them, whose faces they knew best. Miss Fielding, who had come first, taking a long time to walk the long block to the Ransom-Jones house, had been given a wicker chair in the center of things, and sat, withdrawn and polite, smiling pleasantly on acquaintances. "It's very nice to see you so well, dear," she told Johnny Desmond. "I heard you had been ill?"

"No, ma'am," Johnny said uncomfortably. "I hope you are well, too," and slid away, imploring his mother with his eyes.

"Well, *well*," Mr. Roberts said heartily to Miss Fielding, "still the prettiest girl on the block?" and Miss Fielding looked politely astonished, but said, "I hope you keep well, Mr. Roberts?"

The children were still too awed to move freely; they gathered in a whispering, gently pushing group near the house, the Roberts boys and Johnny Desmond, and Harriet Merriam, whose mother was talking to Mrs. Desmond about the wall. Across the street, although none of them knew it, Marilyn Perlman was watching the garden from her front porch, and Mrs. Perlman was watching Marilyn anxiously through the living-room window.

The children were joined gradually by the Donalds, James Donald eyeing Johnny Desmond with uneasy dignity, and then the Byrne children, escaping politely from their parents and the parents of their friends, running the gamut of "How big you are, how tall, what grade are you in, guess you're glad that school's starting soon. . . ." into the comparative safety of the children's group and its nervous giggling.

Mr. Ransom-Jones had laboriously erected, and Mrs. Ransom-Jones and her sister tenderly adorned, a long table garlanded with branches from the garden; it held two punch bowls and trays of food, and the group of children, moving imperceptibly nearer, ascertained through grapevine and passionate speculation that one bowl was intoxicating, one harmless, that on the trays and platters were chicken sandwiches, ham sandwiches, unidentified sandwiches which a vote supported as peanut butter—"For *us*, probably," Virginia Donald said disgustedly; there were also plates of cookies and a wealth of celery and olives—"I bet I could eat a *million* olives, I *love* them," Mary Byrne said; and, finally, the undeniable word went round that later ice cream would be dispensed, in unguessable quantities.

Marilyn Perlman had not been invited; neither had Mrs. Mack, nor George and Hallie Martin; Miss Tyler had entered the plans for the party with the statement, "*Naturally* we will not include the Terrels." It was a very successful neighborhood affair; Mrs. Ransom-Jones had planned on twenty-one guests and had twenty, Mr. Byrne being unfortunately detained on business at the last minute. Mrs. Byrne and Pat and Mary were the last to come; by that time the adult guests, led by Mrs. Roberts, were permitting themselves to be escorted to the long table and were there praising the food and decorations, and renewing their dutiful homage to the garden, before accepting the cup, either intoxicating or non-intoxicating, held out by Mr. Ransom-Jones.

The children, restrained by the eyes of parents, held back until the last, and were then allowed to line up for a non-intoxicating cup apiece, and three sandwiches, and the ice cream, which was strawberry. "Go down to the *very* end of the garden," Mrs. Ransom-Jones said amiably to the children. "All of you children just go down there and play all you want to. The perennials are down there," she explained to her near guests, "and they can't do *any* harm."

"Be careful of the flowers, kids," Mrs. Roberts said immediately, at the same time that Mrs. Merriam was saying, "Harriet, we're courteous with other people's gardens, aren't we?" and Mrs. Byrne warned, "Pat, Mary, don't step on anything."

The children moved off, carrying their plates. They went as far as they thought they should, turned and were waved farther on by Mrs. Ransom-Jones. They proceeded to the end of the garden near the hedge, where, finding that they were where they belonged, they sat down and began to eat, relaxing gradually with distance and food into a completely natural, jostling state, which brought them eventually into a game of tag strictly within the limits of their prescribed area.

"They *are* good children," Mrs. Ransom-Jones observed to

Mrs. Merriam as the children moved away. "I don't know *when* I've seen a better group of children."

"Of course they're well brought up," Mrs. Merriam said. "Harriet and Virginia are very close, and I think Virginia is a very well-mannered child."

"We were just complimenting your daughter," Mrs. Ransom-Jones said to Mr. Donald, passing by. "What a lovely girl Virginia is."

"Charming party," Mr. Donald said, and went on to Miss Fielding. "Good afternoon," He said. "I hope you are well."

"Good afternoon," Miss Fielding said. She had a non-intoxicating cup, which she thought was intoxicating, held in her lap in her best teacup manner, and a cookie in her other hand. "I *am* well," Miss Fielding said. "And you?"

"How *are* you, Mister," Mr. Roberts said enthusiastically from behind Mr. Donald's back. He put his hand affectionately on Mr. Donald's shoulder and said, "Miss Fielding, how are *you*?"

"Very well, thank you," Miss Fielding said, and tasted her cookie cautiously.

"I suppose it's to celebrate the wall coming down, too," Mrs. Ransom-Jones was saying to Mrs. Merriam and Mrs. Desmond. "After all, the old neighborhood will never be the same again."

"You live so far away from it," Mrs. Merriam said. "We've had all that dust, and the *noise*. . . ."

"Caroline and I just came home yesterday," Mrs. Desmond said. She looked down at Caroline, sitting quietly next to her mother, and smoothed the child's hair. Caroline was wearing a stiff yellow frock, with yellow socks and a yellow satin ribbon on her hair; both Mrs. Merriam and Mrs. Ransom-Jones looked down at her and smiled tenderly. "It was very bad for Caroline to be around all that dust," Mrs. Desmond added, and looked appealingly at Mrs. Merriam and Mrs. Ransom-Jones. "She *coughed* so," Mrs. Desmond said.

"I tell Bill they could step right in and stop it if they wanted to," Mrs. Byrne said firmly to Mrs. Donald. "Any time Bill and Mr. Desmond and Mike Roberts and the rest wanted to they could stop it right away."

"It's going to *ruin* the neighborhood," Mrs. Donald said.

"It's too late now, of course," Mrs. Byrne said. "I told Bill."

Mrs. Roberts had got Mr. Ransom-Jones to talking about the ingredients of the intoxicating punch, and Mr. Ransom-Jones said finally, "*This* sort of thing is for old ladies, you know." He looked at Mrs. Roberts and laughed, and Mrs. Roberts said jovially, "Why do you serve it to *me*, then?" and they both laughed, and finally, unnoticed except by Miss Fielding and Mrs. Donald and Mrs. Ransom-Jones and most of the children, Mrs. Roberts and Mr. Ransom-Jones went indoors to the kitchen to find something better to drink. In the kitchen they found Mr. Donald, who had crept there to eat his chicken sandwiches, and drove him outside where he was captured by Mrs. Byrne and given a lecture on not acting in time to save Pepper Street. Mrs. Donald, escorted by Mr. Roberts, presently strolled into the kitchen, where they partook of the refreshments being served there, soon in almost frank rivalry with the table outside.

Mr. Desmond was down among the children, circulating with the plate of cookies and much hilarity, and he observed with pleasure his son and James Donald eating together in silent companionability. "*That's* the boy, Johnny," he said as he went by, and both boys looked up at him and then down again. While Mr. Desmond was walking around among the children Virginia Donald stood up, brushed off her skirt, and began to saunter down the garden toward the grown-ups. After hesitating a minute Harriet got up and followed. Virginia waved cheerfully to her father where he sat with Mrs. Byrne, and went unostentatiously into the house. Harriet, following, was caught by the shoulder, and looked around to see her father, hot and uncomfortable. "Having a nice time?" he asked. "I'll be inside."

Harriet watched her father going toward the house and then went over to her mother. "Dad's gone inside," she said when her mother looked up. Mrs. Merriam smiled and nodded and went on talking to Mrs. Desmond, and Harriet caught Mrs.

Ransom-Jones's eye and whispered, "May I please find out where the bathroom is?"

Mrs. Ransom-Jones said, "Lillian, dear, will you show Harriet the bathroom?"

Mrs. Merriam looked up sharply, and Harriet, agonized at the loudness of Mrs. Ransom-Jones's voice, followed Miss Tyler into the house. They passed the kitchen and heard loud voices, and Miss Tyler, going ahead in her pale dress, turned her head away. After the bright sunlight of the garden, Harriet found it difficult to find her way through the dark rooms inside, and at last nearly ran into Miss Tyler, standing waiting. "It's a lovely party, isn't it?" Miss Tyler said, so softly that she was almost whispering. "The garden looks so pretty."

"It's a *lovely* party," Harriet said.

Miss Tyler leaned forward and put her hand on Harriet's arm. "I knew it was a mistake to have the Roberts people, though," she said. "*She's* very coarse." She shook her head sadly and went on, "I can't imagine why Brad is so polite to her. It's not his nature to be polite to coarse people."

"He's very polite," Harriet said.

"*Always* be polite," Miss Tyler said. She looked at Harriet and said, "You'll never be pretty, of *course*, but you can practice great fascination. The pretty ones always fade, always." Harriet tried to say something, something self-contained, but Miss Tyler went on hurriedly, "Take me, for instance, you wouldn't think now that I was so pretty once."

She tilted her head flirtatiously, and Harriet said, "Yes, I would think so, Miss Tyler."

"Nonsense," Miss Tyler said, and laughed lightly. "His wife is the fascinating one," she said, and when Harriet stared, Miss Tyler said, "His wife, Brad's. My sister. She's always been the fascinating one. You're lucky, you won't ever be pretty."

Harriet knew already that this would keep her heartsick for months, perhaps the rest of her life, and she said thickly, "I'm losing weight right now."

"It isn't that you're so *fat*," Miss Tyler said critically. "You just don't have the *air* of a pretty woman. All your life, for instance, you'll walk like you're fat, whether you are or not."

Harriet thought she was going to cry; her throat was numb, so she said harshly, "Where's the bathroom, please?"

"Oh," Miss Tyler said. She touched the doorway next to them. "Right in there," she said. "I had no idea you were in such a *hurry*."

Harriet went into the bathroom, and Miss Tyler walked slowly through the house to the kitchen. She stopped at the kitchen door and looked through the people inside until she found Mr. Ransom-Jones. When he saw her she waved, and he came over to the door where she was standing, with his glass in his hand and a leftover smile still on his face.

"It's a lovely party, Brad," Miss Tyler said, looking fragilely up at him. "Thank you *so* much for including me."

"Having a good time?" he asked.

"Perfect," Miss Tyler said, "except for—" She waved her hand toward the garden. "She's acting up," she said. "I don't want to carry tales."

"Don't worry about it," Mr. Ransom-Jones said. His eyes began to wander, and he turned his head slightly to look back into the kitchen.

"*I'm* not worrying," Miss Tyler said easily. "Thank you again for the party."

She moved out of the kitchen doorway, down the hall to the garden again. Mr. Ransom-Jones went back into the kitchen, to his place between Mrs. Donald and Mrs. Roberts. They got back to their singing.

Virginia Donald had never been officially at an adult party before. Always she had been allowed to attend, briefly, as a child, to be talked down to and indulged, but now, safely in the kitchen, she passed the initial test of encountering her mother, who waved genially at her across the room, and ended up talking to Mr. Roberts in a corner.

"But I never really had a chance like this before," Virginia said. "Please?"

"I won't take the responsibility," Mr. Roberts said. "Ask Mama."

Virginia giggled, and put her hand on his arm. "You ask her," she said. "She likes you."

Mr. Roberts debated comically, and then turned and called across the room: "Sylvia! Lady with a daughter name of Virginia!"

"I don't have any daughter," Mrs. Donald said, flapping her hand coquettishly. "That's my sister."

Everyone shouted at once, and Mr. Roberts yelled over the noise, "Well, can she have a drink?"

"She can do anything she wants to," Mrs. Donald shouted back.

"Just watch your mother," Mr. Ransom-Jones said, and then amended it, "I mean, your sister."

"See?" Virginia said to Mr. Roberts, "I can do just what I want."

"You better start with a very small one," Mr. Roberts said. "After all, I'm responsible for you."

Mrs. Roberts tried the door of the bathroom three times before she got Harriet Merriam out; as she went past, it seemed to her that Harriet looked upset, but there was really no time to find out. In the bathroom with the door safely locked, Mrs. Roberts, looking searchingly into the mirror, told herself: You're pie-eyed, you're pie-eyed. A giggle caught her, and she steadied herself against the washbasin. You're *pie*-eyed, my girl, she told herself in the mirror: you look so nice, but you're pie-eyed. "I'm pie-eyed," she said out loud, and then was solemn for a minute thinking that someone might have heard her. How much of it did I say out loud, she wondered, and then, looking at herself in the mirror, began to giggle again. Pie-eyed, she thought; pie-eyed, we'll show him, the old fool, the old lady's man, that Donald girl with her father and mother right there, not that the father's any. . . . Pie-eyed, she thought, and began to giggle helplessly.

Outside, Mrs. Desmond said to Miss Fielding, who was getting up slowly, "Caroline and I will walk down with you." She looked around, and Mrs. Ransom-Jones said, "I think she went to find her daddy." Mrs. Desmond's eyes widened anxiously, and she said to Miss Fielding, "I'll only be a minute."

"I'm *so* sorry you have to go," Mrs. Ransom-Jones was saying to Mrs. Byrne with Pat and Mary in back of her.

"It was so nice," Mrs. Byrne said. "We all enjoyed it so much."

"Thank you very much for a very lovely time," Mary Byrne said, and Pat said, "Thank you very much, Mrs. Ransom-Jones."

Mrs. Byrne, followed obediently by her children, began the general departure, and Mrs. Ransom-Jones was saying goodbye to three or four people at once when her sister, beside her suddenly, said, "*He's* in there. Drinking." Her voice had been too soft for anyone else to hear, so Mrs. Ransom-Jones pretended not to have heard it either, and went on saying, "Goodbye, it was *so* nice to have you."

"I can't find my husband," Mrs. Merriam said gaily to Mrs. Ransom-Jones, "and I guess we can't leave without him."

Harriet pulled at her mother's arm. "He's inside," she said. "Let him come later, when he's ready."

"Really, Harriet," Mrs. Merriam said. "Run and get him, dear."

Harriet went with deadly reluctance into the house and toward the kitchen. Right in the kitchen doorway Virginia was dancing with Mr. Roberts, and as Harriet went by Virginia said, "There's Harriet," and she and Mr. Roberts laughed. Harriet found it impossible to ask anyone for her father; Mr. Ransom-Jones and Mr. Desmond and Mrs. Donald and Mrs. Roberts were singing too loud for her to interrupt, and she would have died before speaking to Virginia. Finally Mr. Desmond broke off to say, "Looking for Daddy, Harriet? He's in there." His nod toward the pantry suggested unimaginable horrors to Harriet, but she opened the pantry door and went cautiously in. Her father was sitting alone on an overturned dishpan. He had a full glass in one hand, a cigarette in the other, and his eyes were half-closed. He was humming to himself, and smiling. Harriet said, "Daddy?" and Mr. Merriam jumped and turned around, the smile vanishing.

"Ready to go?" he said. He stood up and put the glass carefully down on a shelf, and came over to Harriet. "I'm ready whenever you and Mother are," he said.

Harriet felt more protected going through the kitchen with

her father, but Virginia grabbed his arm as he went by and said, "Brother Merriam, you haven't danced with me," and Mr. Merriam said pleasantly, "Later," and came out with Harriet into the garden.

He was perfectly sober and perfectly docile, and he said good-bye to Mrs. Ransom-Jones without reluctance, but going down the walk he said to Mrs. Merriam, "You know, I *enjoyed* that party."

"In the kitchen?" Mrs. Merriam said precisely, and they walked home in silence.

Mrs. Donald and Mrs. Roberts were speaking almost sharply to one another when Mrs. Desmond came to the kitchen door. No one noticed her except Mr. Desmond, but the way she looked at him brought him out into the hall immediately. Out of sight of the people in the kitchen Mrs. Desmond took her husband wildly by the arm and swung him around toward her with a violence that shocked him into silence.

"Where is Caroline?" Mrs. Desmond demanded. "Where is she?"

"There's absolutely no question about it at all," Mrs. Byrne said. She felt the outside of her husband's teacup before setting it down. "It's just too hot," she said. "Let it stand a minute. I'm sure I never would have suspected it."

"She was in the kitchen, dancing," Mary observed. "I saw her when I went inside for my coat."

"You never really do know people, even living so near them for years," Mrs. Byrne confided. "Imagine, in the kitchen like that."

"I never like to see a woman drinking," Mr. Byrne said pontifically. "Not the mother of children."

"And out in the kitchen like that." Mrs. Byrne shuddered vividly. "I'm sure I don't know what Josephine Merriam thought."

"Or Mrs. Ransom-Jones," Mary said. "After all, it was *her* husband."

"Mary," Mrs. Byrne said.

Pat Byrne put his glass down suddenly. "I wonder what Miss Fielding thought," he said, and began to laugh.

"I'm glad Dad didn't go," Mrs. Byrne said, and then, "Is that the doorbell? Answer it, Pat."

Pat put down his napkin and got up. "Probably some drunk," he said, and his mother said, "Pat!" as he left the room.

The doorbell rang again before Pat reached the door, and he said, "Oh, shut up," irritably as he opened it. "Yeah?" he said when he saw Tod Donald outside.

"Listen," Tod said. His voice was thinner than usual, and he put out his hand and grabbed Pat's sleeve. "Listen, Pat, we've always been pretty good friends, I want you to buy my bike."

"What bike?" Pat said, surprised.

"My *bike*." Tod's voice was insistent and got higher. "I'm going to sell you my bike. You don't have a bike, I'll let you have mine."

"I don't want your bike." Pat started to close the door, but Tod tightened his grip on Pat's sleeve and said, "Listen, Pat, you *got* to buy it. I'm going to sell you my bike. I've been thinking about it for a long time, honestly."

"You're crazy," Pat said.

"Just about five dollars," Tod said urgently. "Ask your father for it, he'll give it to you. It's a good bike, you know that."

Mrs. Byrne called from the kitchen, "Pat, who's at the door?" and Pat said, "Nothing, no one. Look," he said to Tod, "run along, I don't want your old bike."

"It's a good bike," Tod said furiously, "and it's mine to sell, honestly. James gave it to me, and it really belongs to me. Five dollars, ask your father."

"Pat?" Mrs. Byrne said, from the kitchen doorway. "Who's there, Pat?" She sounded as though she were coming closer, and Tod said, "Please, Pat." He loosened his hold on Pat's jacket and stood poised.

"Go on home," Pat said crossly.

"Don't tell anyone," Tod said, and ran off down the street just as Mrs. Byrne came into the doorway behind Pat.

"Who on earth was here?" she asked. "What's the matter?"

"It was Tod Donald," Pat said. "He acted funny."

"What did he want?" Mrs. Byrne went a step outside the door, looking down the street.

"He wanted to sell me his bike or something," Pat said. "He acted awfully funny."

"Listen," Mrs. Byrne said suddenly. Distantly, from the Ransom-Jones house, they could hear singing. "It's disgusting," Mrs. Byrne said. "Come inside, Pat."

"I didn't see her at all," Miss Fielding said faintly from behind her locked front door. "I'm sorry, I've gone to bed and I didn't see her at all."

"She had on a yellow dress," Mr. Desmond said, his hands flat against the door, his face close to the wood. "A yellow dress and a yellow hair—"

"I'm sorry," Miss Fielding said, even more faintly. "I've gone to bed."

Frederica Terrel said, over and over, "But I tell you I just *looked*. She's in her bed, where she belongs."

"Not your sister," Mr. Desmond said. "I'm not talking about her. This is Caroline, my little girl." He held tight to the side of the door and stood half-turned away, expecting what Frederica was going to say and already set to hurry on.

"Did she have any money?" Frederica asked, understanding in her sudden way. "You know, sometimes if they have money they just go and spend it and then they come back when it's gone."

"This is my little girl," Mr. Desmond said, starting off. "She's only three years old," he called back over his shoulder.

"Oh, my God," Mrs. Perlman said, "the little baby?"

"Three years old," Mr. Desmond said as though it were important.

"Mrs. Desmond," Mrs. Perlman said, "that poor, poor woman. Wait," she said, touching Mr. Desmond's arm lightly, "I'll get Mr. Perlman."

"It's people from outside took her," Mrs. Mack said, nodding her great old head. "People from the other side the wall."

"We think she's just gotten lost," Mr. Desmond said. "She's just lost herself."

"No one from *here*," Mrs. Mack said. "This is a nice neighborhood, not like places where little girls get taken away."

Mr. Desmond was still keeping his voice down, without shrillness or panic. "She's never been lost like this before," he said.

"Well," Mrs. Mack nodded again. "That's what happens," she said, sagely.

"She hasn't been *here*," Hallie Martin said. "You want me to wake Grandma?"

"I thought she might have followed some of the children," Mr. Desmond said. "You know, she might just have followed along behind some of the children."

"Not *this* way," Hallie said. "I could wake Grandma, but I'm sure she isn't around here."

"Thank you very much," Mr. Desmond said.

"It's nothing, I'm sure," Hallie said.

The Merriams walked right into the Desmond house, since there seemed to be no one around to let them in. There was no sign of Mrs. Desmond, Mr. Desmond they knew was going from house to house, but after they had stood in the hall for a minute Johnny Desmond found them and said abruptly, "Has she turned up?"

"We came to help," Mrs. Merriam said.

Johnny spread his hands helplessly. "I don't know what to do," he said.

"Where is your mother?" Mrs. Merriam lifted her chin confidently. "I want to stay with her."

Johnny waved at the back of the house, doors the Merriams had never passed. "She's locked herself in her room."

Mrs. Merriam went in the direction he indicated, straightening her shoulders in spite of the nervous movement of her hands, and Johnny said, "Now she's here I guess I can go help look."

"Perhaps you'd better stay here too, Harriet," Mr. Merriam said. "Johnny and I will go find Desmond and see what we can do."

Harriet looked apprehensively at the part of the house where her mother had vanished. "I'd rather go with you."

She followed her father and Johnny outside and down the block. "When did you find she was gone?" her father asked, and Johnny said, "At the party, when we were leaving."

"Long time," Mr. Merriam said. "That was about five."

"We've been looking since then," Johnny said.

Halfway up the block they met Mr. Byrne and Pat, coats thrown on hastily. "Find her?" Mr. Byrne said.

"Not yet," Mr. Merriam said. The four of them stood uncertainly on the sidewalk, with Harriet waiting nearby. They all had faintly sheepish expressions, as though they were making fools of themselves, talking and acting with dramatic tension over something which would turn out to be nonsense by daylight.

"Can't imagine where she could have gone," Mr. Byrne remarked finally.

"Let's find Dad," Johnny said. "Mr. Merriam, we ought to find Dad."

They began to walk down the street. There were lights in the Roberts house, and Mr. Merriam went purposefully up to the front door and rang the bell. Mrs. Roberts answered; she seemed flushed and nervous, and said, "Oh, it's *you*, Mr. Merriam; have they found her yet?"

"Not yet," Mr. Merriam said.

"I only saw her for just a minute this afternoon," Mrs. Roberts said. "I just caught a glimpse of her. Neither of the boys saw her either. She doesn't play with the children, of course. But we didn't see her."

"We're going to go out hunting for her, I guess," Mr. Merriam said heavily. "I guess all the men had better get out and look for her."

"Oh," Mrs. Roberts said. Then she said, "Oh, you want

Mike, then. Wait a minute." She went indoors a few steps and
called, "Mike? Come here a minute."

Mr. Roberts said querulously from the living-room, "What
the hell do you want now?" and Mrs. Roberts said, "Mr. Merriam wants you. Just a minute," she said again to Mr. Merriam.

Mr. Roberts came to the front door a little unsteadily, walking with his feet carefully put down. His hair was mussed and
he scowled at his wife as he came past her to lean against the
doorway. "Evening, Merriam," he said. "Want me?"

Mr. Merriam was embarrassed. "I don't suppose it's anything, really," he said. "It's just we thought we ought to get
everyone we could."

"The little Desmond girl's gone," Mrs. Roberts said. She
looked at her husband coldly, her smile righteous, her eyes triumphant. "She disappeared this afternoon."

"Gone?" Mr. Roberts said in horror. "Kidnapped?"

Harriet waited on the sidewalk with Johnny and the Byrnes
for a minute, and then said, "Excuse me," and slipped away
up the street. She was surprised to see lights in the Perlmans'
house, until she realized that, late as it seemed, it was hardly
ten o'clock. She ran quickly up the front steps and rang the
doorbell.

"Mrs. Perlman," she said breathlessly, "has Mr. Desmond
been here?"

Mrs. Perlman nodded her head, looking surprised and dis-
approving. "You shouldn't be out so late," she said. "Come in
and wait till Mr. Perlman gets back, and he'll take you home."

"I can't," Harriet said. "No one's home at my house. I
mean," she went on confusedly, when Mrs. Perlman frowned
openly, "I mean, if Mr. Desmond hasn't been here yet you
don't know."

"He was just here," Mrs. Perlman said.

"Everyone's out hunting for her," Harriet said.

"You shouldn't be out alone," Mrs. Perlman said. "Oh, that
poor woman. Come in for a minute, and Marilyn and I will
come with you. Unless," she added, looking at Harriet, "unless

you think your mother would mind if you came in Marilyn's house."

James Donald went to get his mother and sister from the Ransom-Jones house. The front door was open and he went into the hall and called, "Hello?"

Miss Tyler came to him from somewhere, probably her bedroom, because she was wearing a filmy nightgown under a Japanese kimono. "How do you do?" she said formally. "May I help you?"

"I'm looking for my sister," James said, unable to tell this woman that his mother was here too.

"They're all out in the kitchen," Miss Tyler said. She added with a faint touch of malice, "I think they're having breakfast."

"I'm sorry I disturbed you," James said, not thinking of anything except how to get into the kitchen and out again. "Is that the way?"

He started for an open doorway and was halted by Miss Tyler's faint eager laughter. "That's my bedroom," she whispered, and ran past him into the room and slammed the door. "Right straight down the hall," she said from inside. "Naughty man."

James went hurriedly down the hall; as he came nearer the kitchen he heard voices, his mother's shrill. "One quart of coffee coming up," she was saying.

James pushed open the swinging door of the kitchen, and his mother screamed, "It's my son! Look, everyone, here's my little boy!"

They were all sitting around the kitchen table, Mr. and Mrs. Ransom-Jones and Mrs. Donald and Virginia. Virginia and Mr. Ransom-Jones were talking earnestly and did not look up when James came in, but Mrs. Donald ran over and threw her arms around him.

"Come and have some coffee, honey," she said. She looked at Mrs. Ransom-Jones and said unhappily, "Can my honey have some coffee?"

"Mother," James said, regretting the voice that came out boyish, "Mother, I want you to come home. Right away."

"Listen to him," Mrs. Donald said, and Mrs. Ransom-Jones added caressingly, "The dear boy."

"Something *terrible* has happened," James said.

They gathered, eventually, almost everyone, on what was traditionally their forgotten village green—the sidewalk in front of the Donald house. For once the children were not separated from the adults; nearly every mother kept her hands on her children, and stood next to her husband. The children themselves were silent, afraid to meet each other's eyes.

"The poor woman," Mrs. Perlman said companionably to Mrs. Byrne. She had Marilyn in front of her, held by both shoulders. "It's so terrible to think about, that poor woman."

Mrs. Merriam was still at the Desmond house, but Harriet stood very close to her father. "All the men," he was saying, "all the men get flashlights."

"He called the police from our house," Mrs. Byrne said. "I suppose they'll send someone to look for her."

Mrs. Donald and Virginia stood apart from the rest, with James beside them. "If we'd known," Mrs. Donald wailed, "if we'd only *known* in time." Mrs. Ransom-Jones stood beside her, and she turned and said to Mrs. Ransom-Jones, "If we had only known in time."

Nothing that anyone said had any purpose; they were waiting for something, for an act on someone's part that would clarify the situation. No one could do anything at all until the occasion was identified—either it was a great climactic festival over nothing, in which case they would all go quietly home, or else it was an emergency, a crisis, a tragedy, in which case they were all called upon to act together as human beings, to be men and women in a community, the men out on dangerous business, the women waiting, going to the window, wringing their hands.

Mr. Desmond stood in the center; he was frightened, and he said over and over, "It will kill her if we don't find her right away, I don't know what else she wants me to do, it will kill her."

Mr. Ransom-Jones and Mr. Merriam were both trying to take charge. Mr. Merriam was saying, "If all the men get flashlights, we can go around," and Mr. Ransom-Jones was saying, "The police will be right along, I called them again myself."

The prevailing mood was one of keen excitement; no one there really wanted Caroline Desmond safe at home, although Mrs. Perlman said crooningly behind Marilyn, "The poor, poor woman," and Mrs. Donald said again, "If we'd only known in time." Pleasure was in the feeling that the terrors of the night, the jungle, had come close to their safe lighted homes, touched them nearly, and departed, leaving every family safe but one; an acute physical pleasure like a pain, which made them all regard Mr. Desmond greedily, and then turn their eyes away with guilt.

"All the *men get flashlights*," Mr. Merriam said.

James Donald left his mother and came over to Mr. Merriam, saying, "I've got a couple of flashes. I think we ought to start looking right away."

"Good idea," Mr. Merriam said, as though it had never occurred to him. Mr. Desmond said, "Who's that—James?" He put his hand on James's shoulder and said, "It will kill her if we don't find her."

James's voice was, for once, low and steady. He said again, "We ought to start right out."

It looked as if James were going to take charge, with Mr. Desmond on one side of him and Mr. Merriam on the other, both looking at him and nodding. Mr. Byrne said, "Right away," and Mr. Ransom-Jones said, "As soon as the police get here."

In the pale street light, James's head was with the other men's heads, held as tall as most of them, and his voice mingling with theirs in stern masculine comment; Pat Byrne broke suddenly away from his mother's hand, and said loudly, "Did anyone tell them about Toddie?"

"Toddie?" Mr. Desmond said vaguely.

"Toddie?" Mrs. Donald said. She looked around her. "Toddie?"

Suddenly everyone was looking for Toddie; Pat Byrne was allowed to walk over to the group of men forming, and say in his deepest voice, "Tod Donald; he came trying to sell me his bike tonight and he acted awfully funny."

Frederica Terrel stood on her front steps; Beverley was wakeful, and Frederica did not dare leave her house, but she craned her neck to see, and when voices were raised she could hear. She saw Mr. Desmond isolated for a minute, while the group of men stirred, walking up to one another and speaking, and Mr. Desmond was twisting his hands and looking up and down the street eagerly. *That's* no way to find her, Frederica thought wisely; you never find someone who's running away by just *standing* there.

Mr. Donald, next door, was standing in his open doorway. Occasionally he moved a little toward the group in the street and then moved back again. He had a book in his hand, with his finger between the pages marking the place, and now and then he looked longing at his own house, at the lighted living-room window. Why doesn't he go indoors, Frederica thought, they've got enough people standing down there. Suddenly James Donald broke away from the group of people in the street and came up to his father. "Where's Toddie?" he called as he came up, "is he inside?"

Mr. Donald shook his head and James ran past him into the house and came out again after a minute and said, "He's not there." He saw Frederica and said to her, "Have you seen my little brother?"

"I saw him yesterday," Frederica said.

"Today, I mean," James said. "Tonight."

"No," Frederica said. "Not since yesterday."

Suddenly Mrs. Donald raised her voice down on the street. "Toddie," she wailed. "My little baby."

The women standing near Mrs. Donald all moved away from her quickly, and Virginia said roughly, "Be *quiet*, Mother."

Down on the street Pat Byrne stood with the men while James waited in front of his own house. "He acted so funny that I was surprised," Pat said insistently.

Then Mr. Perlman, who had been so quiet until now, waiting with a flashlight in his hand for someone to start off into the dark, said the thing which everyone realized then had been in their minds. "If the two children are together," Mr.

Perlman asked reasonably and softly, "why didn't the boy bring her home?"

They were all silent, realizing that the first person who spoke now would have to say something worse, something else they were all thinking, something which, whether true or not, would be the most horrible thing that had ever happened on Pepper Street.

It was Mr. Desmond, rightfully, who cracked the tense film of comprehension that lay like the pale yellow of the street light over all the people waiting, keeping even the smallest children taut and expectant. "Toddie!" was all Mr. Desmond said. He walked over to the sidewalk and called up to James, standing on his own front walk, "What has he *done* to my little girl?"

Frederica crushed herself back against her own front door. She was afraid to open it for fear the slight noise and the movement would catch Mr. Desmond's attention. The people in the street behind Mr. Desmond had gathered closer together so that it was impossible to single out any one of them; Frederica could see their faces in the light, and their hands, but they were so close together that there were no names for any of the faces, and the hands might be clasped tight in the hands of strangers.

Pat Byrne and Mr. Perlman were with the two policemen who went up to the creek to hunt for Caroline. On the way up there Pat, who was along to show them the way and to tell them what he knew about Tod, walked with long strides, putting his feet down manfully just as the other men did, and he talked using words he would never have dared use before.

It was dark along the road and even darker in the trees around the creek, and Pat had to steel himself to walk alone, ahead of the rest, as though he were really showing them the way, instead of falling back shoulder to shoulder with Mr. Perlman, who seemed faintly nervous and spoke tremblingly when he spoke at all. Once among the trees, Pat was silent; the two policemen communicated in monosyllables, words like "there," or "in here." Mr. Perlman came slowly behind, stum-

THE ROAD THROUGH THE WALL   185

bling. Pat looked more at the darkness, the strange black unfamiliar places; he passed the fallen log without recognizing it
and lost his bearings, so that the steady searching movements
of the policemen lost meaning for him, their voices were rhyth-
mic in their short words, none of the lights ever shone where
Pat could see the way, and he was horribly afraid.

Finally, one of the policemen said, "Down there," and the
other said, "Right," and Pat followed the light blindly, not yet
ready to accept any end to the darkness, an object to the
search. Mr. Perlman, saying, "My God," peering over his
shoulder, made Pat look ahead to where the policemen held
their lights converged, but there was nothing to see except
Caroline Desmond lying on the ground; Pat saw her clearly,
and said, "There's Caroline Desmond."

She was horribly dirty; no one had ever seen Caroline as
dirty as she was then, with mud all over her yellow dress and
yellow socks and, of course, Pat understood perfectly, what
was all over her head must be blood, unconvincing as it looked
in the flashlight. It was absolutely unthinkable at the creek,
not twenty feet from the fallen log Pat could walk across,
and the really dreadful thing, lying right there next to her as
though it might be hers, was the rock with blood on it; part of
the creek, belonging to it, a rock which had probably been
sitting there as long as Pat had been coming to the creek, a
rock he might have stepped over or lifted with his two hands.
Even though Pat had never noticed the rock particularly
before, it should have been left alone.

It wasn't safe behind the wall where a brick might fall on him,
and yet Tod was afraid to move anywhere else, with people
going all up and down the block, flashing lights and talking to
one another. Tod thought they were looking for him, and yet
there had never been this much fuss made over him before in
his life, and the principal reason he had not run out and said
"Here I am," was his fear of the sudden surprise and the
humiliating laughter when they saw him and realized that he
thought they were looking for him.

It was cold behind the wall, and Tod kept turning his eyes

nervously sideways to see if any of his slight movements had loosened a brick that might come plunging downward; it was like the night he hid in the bushes and heard Hester talking to his brother. James was not visible in the street now; Tod had only been behind the wall for a few minutes and so did not know that his family sat within the walls of their house, all together in one room. What did occur to him was that in any case no one in his family would bother to look for him.

He could see Mr. Ransom-Jones, and Mr. Merriam; they had stood together like that, talking, for a few minutes at the party. Tod had left the party without saying good-bye to Mrs. Ransom-Jones; while leaving stealthily was a social error, technically he was still at the party until he told Mrs. Ransom-Jones that he had had a lovely time. For a minute Tod was prepared to step out from behind the wall and find Mrs. Ransom-Jones, and then he cowered back again. He was safer where he was. But it was long past his bedtime.

He heard voices nearby and looked out carefully to see Mr. and Mrs. Roberts going past across the street. "Too damn drunk to go out with the other men," Mrs. Roberts was saying.

It was a long time after that; Tod had finally figured out a way to sit down, and had perhaps fallen asleep with his head against the wall, but he looked out suddenly and the street was empty. Not a person, not a light outside. He waited to see if anyone came, and then slipped out from behind the wall and ran, across Cortez Road and on to the sidewalk again in front of Miss Fielding's, quickly past Miss Fielding's, jumping almost automatically, as he had done so many times before, over the broken spot in the sidewalk, past the house-for-rent, dark and asleep against the heavy pines that almost hid his own house from him; he stopped, horrified, when he saw that there were lights in his house; were they, could they be waiting up for him?

He went quietly around to the back door, hesitated there till he was sure everything was quiet, and then turned the knob cautiously. It opened, and he slid inside through a narrow opening, closed it softly without trying to make sure that it latched, and then eased himself, step by silent step, up the back stairs. Once in the upstairs hall, familiar and lighted and warm and safe, he could not go slowly any longer but raced for his bed, the pillow, the covers over his head.

Downstairs in the living-room James looked upward, said, "Did I hear something?" looked around at his mother, no longer crying, his father reading, Virginia twisting a lock of hair in her fingers, and rose, saying, "Might as well look again." He went upstairs and, outside the door of the room he shared with his brother, said, "Toddie?"

"What?" Toddie said from the bed.

"Christ!" James said, and ran to the head of the stairs, yelling downward, "He's here, everyone! I found him!"

As his mother and father and sister started up the stairs James yelled again, "Virginia, get the Desmonds, hurry!"

The policeman looked like a doctor, like a dentist, like the man at the movie theatre who wanted to know how old you were before he let you in for half-price. Except that he wore a uniform fascinatingly official, he looked at you in the same way, as though he knew things about you he was not going to tell and yet was going to hurt you anyway, of his own accord, whether you wanted him to or not, like the dentist. Or as though there were no way of getting out of it, and he knew best anyway, like the doctor. Or as though he hated everybody who was legally under twelve, the way the man at the movies looked.

Many people had been in and out of the dining-room where Tod sat with the policeman; James looking stern, and Tod's mother and father, and unrecognizable people who looked at Tod as though this were their house and not his. Finally he sat there alone with the policeman—the dentist, the doctor—wondering what was going to happen to him.

"All right," the policeman said finally, leaning back in his chair, the dining-room chair where Mr. Donald sat every night. "All right."

Tod stared; when they brought him into the dining-room he had gone directly to his own chair, and he sat there now, his legs wrapped around the rungs, his hands in his lap.

"All right," the policeman said. "Let's hear all about it."

Tod shook his head numbly; if he opened his mouth the man might start drilling his teeth, if he moved his arm the man might seize it and puncture him with a needle.

"Scared?" the policeman said. "I'm not surprised. Just tell me what happened."

Tod shook his head again, and the policeman looked at him, bright cold eyes waiting. "You're going to have to tell me, sonny," the policeman said. "You might as well start."

You're going to have to. . . . The familiar words stirred in Tod's mind, and he moved as though to stand up, but the policeman held out a hand and Tod sat still.

"Look," the policeman said, his voice a little harder, "about an hour or so ago two policemen and—" he looked down at a piece of paper in front of him—"your friend Patrick Byrne went up to the creek and they found the little girl up there, so we know all about it now. You just tell me what happened."

Patrick Byrne. That would be Pat. Down on the little piece of paper.

"No one wants to frighten you," the policeman said. He leaned forward and pointed his pencil toward Tod, now like, most horribly, the school superintendent. "This is a serious thing. I want you to realize that. Tell me how you killed that little girl."

Tod gasped; once he had been caught copying from his book in an exam.

"Listen, sonny," the policeman said, "we're going to put you in jail."

Without waiting, he stood up after this, and said, gathering his papers together, "Don't try to run away again. I'm going to leave you here for a little while to think about all this. When you decide to tell me all about it you let me know." He went out the living-room door, his big back stern and unforgiving and angry as the door closed behind him.

He was gone longer than he intended, nearly an hour, but Mr. Desmond, crying now, detained him in the hall, and when he came back Tod was dead.

He had taken a piece of clothesline from the kitchen, and his own chair to stand on, the one he sat on every night at dinner. Hanging, his body was straighter than it had ever been in life.

The policeman stood for a minute just inside the door, looking at Tod and flipping his thumbnail across the papers he still held in his hand. "Well," he said in a great gusty breath, and, finally, "That settles *that*," he said.

Harriet Merriam woke up the next morning with a recollection of disaster. Looking around her sunny room with her head still on the pillow, she searched for the source of the flat dead feeling inside her, the knowledge of despair. Something had happened. She remembered slowly; standing in the street she remembered clearly, and coming home alone to bed in the darkness, and, before that, the people in the street, and Mr. Desmond. Mr. Desmond was part of it, she remembered then, and at last it came to her: he was standing laughing in the kitchen when she went by, following Miss Tyler into the house to hear . . . *fat.*

The ugly, the sickening word came back to her, spoken in Miss Tyler's small voice: fat. Harriet looked down at herself under the bedclothes; she was gross, a revolting series of huge mountains, a fat fat fat girl.

She turned her head from side to side on the pillow, her eyes shut so as not to see herself. You'll always be fat, she thought, never pretty, never charming, never dainty. In an ecstasy of shame she searched for every pretty word she knew; she would never be any of them.

Finally she sat up in bed, tears on her cheeks, and looked out of the window. Outside were the eucalyptus trees, like lace against the sky. If it were only possible to lie against them, light and bodiless, sink into their softness, deeper and deeper, lost in them, buried, never come back again. . . .

"Sure I saw it," Pat said. He closed his eyes. "It was awful," he said.

Marilyn smiled involuntarily, and said urgently, "Well, what was it *like?*"

"Awful," Pat said vividly. "All blood, and dirty. It was awful."

"Was the rock there?" Jamie Roberts asked with respect.

"Sure. I nearly touched it," Pat said, and the children sighed, all together. "It was all covered with blood," he said.

"Golly," Jamie said. He folded his arms and stared wistfully. "I *wish* I'd been there," he said.

"Yeah," Pat said scornfully, "you wouldn't have liked it much, I can tell you. Boy," he said reminiscently, "it was sure awful."

"Listen, Pat," Mary said, "listen, was she *awful*? I mean, all bloody?"

Pat made an expressive face. "There was blood all over *every*thing," he said. "I nearly got some on my *shoe*."

"Oooh," Marilyn said, her face all screwed up, "Pat, you're *terrible!*"

Mr. Merriam, walking slowly by the creek in the first dusk, met and recognized Mr. Perlman by the fallen log. They smiled embarrassedly at one another and then stood together, looking out beyond the creek over the golf course.

"I was just looking around," Mr. Merriam said. "I just had an idea I'd kind of like to look around." He laughed uncomfortably. "Suppose the police have covered everything pretty thoroughly," he said.

"I suppose so," Mr. Perlman said. "Doesn't seem quite right, does it?"

"That's what I thought," Mr. Merriam said. "It just doesn't seem quite right."

"He was too small, for one thing," Mr. Perlman said eagerly. "You can't tell me a boy that small could heft a rock that big. Stands to reason."

"No," Mr. Merriam said quietly. "No, I thought of that."

"Just isn't possible," Mr. Perlman said. "And another thing, he came home. Wouldn't have done that."

"You know," Mr. Merriam confided, "Desmond's been saying the kid had blood all over his clothes. Well, now, I was one of the people saw Tod when he came home." Mr. Merriam paused for effect, and then said, "There was not one spot of blood on him. Not a spot."

"Well, then, that's another thing," Mr. Perlman said. "He'd have gotten some blood on him, wouldn't he?"

"You know what I think?" Mr. Merriam said, "I think it was a tramp. Some Godforsaken old bum just hanging around down here. Never did like the kids playing up here, it's a natural place for tramps to hang out."

"Something in that," Mr. Perlman said. "Marilyn's been playing up here; I don't like to think what might have happened."

"My kid too," Mr. Merriam said.

They were both quiet for a minute, looking at the silent trees and the deserted golf course. Then Mr. Perlman said, "At any rate, the whole thing was too hasty. Far too hasty. Everyone jumping to conclusions."

"Take my word for it, it was some tramp," Mr. Merriam said.

"*I* think they're not telling all they know," Mrs. Merriam said. She nodded emphatically, and Mrs. Byrne said in her comfortable voice, "I don't blame the poor people for not wanting any more fuss, after all."

"*I* think," Mrs. Merriam said, leaning forward to emphasize her point, "that when you get a young boy like Tod, who's obviously, well, not *right*, somehow, taking a little girl like that off into a deserted spot. . . . Well." She nodded again and leaned back.

"Really," Mrs. Byrne said. She stirred uneasily, and Mrs. Merriam said, "More tea, Mrs. Byrne?" Mrs. Byrne held up a hand in refusal. Mrs. Merriam gave a muffled little laugh, and said, "You'd think I invited you just to talk about this dreadful affair, Mrs. Byrne, but really I can't *help* thinking about it all the time. It's so fresh in all our minds, I suppose, and then it makes you so *mad* to think of him getting off so easy."

"Easy?" Mrs. Byrne said, startled.

"Well," Mrs. Merriam said, flustered, "you know what I mean. Of course, the way he . . . did it, without telling anything first, is as good as a confession. But they should have gotten the *facts* first."

"He was such a quiet little thing all the time," Mrs. Byrne said. "Seems funny to think about him having gumption enough to go and get the rope, and—"

"Don't," Mrs. Merriam said with a shiver. "I can't even think about it."

"Well, now, Pat, my son, he was there," Mrs. Byrne said. "He went with the policemen that found the . . . that found her. Not that I think he *should* have been along." She looked at Mrs. Merriam, and Mrs. Merriam rolled her eyes in horrified agreement. "Well," Mrs. Byrne continued, "Pat seemed to think it was like an accident. Like she fell against this rock and hit her head, and Tod saw he couldn't help her and got frightened, and no wonder."

Mrs. Merriam said, "No, indeed, that could *not* have happened, Mrs. Byrne. Think about that boy, think about how he acted all the time. He was always strange, I remember myself, noticing how strange he always was. And then think about the facts they're not giving out. Mark my words," Mrs. Merriam said, "even if that killing was an accident, there were other things about it that *were not* accidental." She tightened her lips and looked triumphant.

"'Woe to him,'" Mrs. Mack read, her voice rising slightly as the dog watched her patiently. "'Woe to him that coveteth an evil covetousness to his house, that he may set his nest on high, that he may be delivered from the power of evil! Thou hast consulted shame to thy house by cutting off many people, and hast sinned against thy soul. For the stone shall cry out of the wall, and the beam out of the timber shall answer it. Woe to him that buildeth a town with blood, and stablisheth a city by iniquity!'"

"I am so damn sick of all this business I could scream," Mrs. Roberts said. She sat up in bed and looked angrily down on her husband, barely visible in the darkness. "What the hell do you know about it anyway?" she demanded viciously. "You were too drunk to do anything except fall over your own feet."

"Good night," Mr. Roberts said into his pillow.

"And the way you talked to Mr. Desmond," Mrs. Roberts went on inflexibly, "right there where everyone could hear." She raised her voice to a high mimicry. "'Desmond, I'm so sorry about your little girl getting kidnapped.'"

Indignant, Mr. Roberts rolled over on his back. "What I said—" he began in a voice of cold logic.

"I could have *died*," Mrs. Roberts said. "And his little girl lying there dead."

"Oh, God," Mr. Roberts said. He rolled over onto his stomach again.

"I was so ashamed," Mrs. Roberts continued, her voice dropping almost an octave. "Seems like I always have to be ashamed, when everyone else is out there helping and *my* husband has to be lying there dead drunk, the only one on the block who had to go to a nice party and get dead—"

"Good night," Mr. Roberts said again.

"And dancing with Virginia Donald like a college boy," Mrs. Roberts said. "And the children right there all the time." Sitting up in bed in the darkness she began to cry.

"So." Frederica leaned back and regarded her sister across the round table. Beverley was listening open-mouthed, her hands on the table and her eyes wide. "You see?" Frederica said. "All that I told you is true, every word. You see what happens to bad girls that run away all the time?"

"Tell it again," Beverley begged, scarcely breathing with excitement, "Frederica, tell it again."

The new road was finished on schedule, the following spring, and the first person across it was Hallie Martin. No one ever heard from the Donalds again after they moved out to Idaho where her family lived, but Miss Fielding died very suddenly about a year later and the Merriams went to the funeral, which was badly attended. Mr. Perlman eventually bought the house he lived in on Pepper Street, and put in some improvements, particularly an addition to the garage for the car he gave Marilyn on her eighteenth birthday. The Terrels moved out very suddenly one day and left no forwarding address; no one saw them go.

The Ransom-Jones's cat, Angel, died, and was buried in the garden alongside her three predecessors. After debating for some time, the Ransom-Joneses took another cat, a brown Siamese. The Byrne family finally moved to a home in a fashionable part of San Francisco because Mr. Byrne disliked commuting by train. The Robertses had a third child, another boy, named Francis.

Although the pavement in the new street was fresher and shinier than the pavement on the old Pepper Street block, it was always less satisfactory for roller-skating, being made of some material slightly more slippery. A wide break appeared in the sidewalk the first winter, near the spot where Jamie Roberts had left the print of his hand in the fresh cement.

Mrs. Mack's house remained, a pastoral eyesore, while the neighborhood changed around it. The new boy who moved into the Donald house once ventured in through the apple trees to see the old lady, and she drove him out with a stick.

Harriet Merriam kept house for her father after her mother's death; she never married. The Desmond house was vacant for nearly a year before it was bought by some people from Oklahoma.

The old lady who had owned the wall and the property it enclosed passed away very quietly one night in her sleep. No one was at her bedside when she died.

AVAILABLE FROM PENGUIN CLASSICS

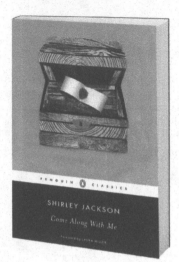

Come Along with Me
Classic Short Stories and an Unfinished Novel
Foreword by Laura Miller

In her gothic visions of small-town America, Jackson, turns an ordinary world into a supernatural nightmare. This eclectic collection goes beyond her horror writing, revealing the full spectrum of her literary genius. In addition to *Come Along with Me*, Jackson's unfinished novel about the quirky inner life of a lonely widow, this book features sixteen short stories and three lectures she delivered during her last years.

ISBN 978-0-14-310711-8

AVAILABLE FROM PENGUIN

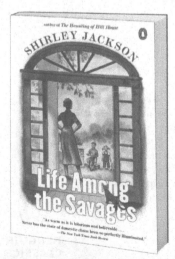

Life Among the Savages

Shirley Jackson was known for her terse, haunting prose. But the writer possessed another side, one which is delightfully exposed in this hilariously charming memoir of her family's life in rural Vermont.

ISBN 978-0-14-026767-9

P.O. 0005399548 20231017